I0522547

Time Magazine called Defiance, Oklahoma, the next great boom town, but Bucky Ontario's about to find out that the community he's chosen for his new home isn't particularly averse to murders...just to the embarrassment of them.

Bucky leaned back, looked up at the stars, and sipped his beer. Yes, siree, his future was looking real bright.

The rear porch light came on, and a screen door banged open. "*Cal!*" Kathy shrieked. "Are you out here?"

Alsop jolted from his chair. "What's wrong?"

Kathy scurried into the yard, her cheeks streaked with mascara. "Miss Iris and Will—an accident! Down the hill!"

"My God!"

"I was right behind them," Kathy said. "We'll take my car."

Bucky jumped to his feet, throwing aside his beer and fried chicken. "I'm coming, too."

They sprinted around the house toward the front.

"I'll call an ambulance," a woman hollered from the porch.

Kathy jabbered hysterically all the way down the hill. "Oh, those poor souls! I think they're dead! The windshield—God, please, no!"

They rounded a bend. Ahead, a car's taillights glowed in the dim moonlight. Will must've missed a turn and gone straight off the road and into a tree. Bucky's stomach shriveled. No one could survive such a wreck.

Kathy pulled over. They all scrambled out into the cold, star-filled night and ran to the scene. The engine, its radiator hissing a dying breath, had rammed into the passenger compartment, crushing both Will and Miss Iris's midsections. Her head had smashed through the windshield, an unrecognizable glob of bloody flesh and shattered bone. A box of Whitman Candies lay scattered at her feet. Bucky yelped, barely dared to glance at Will's skull bashed against the DeSoto's cracked steering wheel. His mind fogged up.

Alsop winced. Kathy put a hand to her mouth and groaned through her fingers then wheeled around and threw up on her red party dress.

"Oh, God!" Bucky exclaimed when his brain kicked in again. "How could this happen?"

Acid crept up in his throat. He worried he would barf, too, but it went away. He shuffled to the rear of the car and stared at the tire tracks in the dirt, following them to the street. *What the—*

He crouched for a closer look. *Holy shit!*

The Internet? Never heard of it. Smart Phones? Who you kiddin'? We're talkin' 1956.

Energetic and eager to make his mark on what *Time Magazine* called the next great boom town, Bucky Ontario leaves his Louisiana home and hops a bus to Defiance, Oklahoma—a town not particularly averse to murders, just to the embarrassment of them.

While helping his friend, Kindra, search for a ring that once belonged to her dead mother, Bucky is told:

"Find the baby, find the ring."

KUDOS for *The Killer Who Hated Soup*

"Like reluctant amateur sleuth Bucky, the reader's lured to and quickly charmed by prospering Defiance, Oklahoma, until the glitz flakes off in the face of murder and mayhem. Brier does a fabulous job recreating the '50s atmosphere as an exciting backdrop for sinister events and shady dealings. He keeps us guessing to the bitter end." ~ Edith Parzefall, author of the *Hangman of Nuremburg* historical mystery series

"Brier's launch of his '50s, small-town Oklahoma mystery series is both chilling and refreshingly different. Filled with fast-paced action and delightful devil-may-care, good ol' country rednecks, this intriguing and oftentimes humorous mystery is one you won't unravel until the end. Get ready to laugh, shake your head, and bite your nails—all at the same time." ~ Pepper O'Neal author of the award-winning *Black Ops Chronicles* series

The Killer Who Hated Soup placed third in the Southwest Writers 2013 contest for mysteries and was shortlisted for finalist in the 2015 Faulkner Creative Writing Competition.

THE KILLER WHO HATED SOUP

THE KILLER WHO SERIES
BOOK 1

BILL A. BRIER

A Black Opal Books Publication

GENRE: PSYCHOLOGICAL SUSPENSE/MYSTERY/THRILLER

This is a work of fiction. Names, places, characters and incidents are either the product of the author's imagination or are used fictitiously, and any resemblance to any actual persons, living or dead, businesses, organizations, events or locales is entirely coincidental. All trademarks, service marks, registered trademarks, and registered service marks are the property of their respective owners and are used herein for identification purposes only. The publisher does not have any control over or assume any responsibility for author or third-party websites or their contents.

THE
KILLER
WHO HATED
SOUP

PROLOGUE

Defiance, Oklahoma, December 1956:

The girl tore through the woods with her baby. Ignoring her bleeding feet, she raced until she slipped on loose leaves and crashed into a shrub, dropping the newborn. Stunned, she lay still in the biting cold and heard her father yelling and bursting through the brush behind her. She snatched up the wailing baby and held her hand to its mouth. Dashing through undergrowth that tore at her bare legs, she broke through onto the road leading to the highway, hesitated, turned, and threw herself across the open stretch and into the shrubbery. She clawed through thick, thorny blackberry bushes, trying to protect the baby as she moved through the brush. She came out onto a narrow path that she knew would lead back to her hiding place in the burnt-out hollow of an oak tree.

Weakening now, she sucked in air with a loud, rasping noise. Her muscles ached, her legs trembled. She heard her father fighting through the blackberry bushes, and, with her remaining strength, she flung herself forward.

She reached the oak and scrambled inside. Pulled up her nightshirt, pressed her baby's mouth to her nipple, and tried to quiet her own breathing. Minutes later, her heart still pounding, she heard the crunching sound as footsteps approached then stopped.

"Come on out, Marybeth. I know you're in there." His voice softened. "Everything's okay."

She peered through tangled branches into the starry sky. "You'll take my baby."

Darkness swept across like a curtain. Hands reached in and wrenched the infant from her grasp.

She scrambled from the tree and clawed at her father's shirt, reaching for her baby held beyond her grasp. "*No. You'll give it away.*"

"God will forgive you, my daughter."

CHAPTER 1

January 1957:

Bucky grabbed his coat and camera, mounted his motorcycle, and headed toward the Chrysler dealership. The cold air stung his face like porcupine pricks, and it felt electrical. He loved the outdoors, and he loved Defiance. It was his kind of town—a town primed for growth. A town where folks were friendly and waved to one another. Where they drove fast in town to show off their cars or pickups and slow on the highway to save gas. Where a cashier would start a detailed conversation about anything from paving sidewalks to building racetracks when someone only wanted to buy gas and enjoy a Nehi pop.

Bucky stopped before his reflection in the showroom window. He pulled a comb from a back pocket, and, with bent knees and an upward turn of his wrist, set his blond hair into a front curl. He blew warm air into his cold and tingling hands, removed the lens cap from the camera hanging around his neck, and padded into the dealership.

He drifted among the cars, pausing to examine a grille, or three, and run his hand across slick leather seats. Would he ever be able to afford cars like these? Right now, he couldn't pay for a new motorcycle. His gaze fixed on the eggshell-tinted Plymouth Fury. He backed up, lifted his camera, and clicked off a shot, then sauntered into the sales office, aware that the owner, Cal Alsop, had been watching him.

Alsop jumped to his feet with a grin that flashed dollar signs. "Good morning, sir. I see you have an eye for fine cars."

"That's why I'm here." Bucky threw out a hand. "My name's Bucky, and I want to sell them for you."

Alsop's smile dropped like the price of last year's Chrysler Imperial. "Well, now, I—I—What'd you say your name was?"

"Bucky, Bucky Ontario."

Alsop cocked his head and squinted. He had a square jaw, black hair neat and trim. Seemed young, barely over thirty. About a decade older than Bucky and with an inch more height, which put him at six feet. "Now I recognize you. You work at Gustafson's Grocery."

"Not anymore. I…um…I was fired."

"Fired! That's hardly a recommendation, then, is it?" Alsop sat down. "You might as well have a seat."

Bucky swiftly did so, in case Alsop changed his mind. He sat straight, his hands on his kneecaps. He really needed this job—the vital next step in his dream of someday becoming the town mayor, a man of influence and value.

"Mr. Gustafson offered to promote me to manager, but when I told him I couldn't accept the position because now that I was twenty-one—my birthday was last week—I'd be quitting soon. So he fired me. You see, I never intended the grocery business as my life's work."

Alsop rubbed one hand on the back of the other. "Is that so?"

"It was a stepping stone to what I really want."

"Mind closing the door?" Alsop withdrew a cigar from a humidor. "Don't want the smell to chase away any lady customers." He struck a match on the side of his desk near a picture of a blonde with a sparkling Doris Day smile. Bucky recognized her from the grocery. "You saw the sign in the window and figured you'd like to sell cars?"

Bucky's heart fluttered with hope. "Mr. Al*sop*—" He felt his Louisiana accent kick in. "—it's more than that. Working at the grocery, I got to know the townspeople and establish myself—I'm pretty sure—in a good light. Now I need to move on. Selling your cars on commission will make me a businessman, not just a salesman."

A faint smile crossed Alsop's lips. He sat back and puffed. "Tell me more."

"There's money to be made selling cars. Next to houses, cars are people's most expensive purchase. On average, they'll buy a new one every three years. Take that Belvedere." On a roll now, Bucky pointed to the showroom. "Quad headlights, dual four-barrel carb. Your Fury beats the pants off GM's Corvette and leaves Ford's T-bird coughing dust. I don't know about your agency, but nationally, Chrysler sales are down this year—due, of course, to lousy marketing and ineffective sales strategies. Fact is, Chrysler makes cars with style and quality." Bucky placed both hands on the desk and leaned in. "Cars I can sell." If only Alsop let him.

Alsop twirled his cigar ash into a piston-shaped aluminum ashtray and smiled but didn't look too impressed. "What's your idea of an effective sales strategy?"

"Statistically, eighty percent of new car sales come from repeat customers or referrals. If I consider every customer a friend, he won't forget me. Volume's the second thing. The trick is to sell more cars than just one at a time." With the weak point of his argument coming up, he gazed at his shoeshine. "Haven't figured exactly how, but I will." He met the man's gaze. "How about it, Mr. Alsop, what do you say?"

Alsop leaned back, squinted again, and puffed his cigar. Bucky studied his face, unable to read a reaction. Finally, Alsop stood. "We'll do a trial basis. You sell three cars next week, and the job's permanent. But I warn you, it won't be easy." He extended his hand. "Be here at ten o'clock Monday morning. You'll work with Sam, an old timer. Been selling cars since the Depression." Alsop scribbled something on a pad and handed the note to Bucky. "Here's my home address. If you're free, drop by this evening. I'm throwing a little party for my shop foreman, Will Chambers. He's just returning to work after having surgery."

"Sure, I know Will. Thanks, Mr. Alsop. I'll be there." A new job *and* an invite to the boss's house the same day. This was going better than he had even hoped! His chest swelled with pride and happy anticipation.

cɔɛɔ

Bucky had a new job and a new sports coat.

He checked his fingernails to make sure he'd removed all the grease after changing his motorcycle's spark plug. The bike was actually a piece of crap, especially with its busted muffler, but it got him around. It was small and had a cartoon quality to it, a wacky, poke-'em-in-the-eye sense of mischief. He threw a leg over the seat, and it creaked like an old saddle. Off he drove, his sports coat fluttering. After two years of clerking at Gustafson's Grocery, he was now a businessman. Step two of his plan to move up the ranks. Sell three cars in one week? He could do that…somehow. He'd always managed to succeed once he put his mind to it, and finding work in Defiance was no exception.

He thought back to that bittersweet goodbye to his daddy and kid sister, Cassidy, and the hot and humid bus journey from Louisiana to Defiance. He'd loved every sweaty minute of it. The miles of open fields of cotton, corn, and wheat; the countless cattle ranches, like those he'd seen only in movies. The temperature had reached ninety-nine in Defiance when he jumped off the Greyhound bus, shirtless, his chest golden as a new penny. The very next day, his new neighbor, Miss Iris, landed him the job at Gustafson's.

It would be great meeting Alsop's wife at his party, getting acquainted in a social atmosphere, where people are relaxed. Dale Carnegie said in his book, *How to Win Friends and Influence People,* that a successful businessman is friendly to everyone, especially the boss's wife. It probably didn't say the wife part, but just the same, it was good advice.

Cars lined the street and clogged the driveway of Alsop's single-story redbrick home. Above the entrance hung a banner: *Welcome back, Will.* Bucky parked on the street's steep downhill slope behind a nicely polished '52 DeSoto the color of canned peas. A "for sale" sign sat on the back seat.

Bucky jaunted up a walkway lined with flowers. A sign on the door said *Come on in.* Bucky restyled his front curl and stepped inside the living room crowded with people and chatter. Toasty air carried the scent of sweet pine from the fireplace.

A woman approached him, a friendly smile lighting up her peach-colored cheeks. "Welcome to the party. You must be Bucky."

"And you're Mrs. Alsop." She really did look like Doris Day. He flashed his best smile and handed her one of the two boxes of chocolates he'd bought at Woolworths. "The other box is for Miss Iris. A surprise."

"Why thank you, Bucky. Call me Jo-Dee. I understand you know Will through his sister, Miss Iris."

"We live in the same building. Often we sit out in the backyard together, and I teach her birdcalls. She's really good. On Sundays, she cooks dinner for Will and me."

Jo-Dee looked at the camera hanging from his neck. "How nice—you'll take pictures. My ear tells me you grew up farther south. Louisiana, maybe?"

Bucky nodded. "Gulf Coast. My daddy's a fourth generation shrimper. I would have been the fifth, but the big boys have taken over the industry. That's why I left." And with a heavy heart.

Bucky sprouted from a proud family who rode the bayous and coastal waters of Louisiana the way cowpunchers rode the Oklahoma range. His momma wore white fishing boots under her wedding dress.

Jo-Dee smiled again. "I like it when men call their fathers daddy. I'm from Mississippi. How did you happen to settle here, in Defiance?"

"*Time* magazine had a list of the next six boomtowns. So I closed my eyes and picked." A gentle hand touched his shoulder.

"Howdy, neighbor," came a familiar high-pitched rusty voice, followed by a warm and hardy laugh.

Bucky turned to see Miss Iris, round faced and rosy cheeked. "Well, fancy meeting you here," he said and winked.

If Joe-Dee looked like Doris Day, Miss Iris looked like Ma of *Ma and Paw Kettle*. Brown hair parted down the middle and curled up in front. She had on a blue flowered dress that fit her five-foot, square body like a colorful gunnysack. As always, she looked full of good spirit. He handed her the box of chocolates.

"Why, thank you, Bucky." She glanced to be sure they were creams only. She didn't want her false teeth broken to bits on walnuts or anything. "I'll share them with Sunday's Bible class."

Bucky had read the Bible growing up, and it offered lots of good advice. So did the Dale Carnegie book his daddy had given him as a going away present. The book said the cornerstone of winning friends and influencing people was being honest and sincere. Bucky had made that one of his life's goals. It was probably in the Bible, too.

"Cal's serving drinks at the bar, and there's plenty of food in the kitchen," Jo-Dee said. She left.

Miss Iris leaned in close to Bucky. "Will told me that Cal was impressed with how you handled yourself in the interview this morning. Also, don't tell Cal, he'll find out soon enough, but just today, Will bought a used car," she whispered. "Private party."

"How's he doing? You know, his prostate operation and all."

She closed her eyes, shaking her head. "He's doing fine. It's his drinking I worry about."

Bucky wandered into the den where Alsop poured drinks for an invigorated group. Maybe his booze had more kick than the backyard brew Bucky's daddy whipped up at parties.

"Glad you could make it, Bucky," Alsop said. "What can I do you for?"

"A Hamm's would be great." Bucky liked the beer commercial on TV and tapped out a drumbeat on the bar. With his beer, he ambled into the living room where Will had undone his belt buckle and was showing off his scar to a group of wary onlookers. Miss Iris was old, but her brother was *really* old.

"Lost a hell of a lot of blood," Will slurred. "Picked me up a bladder problem along the way." He grabbed his bulging crotch. "That's why I wear this here diaper. No more beer for me, thanks. Already had ten." He laughed with his mouth as wide as it would go, and everyone lurched back like he was radioactive. He looked at Bucky but was too drunk to recognize him.

Miss Iris took Will's arm. "Let's get you some hot soup and then we'll leave."

Bucky followed them into the kitchen to take pictures. It smelled of clam chowder and fried chicken. Those drinking the most, mugged the most. He snapped a shot of a man with a chrome hook for a hand and still managing to hold his beer with it, then he turned his camera toward Kansas, another fella he knew from Gustafson's, who was standing near the back door and scratching his ass like a baboon.

"Get that goddamn camera away from me!" Kansas growled, stepping closer, waving his beer and splashing it. "Who the hell are you to get up in my business?"

"Relax, Kansas," the man with the hook piped up at Bucky's elbow. "He's just taking pictures of the party."

"Well, he better take pictures of someone else, or I'll put the camera where the sun don't shine."

"Hey! It's not a big deal," Bucky said, feeling his own temper rise but refusing to let it get the better of him. He couldn't get involved in a scene here at his new boss's house.

A fireplug sort of man waddled up. "Don't worry about him none. He's always a pain in the ass. You must be Bucky. I'm Sam. Glad to meet you."

So, this was his new cohort, fleshy and pink-faced. Alsop had said he'd sold cars since the Depression.

Sam threw out a hand that Bucky caught. The smell of whiskey wafted from his mouth on a stream of words. "Welcome aboard, son."

"Thanks, Sam. Some party."

"You ain't seen nothin' yet. Listen, young fella. I'll

tell you a trade secret." He planted a forearm, heavy as an iron bar, on Bucky's shoulder. "In the car business, there's no such thing as browsing." He downed a gulp of drink. "And another thing, comparison shopping is counterproductive. So are principles. Try to keep those to a minimum."

Bucky felt embarrassed for Sam being so open about unscrupulous trade secrets, but what the hell—good stuff to know. "I'll do my best." He backed up, freeing his shoulder and trying to extricate himself from the room, but Sam kept talking.

"One more piece of advice, Buck. Never talk about the price of a car. Break the numbers into easy-to-digest monthly payments. Stating the price only weakens your position. And if the car is used, your position is already weakened by having to show it to the customer up close—don't make things worse."

Jo-Dee walked past, balancing a tray of empty glasses. "I'm sure he'll figure it all out, Sam."

Sam staggered toward Bucky with an eye on his shoulder. "Did you hear the one about the guy who goes into a bank and says, give me all your money, this is a—"

Banging erupted from down a hallway. "Let me outta this bathroom, goddamnit!"

"Oh, my gosh!" Jo-Dee exclaimed, darting from the kitchen.

The banging became violent. "Open this damned door," a thick voice bellowed from inside, "or I'll kick it open."

Bucky followed Jo-Dee in case he could help. The door shuddered as if being throttled by a demon inside. She turned the knob and opened the door. "Josh! Are you all right?"

A bug-eyed man with hair like Einstein's grandmother came stumbling out. A woman appeared from the hallway, her face a mask of worry. She draped a gentle arm around his shoulder, as if comforting a frightened child. "It's me, honey. You've just had too much to drink." She turned to Jo-Dee. "He'll be fine," she said softly before leading him down the hallway.

Jo-Dee leaned against the wall, hand to her forehead. "Cal has *got* to fix that doorknob."

The man with the hook spoke up, "Thought I fixed it earlier, but I guess not. Josh served in the marines. Korea. Spent six months in a hole. No wonder he doesn't take to locked doors."

Looking stricken, JoDee headed toward the kitchen.

Bucky paced back into the den, shivering at the thought of being locked in a hole. He introduced himself to Kathy, Alsop's secretary, complimented her on her red dress and caught himself eyeing the top of her bulging breasts.

"We look forward to having you with us." She glanced at her watch and sighed. "Still early, but I have to leave. Nice to meet you, Bucky."

For a moment, he wondered if his stare had scared her away, but a woman like Kathy, dressed so invitingly, had to be used to them. Then he swung by the kitchen to fix a plate of fried chicken and potato salad before dropping by the bar for another Hamm's. Pretty good turnout. He'd see what the backyard was like. He opened the door and stepped out onto the moonlit porch.

Someone whistled. "Bucky, over here." Alsop was sitting by the garage with a bowl of soup.

"Oh, there you are." Bucky snagged a lawn chair and dragged it alongside.

Alsop lit up a cigar. "Care for one?"

"No, thanks. Tried one once on my daddy's shrimp boat before heaving over the side. He said I turned green."

Alsop chuckled. "He gave it to you, did he?"

"I was nine."

A coyote made a long plaintive cry in the distance. Alsop rolled his cigar between his thumb and finger, staring at the glowing tip. "Sorry about Kansas giving you a hard time in the kitchen. Heard the ruckus even in the den."

Bucky was used to Kansas. He'd limp into the store with Marybeth, his young teenage daughter, park her in the magazine section, and throw out orders. Fetch five pounds of potatoes, get this, get that. Bucky had always felt like telling him to shove it, but that's not exactly the way to win friends and influence people.

Alsop puffed his cigar and blew out a thin stream of smoke, then said, "He had his hopes on becoming shop foreman."

Bucky took a swig of beer. "Don't tell me he was hoping Will would die from his prostate cancer."

"Was counting on it. Made a bet with Josh, another mechanic, that he'd be gone by Thanksgiving." Alsop eyed the camera hanging from Bucky's neck and nodded. "That's a quality camera you've got there. Don't see many of those; mostly everyone has Brownies. You any good with it?"

"I've had lots of practice. Had a paper route when I was in junior high and saved up. Bought this camera and been taking pictures ever since. Won a photo contest once. Even have my own darkroom."

Alsop scooted his chair closer. "Listen, it'll be the state's fiftieth birthday soon, and the mayor and I are planning a special ceremony. It's not official, and I haven't cleared it with the other council members yet, so I can't divulge details. But if you'd be interested in documenting the event with photographs, I'd front your costs."

Bucky's heart pumped like a piston. "Absolutely.

What do you mean, clear it with the council?"

"We're meeting on Monday. The entire plan hinges on selling it to my council cohorts." He put a finger to his lips. "Not a word. But I'll tell you this, if my resolution passes, your pictures will be famous one day."

Bucky leaned back, looked up at the stars, and sipped his beer. Yes, siree, his future was looking real bright.

The rear porch light came on, and a screen door banged open. "*Cal!*" Kathy shrieked. "Are you out here?"

Alsop jolted from his chair. "What's wrong?"

Kathy scurried into the yard, her cheeks streaked with mascara. "Miss Iris and Will—an accident! Down the hill!"

"My God!"

"I was right behind them," Kathy said. "We'll take my car."

Bucky jumped to his feet, throwing aside his beer and fried chicken. "I'm coming, too."

They sprinted around the house toward the front.

"I'll call an ambulance," a woman hollered from the porch.

Kathy jabbered hysterically all the way down the hill. "Oh, those poor souls! I think they're dead! The windshield—God, please, no!"

They rounded a bend. Ahead, a car's taillights glowed in the dim moonlight. Will must've missed a turn and gone straight off the road and into a tree. Bucky's stomach shriveled. No one could survive such a wreck.

Kathy pulled over. They all scrambled out into the cold, star-filled night and ran to the scene. The engine, its radiator hissing a dying breath, had rammed into the passenger compartment, crushing both Will and Miss Iris's midsections. Her head had smashed through the windshield, an unrecognizable glob of bloody flesh and shattered bone. A box of Whitman Candies lay scattered at her feet. Bucky yelped, barely dared to glance at Will's skull bashed against the DeSoto's cracked steering wheel. His mind fogged up.

Alsop winced. Kathy put a hand to her mouth and groaned through her fingers then wheeled around and threw up on her red party dress.

"Oh, God!" Bucky exclaimed when his brain kicked in again. "How could this happen?"

Acid crept up in his throat. He worried he would barf, too, but it went away. He shuffled to the rear of the car and stared at the tire tracks in the dirt, following them to the street. *What the—*

He crouched for a closer look. *Holy shit!*

CHAPTER 2

Bucky's eyes flicked open wide. He sat up and stared ahead, his T-shirt soaked, his pulse pounding in his ears. He'd rolled around all night, dreaming he was at a carnival looking through a peephole into a box with a crank. As he turned the crank, a succession of pictures flashed by. Horrible, grisly pictures of Will and Miss Iris, dead in their car.

He shook his head to clear his mind of the gruesome images, got up, splashed water on his face, and turned on the heater. Warming up, it started a deafening symphony of clangs and rattles, as if a colony of mice had constructed a high-speed rail network in the hot water pipes. Clang! Clang! Clang!

He lived in a two-story, turn-of-the-century, clapboard boarding house on Lower Fifth Street. City councilman Maynard Johnston had bought the large home after the war, and it hadn't seen a lick of paint since the Battle of the Bulge. Johnston divided it into eight equal size units. Like a piece of paper folded three times and then opened and laid flat. Bucky's unit occupied the converted downstairs rear kitchen. Miss Iris lived in the lower front.

Bucky stared out the window. Two newspapers lay in the driveway. His and Miss Iris's. He had always picked up both papers and dropped hers onto her porch. Oh, God! How the hell could such a thing happen? She was like a grandmother to him. Made him cookies and…and like his real grandma met a grisly, violent death. He wiped the tears starting to roll down his cheeks, shuffled to the sink, and poured a glass of water. Drank it and glanced at the phone. *The police. Maybe they've learned something.* He took a deep breath and dialed.

"Chief Parker's office. Mrs. Rheingold speaking."

"Mrs. Rheingold, this is Bucky. You know, from Gustafson's. Is the chief in?"

"Hello, Bucky. Such a tragedy. I know you and Miss Iris were very close. I'm so sorry." Her voice cracked, and she cleared her throat. "I'll put the chief on."

"Chief Parker, here." He sounded very official.

"Chief, this is Bucky Ontari—"

"I know who you are, Bucky. What can I do for you?"

Bucky's throat tightened. "I'm wondering what you've learned about the accident. You know, last night."

"Nothing yet. We had a big rig jackknife on the Eighty-One early this morning that's kept us busy. I'm going to the coroner's soon. I'll let you know what I find out."

"I'd like to come along if you don't mind."

"Won't be necessary," the chief said, not sharp but quick. "I'll keep in touch."

"Well…okay." Bucky wanted to tell him he'd like to go anyway, but didn't think the chief would let him. "Up at the crash site, did you notice there were no skid marks?"

A pause. "You sure? It was pretty dark out there."

"I'm positive. I checked closely." Crap! Shoulda taken a picture.

"I'll go back up and check again in the daylight."

"I'd really appreciate it if you'd let me know when you learn something."

∽∾∽

Bucky had spent the rest of Saturday sticking around the house, working on his motorcycle, and feeling pretty shitty. By Sunday noon, he needed to get out and do something. Earlier that morning, he had developed and printed the party pictures. Two shots were left on the roll, and rather than waste them, he decided to head out and find an interesting subject to photograph. Getting out of the house would also keep him from obsessing about his departed neighbor, and taking pictures always made him feel good, especially when he was out in nature. He could focus his mind on the shot in front of him and float away from his everyday problems.

Bucky always kept a sharp eye out for interesting subjects to photograph. A shot of a Nash Rambler had earned him first place in a contest. It showed two cows sticking their heads out the car's rear window.

Riding along a country road under a rose-colored sky, Bucky remembered a couple of shots he hadn't yet printed: a bum behind the bus depot gulping from a brown bag, and a city worker taping off a rectangular shape on the courthouse lawn. He'd print them along with those on the current roll.

He cruised passed an abandoned roadster. A mile or so later, he came upon an energetic stranger in a dark suit walking along, whistling, arms swinging. For the hell of it, Bucky pulled alongside. "Howdy, mister." The man must have been in a hurry, but mischief prodded Bucky to add, "Out for a stroll?"

The lanky man stopped and cupped his ear like he was standing next to an airport runway.

Bucky killed his fiery engine. "I said, enjoying the outdoors?"

"Oh," the man said, removing his fedora and running a hand through a thick crop of curly brown hair. "Hate to admit it, but I ran out of gas."

The fella had probably been listening to the radio and forgot to keep an eye on his gas gauge. "There's an old 'thirty-five Ford Roadster parked back a ways. That yours?"

"Yep, and I'm looking for a filling station."

"There's a Texaco just up the road." Bucky introduced himself and offered his hand. As an up-and-coming businessman, he had studied the correct firmness of a handshake. Too light, and one appeared wimpish. Too hard, brutish. Too short, disinterested. Holding too long made the person question the guy's motives.

The man reached out a long arm. "Peter Thomas, reporter, *Oklahoma City Free Press*." He shook hands like he was pumping water, but the firmness felt okay. He spotted Bucky's Rolleiflex hanging from his neck. "Some camera you've got there." The man rubbed his arms in the cold. "Mind if we keep moving?"

Bucky would have offered him a ride, but his 125cc Norman motorcycle was too small. He wasn't in a hurry, and since this stretch was downhill, he'd coast along and shoot the breeze. "What brings you to town, Peter?"

"I'm covering your Defiance's commemoration."

"Commemoration? Never heard of it." While the words tumbled from his mouth, Bucky realized that must be the secret ceremony Alsop wanted photographed.

"Well, you will," Peter said. "But keep it under your hat. This is my first out-of-town assignment, and I don't want to get in trouble. I got a tip Friday from your mayor that they're going to bury a time capsule. That's all I can say."

Bucky's heart sped up. *A time capsule—cool!*

"Any good motels around?"

"Holiday Inn up on Simpson Road might be okay. Pretty new. TV and rust-free water. Probably no bedbugs yet."

They reached the station, and Bucky took a picture of Peter filling a gas can. The reporter held his head back, like he was allergic to fumes. Bucky mounted his motorcycle and waved *so long*. A nice guy.

Burying a time capsule, were they? He wondered where. Alsop said he had to sell the project to the council at tomorrow's meeting. Bucky would keep his fingers crossed.

With one picture left on the roll, he decided to take a new route home. Following Valley Spring Lane along a creek for about a mile, he turned onto a narrow road, expecting it to loop back but found himself on the upper ridge of a wooded area of old oak and red cedar.

He got off his motorcycle and gazed down the slope. The orange rays of the setting sun cut through the trees. The air held a faint scent of burning wood. He'd climb down and maybe find a roosting screech owl. Back home, he'd explored all the time. Liked drifting along the bayou in his canoe. You saw lots of interesting sights, just drifting. Once he witnessed two alligator snapping turtles mating. They could weigh over a hundred pounds and had such good smellers they were used to find human corpses. Usually murdered—usually colored. But ever since his grandmother died, he didn't even like hearing the word gator.

The wind picked up, and he was thankful for his coat. Sheila, his old girlfriend from back home, had given it to him for his eighteenth birthday. He appreciated the fur lining. In return, she'd used his old jacket to line her dog basket.

Leaving his motorcycle at the roadside, he descended the soggy slope with its pungent smell of decayed leaves and passed through pockets of cold, still air. About a hundred yards ahead, behind trees and foliage, sat a cabin. Smoke oozed from its chimney. Still no owls, but the cabin looked interesting.

He buttoned his collar and ambled on, stepping carefully on slippery leaves. He inched his way between gnarly patches of blackberry bushes. Grackles squawked overhead, black dots against an orange sky.

Weeds blanketed the cabin's front area. A shovel and girl's bicycle lay in the dirt near the porch. Between the house and a neglected garden, a girl knelt on the ground, her back to him, shoulders trembling.

He maneuvered his way behind a thick oak, only a few feet from her. *Well, blow me over.* It was Kansas's teenage daughter, Marybeth. And she was crying. She looked different out here than in the store reading magazines. In the sun's low rays, her red hair seemed brighter, as if on fire.

She propped up a small stuffed giraffe onto a mound of dirt, and tears dripped off her nose. What a cool shot. He quietly opened his camera's viewfinder, his finger on the release. He hesitated. It seemed so personal.

"Hey!"

Bucky flinched and clicked the shutter.

"What the *hell* you doin'?" boomed a voice from behind. Bucky whirled. It was Kansas, Marybeth's father. Stern and unshaven to the whites of his eyes, he held a rifle and a dead rabbit by its ears.

Bucky's heart leaped to his throat. "I—I just happened by, and—"

"You just happen your nosy ass off my property." Kansas cocked his rifle. "And don't come back or you'll spend the rest of your life dead."

Marybeth bolted toward the house like a deer.

"Sure, Kansas." Bucky sidestepped around the man's bulk and scurried up the slope. He glanced back to see Kansas scowling, the rifle held level at his hip.

Bucky rode back over the pebbled road, fenders and nerves rattling. When caught off guard, Kansas could be downright scary. But the weird part was Marybeth. Long after he left Kansas's property behind, he still couldn't get the image of her crying out of his head.

CHAPTER 3

alf Chance Bridge lay ahead, short and narrow. Bucky had read that in the '30s, President Roosevelt's Civilian Conservation Corps had replaced the original footbridge built by local Cheyenne Indians entirely of bark rope and wood. Back then, it lacked hand supports, and travelers in gusty winds had half a chance of tumbling into the river.

Crossing the bridge on this Monday morning under a dome of blue sky, Bucky spotted a policeman on the other side, standing by his motorcycle and pissing into a winterberry shrub, only partially sheltered by willows. The officer glanced over. Bucky waved and sailed past.

"Hey! Hold up, you!"

Bucky turned his head, and the cop motioned him back. Damn! That's all he needed, a speeding ticket on his first day at a new job. There wasn't even a posted speed limit. Maybe he could talk his way out of it. He made a U-turn and pulled up alongside the policeman zipping his pants. His badge said Deputy Chief Harman, and his motorcycle was civilian. About thirty and skinny, he wore tight-fitting blue slacks and a flat face.

"And where might you be rushing off to, lookin' all polished for the dance?"

Bucky didn't care much for the officer's sarcastic attitude, but he flashed a friendly smile anyhow. "No dance. Just off to work."

"Ain't that a coincidence? Me, too."

"Salesman. First day. Alsop Chrysler Plymouth Motors."

The cop made his eyes big. Very dramatic. "Well, aren't you special?" He circled Bucky's motorcycle, strutting, checking it over.

Bucky rubbed a perfectly circular area of smooth skin on his face. A marsh mosquito had bitten him there, and ever since he'd never had to shave it. Occasionally he found himself rubbing it when he felt uneasy about someone.

"I'm afraid I'll have to write you up for—"

"There's no posted speed limit."

"Mind—if—I—finish?" The officer emphasized each word with a hard tap to Bucky's chest. "Write you up for operating a motorcycle without proper noise abatement."

Bucky blinked. "You mean the muffler?"

"You can't ride around disturbin' folks. Hurts their ears. Besides, we got laws, and it's your civic responsibility to follow those laws."

Like those prohibiting public urination? Bucky glanced at his watch's florescent dial. Ten to ten. He needed to get going. "You're right, Officer. The thing is, the muffler just recently developed a hole, and I haven't had a chance to fix it. But I will, promise. Maybe you could consider this a warning, and I'll be on my way?"

The cop threw his head back and looked down his nose at Bucky. "I suppose I could let it slide this time." He raised a finger. "But you're on my radar, so I suggest you get on it pronto. And, just so we're clear, I'm not asking. Just being nice about it. Now here's a piece of advice. Don't get too chummy with your co-worker, short-eyes Kansas. I'll be puttin' the gimp away soon enough."

"Short-eyes?"

Harman grinned. "Child molester."

Child molester! Why, Cassidy was only twelve. The thought of anyone hurting his sister—or any little girl—churned his stomach. "How do you know that?"

"I've got evidence," Harman said assuredly and puffed out his chest.

Bucky wanted to learn more, but a glance at his watch warned him he'd be late if he didn't get moving. He bid goodbye to the officer and jumped back on his motorcycle, careful to be extra aware of the rules of the road until he was out of the cop's sight. But what Harman had said lingered with him. Short eyes. Child molester. Maybe he made it up just to look good. But what if he was right, and Marybeth had been crying last night because of what her own father did to her?

❧❧❧

Bucky parked his motorcycle in back near a stack of old tires between the showroom and the service department. The bike looked pretty crummy with its rusted fenders and all. Best to keep it out of customers' sight.

He paced around to the front entrance, thinking of Deputy Chief Harman. He probably didn't even have his ticket book with him since he was on his way to work. So full of himself. That was something, though, him saying Kansas was a child molester. If the cop wasn't such a jerk, Bucky might have told him about Marybeth crying.

Bucky checked his reflection in the large glass door. Shoes shined, tan slacks, neat and pressed, front hair curl, perfect. He unbuttoned his green and red plaid sports coat and strode inside.

The showroom smelled of fresh paint, new tires, and

something new in luxury cars—leather seats. He weaved his way through the sparkling vehicles toward the back. Alsop's office light was off.

"Hello, Bucky," came Kathy's voice from down a hallway. Her high heels clicked on the polished concrete floor. At the accident, her face had been as white as her gleaming Pepsodent teeth. She seemed okay now.

"Hi, Kathy."

"Oh, Bucky. I still can't believe it." She shivered. "Awful, just awful. How are you doing?" She placed a hand on his back and directed him down the hall.

"It's hard, but I'm okay. Thanks."

Inside her office, she said, "Have a seat," and pulled employment forms from a cabinet.

"I'm mighty pleased to be working here," he said.

"Sam's mighty pleased, too. He prefers working part-time to retirement."

"What time's he come in?"

"He decided to take Mondays off, so you're on your own. Cal will be around, though."

The phone rang, and Kathy grabbed it. "Alsop Chrysler Plymouth Motors." She slid the forms in front of Bucky and jiggled them. "Yes, Mr. Mayor. I'm sorry, Mr. Alsop's not in. He—" She reached for a *While You Were Out* pad, scribbled and said, "—call you immediately after the council meeting. Got it."

On the wall, a picture showed Alsop accepting an award from the Chamber of Commerce for his accomplishments in *Driving the Town Forward*. Maybe he could teach Bucky how to move forward and become a councilman. One step short of becoming mayor, like his Uncle Rupert back home.

"Yes, sir," Kathy said. "The moment he gets in. Good day to—" She looked at the phone and stuck out her tongue, then hung up and patted her ash blonde hair. It swept up about four inches above her forehead and appeared glued in place.

The sound of heavy footsteps rumbled in the hallway. "Oops, that's him. I'll be right back." She tore the message from the pad and dashed off.

Bucky was digging through his wallet for his Social Security card when Alsop came in. "Mornin', Bucky. Welcome aboard." They shook hands quickly. "A goddamn tragedy. I still can't believe it. How you doin'? You okay?"

"Yes, thanks. I'm eager to get working. Helps keep the accident out of my mind."

Alsop took Bucky's shoulders and squeezed. "All right, then." He led Bucky to a small corner desk in the showroom. "This is yours. In the drawers, you'll find brochures, sales forms, prices, everything you'll need. See me or Kathy if you have questions."

Bucky sat down and ran his hands up and down his thighs. He had to start selling cars. Fast. He opened a phone book and was still flipping pages when Chief Parker tramped through the door, wearing sharply creased pants, a starched blue shirt, and a grave expression. Bucky's heart did a little rhythm. Maybe the chief had something to report.

"Hello, Bucky," the man said, his forehead creased like a washboard. "I understand you knew Miss Iris pretty well. That right?"

"Fairly well. We lived in the same building."

"Come with me, I want to talk to you and Cal."

Bucky trailed after him into Alsop's office. His new boss gestured for them to sit and raked a hand through his hair, his face crumpled. "I should never have let Will drink so much."

The chief frowned. "Alcohol didn't kill him," he said and removed his hat. "He and Miss Iris were murdered."

Bucky blinked. "*Murdered!* Jesus!"

"Someone cut his brake line. By the time he reached the steep stretch down the hill, the line was empty, and the brakes were useless."

Bucky felt a deep hard thud in his heart. "That's— that's unbelievable. I mean, who would do such a thing? And—and why?"

"Those are things I aim to find out. Cal, you knew him. Who had it in for him?" The chief pulled out a note-pad and ballpoint pen from his shirt pocket.

"Hell, I don't know."

The chief clicked his pen. "He worked for you, for chrissake. *Think.*"

"Will could be outlandish, but people liked him okay. I—I can't imagine."

"What about Kansas?" Bucky said. "You said he wanted Will's job."

"That's true. But to kill him for it?" Alsop sucked air between his teeth and shook his head.

"I'll note that," the chief said. "If he did it, I'll find out. Bucky, what about Miss Iris? She have any enemies, you know of?"

Enemies? He couldn't imagine that. "I doubt it. Do you think someone wanted her killed?"

"Anything's possible. Someone after an inheritance maybe. Like relatives. Know of any hanging around."

He raised his palms. "I—I—really wouldn't know."

"Cal, anyone else who could benefit from Will's death? Someone who knew how to tamper with brakes?"

Alsop shrugged.

"I'll check all that. Either of you see anything suspicious during the evening?"

Bucky and Alsop shook their heads.

"Cal, I'll need a list of everyone at your party, and I want to examine where Will parked his car."

"Across the street," Bucky said. "Right in line with Cal's front door. I parked behind him."

The chief stood and clicked his pen closed, tucking it away with his pad.

"Don't you want to question Kansas?" Bucky asked. "He was at the party, too."

"In due time. If either of you think of anything else, get back to me. So long, gentleman." Donning his hat, the chief marched out the door.

To Bucky, Kansas figured to be a prime suspect. "I'm just wondering," he said to Alsop, "did Kansas arrive before or after Will?"

"Before. He was one of the first to show up. He lit the fireplace."

"Who left first?"

"Will and Miss Iris. At the door, Kansas made a comment about Will having to change his diaper."

"Kansas might have left during the party, cut the brake line, and gone back in."

Alsop thought a moment. "Good point." He grabbed his armrests and pushed himself out of his chair. "I'm going to talk to him right now."

"I'd like to come along," Bucky said, getting up. This was no time to feel intimidated by a mechanic. Bucky was no longer a grocery clerk, taking orders from demanding customers. He'd stand up to him, if necessary.

They trooped out back to the repair shop. Dark rain clouds on the horizon would soon be rolling in.

Inside the shop, they almost collided with Kansas stepping out of the can and working the zipper of his pants.

"I want to talk to you," Alsop said.

Kansas frowned, his fuzzy eyebrows arching like a caterpillar. "Oh?"

Alsop pointed to a chair. "Sit down and stop making faces."

Kansas dropped into a chair at a desk cluttered with grease-smudged manuals, service orders, and a picture of Marybeth smiling and holding her junior high school diploma. Alsop dragged a chair over and sat.

Bucky, remaining on his feet, said, "Chief Parker paid us a visit a few minutes ago."

Kansas yanked out a rag from his pocket and wiped his hands. "He learn anything about the accident?"

Alsop narrowed his eyes. "It wasn't an accident."

Kansas's face tightened, impossible to read. "Whadaya mean?"

"I mean," Alsop said, "someone did surgery on Will's brake line."

Kansas pursed his lips. "Chief Parker say who?"

"He doesn't know," Alsop said coldly. "Yet."

Kansas clenched his jaw, and a muscle twitched near his temple. "I know what you think. I wanted Will's job. Wanted it real bad. Still do, but I'd never kill him for it. You've gotta believe that."

"Chief Parker's got to believe that," Alsop said. "As for Will's job, it stays unfilled for now."

Kansas was sounding pretty believable. Trying to think like Chief Parker, Bucky asked, "Do you know if Will had enemies?"

Kansas's fuzzy eyebrow arched a little higher this time. "Who asked you to stick your face in?"

"My face has nothing to do with it. My friends' murder does, so I'd appreciate an answer."

Kansas snorted like a horse clearing its nostrils. "Enemies? Who would hate an old fool like him?"

"The chief will question everyone at the party," Alsop said. "He'll ask you when you arrived. I know it was about fifteen minutes before Will. I also saw you leave after him."

"There you go. I couldn't have done it."

"Not so fast," Alsop said. "Did you leave the house anytime during the party?"

Kansas scowled. "You're poking your stick in the wrong hole."

Alsop narrowed his eyes again. "Are you saying you didn't leave the house?"

"Absolutely."

"Okay then," Alsop said. "Thanks for your help." He turned to Bucky and cocked his head toward the door.

On their way back to the office, Bucky said, "Kansas has a pretty solid story. I guess there's nothing anyone can do now except wait for Chief Parker to learn something. He any good at solving murder cases?"

"Tenacious as a fox at a rat hole. If he doesn't solve this one, he'll die trying."

Bucky found that comforting, in a grim sort of way, but right now, he had to get busy and meet this week's three-car quota.

And he knew just where to start.

CHAPTER 4

It was ten a.m. Monday when Alsop bounced up the courthouse steps and entered the second-floor jury room to attend the last city council meeting before the upcoming election. No pictures adorned the walls, as if a jury shouldn't be distracted from horrible crimes by pretty sights.

Alsop was the newest council member, but he had the oldest Oklahoma roots. His grandfather had settled here from Missouri when the state was spreading out and filling in. Defiance didn't have a council back then. Didn't have much of a police department, either. The only crimes to speak of were committed out of desperation. No one would arrest a man for stealing a loaf of bread to feed his family.

Oklahoma's fiftieth anniversary of statehood would arrive soon, and the council had wanted to celebrate the occasion but had dithered over ideas for months. No surprise there; these were the same men who'd held up a parking project for six weeks as they argued over parallel versus diagonal parking. Finally, Alsop had a brainchild that he ran by the mayor, who would have smiled if he knew how.

His popularity had slipped, and this event could generate enough publicity for Collins to win reelection and make the town famous.

The conservative council members, though, would chew rusty nails to prevent four more years of *commie-leaning* Jimmy Collins. That meant Alsop had to keep secret the $2,000 contribution the mayor made toward the project by tapping into his reelection fund. He'd pay it back soon enough, so there would be no harm done. It just wouldn't look good if it came to light right now.

Alsop, as rotating chairman, called the meeting to order and asked Lamar Fromm, secretary and local undertaker (or funeral director, as he preferred to be called), to read the minutes of the previous meeting. Doc Little resubmitted a motion for adding cement sidewalks on Upper Fifth Street. All but Maynard Johnston, landlord, owner of the Johnston Ranch, and sporting a bolo tie, seconded and approved it.

"But Maynard," City Manager Benjamin Horning said, "work will later commence on Lower Fifth Street."

Alsop smiled, knowing Johnston owned property there.

Johnston threw up his hands. "Okay, if it's that important to everyone, aye."

"Any other old business?" Alsop asked. After headshakes by everyone, he cleared his throat. He knew convincing the others might take some creativity, but he reminded himself that his plan was not just for the mayor, but also for the good of the whole town.

"Gentlemen," he began. "One unresolved issue remains on our agenda. The celebration of our state's birthday. Every city in Oklahoma will make a hullabaloo of this historic occasion and vie for the most press. I propose we top them all with something so spectacular that Defiance will be recognized as a town ahead of the times. A town with vision. We'll not only commemorate our fiftieth year of statehood, but arrange for its hundredth."

Lamar Fromm's head shot up from his note taking. "Huh?"

"We'll bury a time capsule in front of the courthouse, to stay sealed for fifty years. The site's already been staked off. The event will be noted with fanfare and ceremony. Drape a huge banner across the courthouse with a mass of balloons. The high school band will parade in their new uniforms. I'll contact the governor and—"

"Hold your horses," Maynard Johnston said. "What the hell do you mean, time capsule?"

Alsop grinned. "Thank you, Maynard. Got a little ahead of myself. Encased in this capsule will be a symbol of our great country, and there's no better symbol than an automobile. The 1957 Plymouth Belvedere will still be in style a half century from now."

Doc Little shook his head and grumbled, "Doesn't seem practical."

Horning, who'd been listening with eyebrows ready to rise, chimed in, "Let's get past the noodles and right to the meatballs. How much money we talkin'?"

"Detroit will practically donate the car," Alsop offered. "Cost us under a thousand dollars. We'll dig a hole and encase the car in concrete strong enough to withstand a damn Russian nuclear bomb. Hell, maybe we'll strike oil." A few chuckled. "We'll get newsreel cameras. Invite *Life Magazine* and maybe get our pictures on the cover."

"The pictures will be of Caddo people holding protest signs," Johnston grumbled. "They're troublemakers. Any chance those Indians get to demonstrate against our taking '*their*' land, they'll do it."

A. J. Farnsworth, editor of the *Prairie Duster,* countered, "Chief Parker's always done well keeping the Indians in line."

"This whole idea is practical as a Mayan handball

court," Johnston fired back. "The car will be a rust bucket in fifty years."

Fromm raised a forefinger. "Not if we weld the seams."

"We'll need to stimulate public interest," Horning said. He gazed at the ceiling in thought. "What about a contest? We get the townspeople to write down their guesses of something that won't be known until 2007."

"The town's *census*," Fromm yelped, his butt rising from the chair. "Everyone writes their guess on a post-card. They'll be sealed in the car, and the person with the closest one wins the car."

Horning guffawed. "More likely, the winner's next of kin."

Alsop could have kissed Fromm and Horning. "The car will rest on steel skids that my mechanic, Kansas Karradine, will build. He'll also wrap the car in a protective covering. Any other suggestions?"

Grocer Gus Gustafson spoke up, "We could place a few contemporary items in the car, a woman's purse, bobby pins, and um…"

"Tranquilizers," Doc Little suggested. "Always popular with the ladies."

"I know, I'll throw in a case of Falstaff," Gustafson offered.

"Hold on," Horning insisted, jumping back in. "Fifty years is a long time from now. Petroleum may be a thing of the past. I advise including an extra ten gallons of gasoline."

"I think we're ready to vote," Alsop submitted, riding the wave of enthusiasm.

"So moved," Horning said.

"Seconded," Farnsworth said.

"All in favor?"

"Aye," four men chimed.

"All opposed?"

"Hold the music," Johnston said. "No more gasoline? Poppycock. I suppose everyone here thinks folks in 2007 will fly around in jetpacks. Nay."

"The motion passes, meeting's adjourned." Alsop stood. "Good day, gentlemen." Now his only worry was Johnston getting a wild hair up his butt and causing trouble. But he was confident he could deal with that. The important thing was that his idea had passed. This would be great for Defiance. Folks were going to be talking about the event for a long, long time.

☙❧☙

Alsop had just smoked the last cigarette in his pack when the phone rang. Probably the mayor, eager to know if the proposal passed. Alsop answered in his distinct manner, "This*ss* is Cal."

"Did it pass?" Jo-Dee chirped.

"Enthusiastically. Johnston's unhappy, but we expected that."

"How wonderful. Would you please pick up two bottles of Squirt on your way home? We're all out."

"I planned to stop anyhow for—" He glanced at his empty cigarette pack. "—for charcoal."

"Oh, and Cal, you've *got* to replace the bathroom doorknob. It's acting up again."

He sighed. "The damn setscrew keeps loosening. That's why the knob spins on the shaft."

"For goodness's sake, buy a new one. Mother won't visit. And Josh—oh, that poor man being trapped in there."

"All right. I'll replace the goddamn thing." Alsop scribbled himself a note. "By the way, Will and Miss Iris's funeral is the day after tomorrow. Uh-oh, the mayor's here, got to go."

Jimmy Collins often strolled into Alsop's office and, a minute later, he'd have one butt cheek planted on the corner of Alsop's desk. This time he didn't stroll in—he stomped in, neck veins swollen like blue ropes. He shut the door and hissed, "Johnston's accused me of misappropriating campaign funds. How the hell'd he find out?"

Alsop raised his hands. "Beats me. Take a seat. We're going to have to think about this."

"We'll have to do more than think." The moon-faced mayor dropped into a chair. "Johnston told an Oklahoma City reporter to pack it in and go home, that I'd cooked up the commemoration only to bolster my reelection chances, and that the council would reconvene at six o'clock to shitcan the project. The whole county will have to be hosed down to clean up the mud he'll sling at me."

Alsop regarded the one-time cowboy, who attended press conferences wearing his good-luck silver spurs given to him by Vice President Nixon. The mayor was right. If they didn't turn this around, Alsop could stop dreaming of becoming mayor in four years, and Jimmy Collins could use his bolo tie for a rope and go back to punching cows.

"We have to accept that Johnston knows you kicked in a large sum toward the Belvedere's purchase. If you deny it, it's you who'll be buried."

"Jesus *key*rist. I can't admit a thing like that."

"You can if the money came from you personally."

The mayor seemed to have trouble swallowing.

"Don't look so glum. When you're governor, you'll think back and laugh. If you mishandle this, you can bet your fancy spurs that Johnston will say the idea was a gimmick to get you reelected. Politics, pure and simple."

"Humph."

"If Johnston fails to squelch the commemoration, you'll be as popular as Eisenhower and retain your seat. But first things first. You need to call a press conference immediately and explain that the council had already refused the purchase of a new fire truck and certainly wouldn't pay for a brand new automobile only to bury it."

"But won't I seem exceedingly generous?"

"Relax. Everyone knows you're a rich ex-cattle rancher." Alsop stood and guided the mayor to the door. "You need to call that press conference, and I need to find that reporter."

ભૈભ

Kathy made some calls and learned that the out-of-town reporter was staying at the Holiday Inn. Alsop sailed into the motel office and smacked the bell. "What's Peter Thomas's room number?"

The clerk, his back to Alsop, flinched and turned around, lighting a pipe. He had a high forehead and a low part. His hair swept from one ear, over his head, to the other ear. "He's not here," he said, shaking out a match.

Alsop gulped. "How long ago did he check out?"

"He didn't. He left about twenty minutes ago with some guy in a fancy new car."

"Guy? What guy?"

The clerk shrugged and puffed his pipe.

ભૈભ

Back at the dealership, Alsop found Bucky huddled over a purchase contract with a curly-haired fella in his mid-twenties. Bucky caught his eye and waved him over. "Cal, meet Peter Thomas. Peter, Cal's our headman here."

Alsop shook hands, wondering what the devil was going on. "You're the reporter from Oklahoma City."

"And proud owner of a new Fury. Your man, Bucky, is quite a salesman. He called me at my motel. Said he had a new job and promised me the deal of a lifetime."

Alsop looked at Bucky in disbelief.

"He wouldn't say what it was," Peter went on, "just that he'd be right over." He gave Bucky a friendly pat on the back. "I was just about to leave town. Sure looking forward to my drive home."

"That's wonderful, Peter," Alsop said, hitching up a chair. "You've made a wise investment. Now, about this business of you leaving town…"

CHAPTER 5

If Johnston wanted to play hardball, Alsop would pitch him a knee-buckler. He pulled up to the Johnston Building on Main Street where cars parked nose to the curb. Before the war and before Sears came along, Johnston had bragged that his three-story building was the town's tallest. His office occupied a corner top floor. Beneath were rental offices and the Ellis movie theater.

Alsop entered through a side door, paced past an elevator and hit the stairs two at a time. He shoved open Johnston's door and marched in. The place had the warmth of a bunker. Johnston sat slouched at his bed-sized desk looking grizzled and stone-faced, the phone pressed to his ear and a cigar stub clenched between his oversized teeth. Behind him hung two floor-to-ceiling flags—American and Confederate—the latter, a reminder of his great-grandfather, Joseph E. Johnston, the Civil War general. On the wall, there was a picture of Johnston wearing an OU football uniform and sacking a quarterback. The caption read *Mad Dog Johnston. Five pounds of dynamite in a four-pound box.*

"Cal just walked in," Johnston said into the phone. His jowls jiggled, and he looked more dog than mad. He crushed his cigar in a dinner-plate-sized ashtray. "I'll handle it." He shot a nervous glance at Alsop. "See you at six."

"Like hell, you'll handle it," Alsop exploded before the receiver hit home. "How dare you go behind my back? You're sabotaging the very thing this town needs. We agreed to it."

Johnston pulled out a fresh cigar from a drawer and gave it life with a boot-shaped table lighter. "Not *every-one* agreed. Besides, that was before your cozy arrangement with the mayor came to light."

"The mayor just explained all that at his press conference. This has nothing to do with what you would call the mayor's liberal policies.

Johnston pinched a piece of tobacco off his tongue and examined it intently. "Communistic is a better term." He flicked the speck away. "Do you want your business run by unions?"

"No, I don't. And if you want to run a campaign to unseat the mayor, that's your business. But do it in a way that doesn't ruin Defiance's chance of making an historic mark."

Johnston drew several short puffs on his cigar. He held it in front of him, exhaled, and examined the glowing tip through the smoke. "Come on, Cal, you're talking to me. I know how you stand to gain."

"You're damn tootin' I'll gain. I'll sell cars, sure, but it cuts two ways. The town will get national recognition and might even host the next County Fair. You, on the other hand, along with your pal Overstreet, sold the town out with your secret deal to build the racetrack in Tulsa County. That racetrack belongs right here in Garfield County—smack between Tulsa and Oklahoma City." Alsop jabbed his finger at him. "And *you* know it."

"Don't know what you're talkin' about," Johnston muttered.

"Hell you don't. All pure and self-righteous. Espousing the evils of gambling, yet having a real estate interest in Tulsa County. Precisely where the racetrack's to be built if the governor signs the bill, and you become richer than anyone deserves." Alsop leaned over the desk. "I know all about you and Overstreet under the covers. And if you want *that* dirty little secret, plus a whole bunch more, to stay under this—" He tapped his fedora. "—you'd better cancel that six o'clock meeting." Alsop turned and strode out.

꽁꽁꽁

Alsop returned to the office and called Jessie from Jessie Smith Construction, telling him to get to the courthouse and start digging. An hour later, Alsop arrived at the site to see Jessie unloading his backhoe. "Dig until dark," he ordered. "Then continue first thing in the morning. And I *mean* first thing." He held up two fingers. "Two days, like the contract says, then I want cement poured."

Alsop left with mixed feelings. On one hand, they were breaking ground and finally underway. On the other, there was that scoundrel, Johnston. He didn't retreat, he reloaded. Six months earlier, he'd bullied a reluctant council into passing bicycle license fees in spite of the Children of Defiance Petition of Protest. Johnston's response had been, "If they don't like it, let 'em walk."

Johnston had a point about the publicity helping Alsop sell cars, but Alsop would have buried a tricycle if it meant boosting the town's status. Defiance was on its way up, and so was Alsop.

Businessman, councilman, mayor, governor, and who knows? Perhaps in fifty years, grand officiator of the time capsule opening. Lots of people lived to be eighty-three.

CHAPTER 6

Noontime, and a horn blasted outside. Bucky peered out his office window at a white-paneled truck rumbling onto the lot.

"Roach coach," Kathy sang and swept out the door.

Bucky assumed that meant food and not cockroaches. He stepped into the sun and cool breeze and waited in line behind Kathy. An Indian in a cowboy shirt swung open the truck's wide panel, revealing a chrome counter and an ice tray crammed with drinks. Far out! A restaurant on wheels. A lot different than back home, where vendors sold rattlesnake, watermelons, and strawberries off the tailgate of a pickup truck.

Bucky ordered a patty melt and milk. While waiting, he gazed beyond the service department to a stream and thought of his bayou with all the varied colors running into each other. Of the angular cypress trees draped with silvery Spanish moss like tinsel on a Christmas tree. He thought of the canoe rides with his daddy: him paddling, his daddy stretched out, floppy hat shading his eyes, while he read aloud Thoreau, Whitman, Emerson.

Loneliness crept through his bones.

"Ontario! Your food's ready."

Bucky jolted and turned around.

Kansas scowled at him, his mouth bent iron.

"Oh, thanks."

"Seventy cents," the vendor said.

Bucky fumbled with his change and dropped a quarter between Kansas's feet. Bending down, he noticed Kansas wore a thick shoe. Probably something to do with his limp. Bucky picked up his coin and wandered to the back.

What a neat place. Trees, a couple of picnic tables, and a horseshoe pit. Kathy sat at a table reading a book. Kansas would probably join the three mechanics in blue work shirts at the other table. Bucky didn't want to bother Kathy and definitely didn't want to be around Kansas. He'd sit on a rock by the stream.

Earlier, when Kathy introduced him around, he made a point of memorizing everyone's name. Dale Carnegie's book said *Remember that a person's name is to that person the sweetest and most important sound in any language.*

Kansas carried his food to where the men sat, and the laughing stopped. Hector, the man with the hook from Alsop's party, scooted over to make room. Bucky had learned from Kathy that a Hudson engine had fallen on Hector's hand back in Detroit. When he moved to Defiance, Doc Little fixed him up with the hook. Funny watching him from up on the rock. He held his sandwich on the hook and with his regular hand squeezed ketchup out of a packet.

Kansas plopped down, and his butt drooped over the bench, showing his crack. He wiped his hands with a rag from his pocket. No one spoke until Kansas, in a thick voice that carried well in the crisp outdoors, relayed his adventures of weekend rabbit hunting.

One of the other mechanics, Josh, had an anvil-shaped head and a haircut that could land aircraft. He spoke softly. Not like that time he got trapped in Alsop's bathroom.

Poor guy. Six months stuck in a Korean hole in the ground. It sounded like he said "goddamn," and Kansas snapped at him like a water moccasin. "Use God's name in vain, and you might as well kill your fellow man or steal his wife."

Josh apologized and mentioned his hunting dog.

"Two things I've always lived without," Kansas interrupted. "Cooked vegetables and dogs."

"No animal's safe with Kansas," Hector said, chuckling. "Guns down anything with four legs."

And, Bucky thought, likely anyone with two legs that trespasses on his property a second time.

"You ain't jus' whistlin' Dixie," Kansas agreed. "Don't even own pets. Did I ever tell you boys about the cougar I bagged when I was eleven?" He launched into his story, and two of the men shifted uneasily. Hector got up and headed toward the bathroom, his neck sticking out and bouncing up and down like a chicken's.

Bucky stopped listening and went back to his sandwich. He didn't care at all about Kansas's hunting story, but he did care about whether he had caused Will and Miss Iris's death just to get Will's job. That was something he was *very* interested in—and one way or another, he was going to find out.

ↂↄↂↄ

"Bucky," came Kathy's voice from a box on his desk. "Are you there?"

"I'm here." He waited. Confused, he pressed a lever, and a red light glowed. "Hello, hello," he said and released the lever.

"Cal wants to see you in his office."

Bucky pressed the lever again. "Be right there." Cool! An intercom. This would be a good time to ask if he could buy Peter's old car. With payments, of course.

"You wanted to see me, Cal? Um, I hope it's okay to call you Cal."

"Sure," he said, unsmiling, "unless Peter Thomas's check bounces." He cocked his head toward a chair. "Initiative is an excellent quality. That's what the Winnebagos meant when they said, 'A man must make his own arrows.' Now then, about our commission structure."

"Actually, I was wondering—"

"Of course, you were. Salesmen are paid ten percent of profit per car. Same for volume rebates. Plus twenty percent for extras—heater, radio, whitewall tires, and such. Now, in this case," he whipped out Peter's purchase contract and slapped it on the desk, "we have a problem." He spun the contract around to face Bucky. "The car you sold had a radio. Do you see a charge for a radio in this contract?"

Bucky glanced at it. "No."

"What about a heater charge? Car had a heater, didn't it?"

Bucky swallowed. "I screwed up."

"The car also had whitewalls."

Bucky slumped.

"That's okay, they come standard on this vehicle. Now, those extra costs must be eaten."

Bucky inhaled deeply. "Guess we'll have to."

"Not we—*you*. But save your regrets for things important. You made a good markup, so you'll do fine."

"Cal," Kathy's voice came over Alsop's intercom. "The mayor's on the line. Says it's urgent."

"Put him through." Alsop placed his hand over the phone and said to Bucky, "Remember what the Creoles said. 'One rain doesn't make a crop.' You've got two more cars to sell this week. Otherwise…" He raised his dark eyebrows and shrugged.

CHAPTER 7

Hello, Jimmy," Alsop said into the phone. "What's so urgent?"

"You mean you haven't heard?"

Alsop's heartbeat forced its way into his temples. "Heard what?"

"Your man dug up an Indian burial site, and the Cheyenne demanded an immediate stop to the digging. They've even stationed guards to keep everyone out. Afraid you'll have to find a new site."

Alsop's temples pounded. "That won't work. This whole thing's already on thin ice. Any delay and Johnston will convince the council to quash the entire plan."

"This is your baby, Calvin boy. I'm leaving town for the mayors' conference, and I'm counting on you to straighten this out."

Alsop slammed down the phone. This was all Johnston needed to ruin everything. Well, not if Alsop had anything to say about it. Johnston or no Johnston, Cheyenne or no Cheyenne, he was going to bury that damn car!

❧

She had a pink angora sweater pulled tightly over her

breasts, dark, rocking-horse eyes, and thick honey-blonde hair that spilled down her chest and shoulders.

Deputy Chief Harman gazed at his palm in Sylvia's soft hand while she traced lines with her turquoise fingernail. "This signifies intuition," she shouted over the sound of live rock and roll. Her finger slid to another line. "This wiggle means strong insight."

Uncle Lewy's silver-haired lady beer puller slid two Falstaff beers across the bar to them, froth oozing over the tops. It was their third. Sylvia wasn't a guzzler, but she was persistent.

Harman hated the band. It had a wimpy name, and the singer looked like a fag in black-framed glasses. *Buddy Holly and the Crickets.*

"Strong insight, huh?" he said. "What about this one?" He pointed to a line across the middle of his palm. He didn't believe any of this crap, but chicks dug it.

"That's the head line, different than the life line. It shows adventure and enthusiasm for life. And this?" She traced a thin line under his little finger. "It's the marriage line."

"Uh-oh, what's the verdict?" If marriage was imminent, no bueno. Anything else meant she was hot to trot.

She squinted at him through swirling cigarette smoke. "Aren't you cute? Won't happen anytime soon."

Yahoo!

"However, these little lines right here." She raised her finger high in the air, made a circling motion, and landed it near the middle of his palm. "They mean romance."

"Call me Mister Romance." Should he screw her in the backseat in the parking lot or drive over to old man Gustafson's catfish pond? He put his hand on her thigh and nuzzled his nose deep among those wispy curls behind her ear.

A hand gripped his shoulder from behind, nearly

squashing it like a ripe banana. "Party's over, kids."

Harman wrenched free, turned to see the chief, and gulped.

Parker tugged Harman's coat off the back of his barstool and tossed it in his lap. He turned to Sylvia. "Sorry, miss, my deputy has business to attend to."

Outside, Harman said, "What's the matter, Chief? I'm off duty and on a date."

"You're now on duty with two dates."

やのやの

Alsop couldn't reach Jessie to find out what the backhoe operator had unearthed, so he left word for him to call, then drove to the site.

He arrived at the courthouse lawn to see that lights had been set up and the dig area cordoned off. It smelled of freshly turned soil. A curious crowd of onlookers milled about. Two well-fed Indians with long hair sat on lawn chairs inside the ropes at opposite ends of the hole, each in western shirts and cowboy hats. The deputy chief stood nearby with a toothpick between his bent down lips.

By most accounts, Deputy Chief Raymond Harman was a competent officer. He had a pleasant personality when it suited him, and he gave a twice-yearly civics lesson to high school seniors. He'd put two years in the Army as a private—'45 to '47. Too late to fight the war, he cooked for field artillery cadets at Fort Sill in Lawton, Oklahoma. At the time, he had no experience in law enforcement, but he did have an uncle named Chief Parker.

Alsop strode up to him. And he didn't look happy. "What do you know about this, Ray?"

"Ah, they dug up some injun relic, is all."

"Well, it's good you're here. Learn anything?"

"Heard they got some mucky-muck archeologist coming up from OU in Norman to take a look-see."

"What'd they find exactly?"

The deputy chief pointed to one of the Indian guards. "Ask ponytail over there."

Alsop stooped under the rope, and the man sprang from his chair. "Sir, stay outside the ropes."

"Who sent you here?"

The man pointed a thick finger near Alsop's chest. "*Out.*"

Alsop knocked his hand away. "I'm Councilman Alsop, and I asked you a question."

He stared at Alsop, jaw tight. Finally, he said, "Dan Lightfeather Brown."

Alsop thanked him, stepped outside the ropes, and left. With plenty of fight left, he knew just who to see.

⌘

He pulled into the Speedy Mart's gravel parking lot to pick up some items, including Jo-Dee's bottles of Squirt, and to talk to Tony, a young Indian clerk with almond eyes and the shading and bone structure of the Cheyenne. Tony would often pass along tribal gossip that Alsop often found interesting. If the information related to city business, he'd share it with the council. Tonight, Alsop wanted a line to Tony's grandfather—Dan Lightfeather Brown. He grabbed a bag of charcoal near the hot soup and headed to the soda pop section. Two elderly women were talking about the Peeping Tom on the loose that everybody had heard of, but nobody had seen. He grabbed his Squirt bottles and went to the register.

"Tony, what's the difference between a pickpocket and a Peeping Tom?"

Tony shrugged, and with his hands, flicked his thick black hair behind his shoulders.

"The pickpocket snatches watches. Give me a pack of Luckies."

A smile played at a corner of Tony's lips while he rang up the items. "Why do you always buy single packs, never cartons?"

"The wife wants me to quit. I will—someday. Thing is, nobody serious about quitting would take home a carton." Alsop nodded toward a box of Havanas. "Throw in a couple o' those." He liked cigars but, in deference to Jo-Dee, only smoked them when he had serious thinking to do, and never inside the house. He laid three bucks on the counter and glanced around to ensure they were alone. "Your grandpa, Dan Lightfeather Brown. He's your tribal chief chairman, right?"

"Ever since I can remember. Why?"

"Have you heard about an Indian burial site discovered today?"

Tony handed Alsop a fifty-cent piece and a nickel. "Where's that?"

"The town is planning a big celebration of statehood that requires digging in front of the courthouse. And maybe, *maybe*, an Indian burial site has been discovered. If so, I can assure your grandfather, and every other Cheyenne, that as a city councilman, I will see that we respect your ancestors."

"Want me to tell my grandfather that?"

"Just find out what was buried there. Also check with anyone else who might know." Alsop pulled a ten-spot from his wallet and laid it on the counter. "Call me when you learn something."

That evening, Alsop got a call from Jessie. "Two hours into digging, my backhoe operator dumped a bucket of dirt that included a bone the size his dog would've killed for. Naturally, I had to report it."

"So that's it. Sit tight until I get back to you."

Alsop would take care of this, one way or another.

CHAPTER 8

Bucky arrived home after work and parked his motorcycle beside the back porch. A large pine tree with a white bench around its base dominated the yard. During summer afternoons, Bucky stretched out in the tree's hammock, taking in the heavy scent of pine, and practiced birdcalls he'd learned from his daddy. The same calls he'd taught Miss Iris. During the first red streaks of sunset, he'd call in hawks that would drop gently onto treetops, as though on sore feet. As the sky's colors faded, he'd imitate meadowlarks, towhees, and finches. And they came.

He trailed inside his one room rental, threw his coat somewhere, and dropped into a chair at the kitchen table cluttered with dirty dishes, car magazines, and photographs. That was the good thing about living alone: things could be messy if you wanted. He would return from the Laundromat and not bother to remove clean clothes from his duffle bag until he needed them. Of course, his shirts and pants would be wrinkled as a newborn turkey vulture, but he knew how to wield an iron.

He'd ring up Chief Parker and see how the investigation was going.

"Hi, Mrs. Rheingold. Bucky here. The chief in?"

"Hold on. He's just about to leave."

Moments later, "Hello, Bucky. Nothing yet to report."

"Any clues at the crime scene? You know, where they cut the brake line. You were going to check it out."

"Came up empty. Nothing but brake fluid and gravel."

"What about footprints?"

"Like I said, brake fluid and gravel."

"How about the crash site? Learn anything there?"

"Afraid not."

"Maybe there was a witness. It was pretty bright out there with the full moon. Have you asked around?"

"We're working on it. Trust me, this isn't my first investigation. Have a good night." The chief hung up.

Bucky laid down the receiver. *Tenacious as a fox at a rat hole?* Seems like the rat has little to worry about.

He pawed through the black-and-white pictures he'd just printed. Two were no good. The wino appeared to hold a bag over his head instead of drinking from the bottle inside, and the accidental shot he took of Marybeth was too bright. The light streaming through the trees burned out her hands holding the stuffed giraffe. He started to toss the picture aside, but something caught his eye. He reached for his magnifying glass. A cross. Marybeth had propped the giraffe against a cross stuck in a mound of dirt. Maybe it was a grave for a pet dog or cat. But the giraffe being there seemed weird. Then again, as a kid, he'd owned a three-legged pet raccoon named Tripod who played with a stuffed squirrel.

He grabbed his coat to go check for clues at the crash site, when he heard a car crunch up the drive past the window. It was Kindra, the granddaughter of his former boss, Gustafson. She was a high school senior who worked at her grandfather's store, running the register and manning the gas pumps out front. Bucky had photographed her sweet sixteen party almost two years ago, and ever since, she'd considered him her "big brother."

He quickly cleared the table of dishes and tossed his coat and duffle bag in the closet. Her knock came, and he opened the door just as lightning lit the horizon with an eerie glow. "Hi, Kindra. Fancy seeing you here."

"Are you all right?" Her eyes were big, like green saucers.

"Why wouldn't I be?"

"The accident. You were there, you saw everything."

"Yeah, it was pretty bad, but I'm okay. Wanna come in?"

Her face brightened with that idea. "Gee, thanks. But only a minute." She pranced past him. "Wow! Small and compact, but nice."

"How'd you find out? You know, about the accident?"

"Grandfather told me." She bopped to the sink and started reading labels of photographic chemicals. "I'm glad you're okay."

"I've always been okay. I wasn't in the accident." He gathered loose photos on the table together.

She picked up a developing tray, as if checking its weight. "I'm glad you're working for Mr. Alsop."

"I'm glad, too. It's the next step in my plan."

"Just like your book said, two years at the store, then become a business politician."

"You're mixing everything up. My daddy said to become a businessman and go into public service, the Carnegie book said how to work with people, and *I* said two years at the store."

"Why do all that?"

"My daddy always said we've got to leave the world better than we found it. That means I can't waste my life doing something pointless. I want to help lead our town to do great things, things for people, not corporations like the ones taking over the shrimping business and ruining it for the little guy, such as my daddy. Someday I want to be on the city council, then become mayor. I could do important things, like my Uncle Rupert. He was the first mayor in the country to integrate Negros into the police department."

Kindra now peeked into the partially open closet. Obviously, she used the accident as an excuse to check out his room. At the store, she would say stuff like, "You're so lucky to have your very own place." And she'd ask personal questions. "Have you ever thought of becoming a vegetarian?" As for the art of suggestion, she was a master: "I love rock and roll. Uncle Lewy's sounds like *so* much fun." Hint, hint.

Uncle Lewy's was a beer joint where Bucky photographed performers such as Jerry…Jerry something Lewis. He'd sing and pound the piano like a madman.

Her poking around was getting on his nerves. "Want a Nehi or something?" Anything to settle her down.

She beamed all over. "*Sure*." Her forehead crinkled. "But, if I'm keeping you—"

"Well, I was—"

"Okay, a Nehi. A quick one."

The thought of leaving went out the window. Kindra did a few twirls and dumped herself onto a loveseat. Her legs shot up about three feet in the air, like a little kid's. She picked up a picture on the end table. "Who's freckle face?"

"Just someone I know." He took it from her and put it back. No way was he going to talk about his old girlfriend back home. Kindra would have a million questions. He opened two Nehis and they sat at the kitchen table.

She began pawing through his stack of photos, tapping the one of the courthouse with her finger. "That's where they're going to bury a car."

"A car?" He grabbed the picture. That must be the time capsule Peter talked about. "How do you know?"

"Grandfather told me." She stared at another photo. "Good old Marybeth."

He told her how Kansas had freaked out when he took the picture. Kindra kept glaring at it. "What?" he said.

"She ran away."

"*Really?*"

"She told me she was going to. I warned her that her father would kill her. The next day, Kansas came in the store totally freaked out. I kept my trap shut."

"Where'd she go?"

"It's a secret. She doesn't want her father to know. He'd beat her and then read the Bible to her. I'll tell you something, but you have to promise not to blab to anyone."

"Okay."

"She had a baby," Kindra whispered.

"No way! I'd have known if she was pregnant. She came in the store all the time."

"I got suspicious when she started wearing loose-fitting clothes. Since I'm going to be a nurse, I notice those things." She took a swig of drink. "One time I heard her throwing up in the bathroom. When she came out from the toilet, I gave her a paper towel. She said she'd been doing it a lot. That's when I put two and two together. Baggy tops, throwing up."

"Didn't know you guys were chummy."

"I only know her from in the store."

"But where's the ba—my God, she ran away with it?"

Kindra sipped her drink. "Took it somewhere to be adopted."

"But, why run away?"

"Afraid of her father."

Bucky shook his head. "How could Kansas—I mean, he must've known she was pregnant."

"She said he didn't."

"Who's the father?"

Kindra took another swallow. "Vester Overstreet."

"*VO.* That twerp?" Wait a minute! Wasn't Kansas the father? The deputy chief said he was a child molester. Bucky couldn't tell Kindra that.

"That's who she says."

"Where'd she run off to?"

"VO's house. She's hiding there, and I need to go and get my mother's wedding ring back."

Bucky knew Kindra's mother and father had died. That's why she lived with her grandparents. He raised the drink to his lips and stopped. "What's she doing with the ring?"

"I lent it to her so she and VO could pretend to be married when they went to the adoption agency."

He took a gulp. "Pretty stupid."

"Made sense to her. She only just turned sixteen."

He burped. "I meant of you. Shouldn't a told her about the ring."

"She promised to give it back. '*Cross my heart and swear to God.*' Oh, Bucky, my mother's ring is the most important thing in the world to me. Will you come with me to VO's?"

Bucky didn't want to get involved. If Kansas would shoot him for trespassing, what the hell would he do for getting mixed up with his runaway daughter? "Sorry, have to pass."

"But I can't go alone."

"Look, I'm sure she'll come back once the baby is taken care of and give you the ring." No wonder she wanted to put the baby up for adoption if her own father got her pregnant. He suppressed a shudder.

Kindra grabbed his arm, her eyes droopy, like that dog whose breed he couldn't remember. "But she said VO has it and won't give it back. He'll have to if you're there. Let's go now. *Please*."

Bucky clomped to the window. "Look." He pointed to thick dark clouds. "It's going to rain any minute." No way did he want to face Kansas and accuse him of child molestation.

"I don't give a darn. I'll drive."

Bucky thought of Marybeth all scared and hiding. Maybe he could do something to help. "All right, but first we need to make a stop."

CHAPTER 9

Kindra slewed from the curb, headlights on. Thunderheads had erased the sun from the sky. Bucky pointed ahead. "Turn right at the light. I want to check out the crash site."

Twenty minutes later, Kindra pulled up near where Will's car had hit the tree. They got out, and Bucky studied the area where the Desoto had run off the road.

"See, I was right," he said. "No skid marks." He paced back to the tree and inspected its new scars. A shard of glass from Will's windshield still posed in the bark. Broken glass dotted a damp spot on the ground. He put his finger to it and sniffed. "It's oil." He stuck his finger under Kindra's nose. "Smell."

She sniffed. "No it's not. It's brake fluid."

He thought a minute. "I guess you should know, being a grease monkey." They got back in the car and Kindra headed toward VO's house. "Go the other way," Bucky said, hitting on an idea. "I want to see the spot where Will parked his car. There might be evidence."

"Didn't the police already check?"

"Yeah, but I want to look anyhow." No telling what Chief Parker may have missed.

"But it's out of the way. Let's do it coming back."

Bucky peered up through the windshield. "We have to go now before it rains."

She sighed and whipped a U-turn.

Bucky wondered what the killer had used to cut the brake line. The tool must have been small. The guy couldn't very well haul around bolt cutters. Maybe a pocketknife. One of those Swiss Army ones. Lots of guys carried those.

The Olds rolled up the steep road leading to Alsop's house, as raindrops struck the windshield like tiny dots. Kindra parked in front. They got out and tramped across the street.

"This is where Will parked his Desoto," Bucky said. "I know, because I pulled in behind it."

Kindra bent down and put her finger on a dark patch of gravel. She sniffed her finger. "Smell this," she said.

"I don't have to. It's the same brake fluid we smelled earlier." Bucky scoured the area for clues. Cigarette butts, clothing lint, dropped items. Anything. But like Chief Parker, he came up empty. *Nothing but brake fluid and gravel.*

They got back in the car, and Kindra started to pull away.

"Wait a minute," Bucky said. "Just thought of something." He got out and walked along the berm, examining the slope below. Brake fluid must've coated the perpetrator's hands. Maybe he'd have wiped them on something he threw away. It would've been too smelly to carry around in his pocket.

The area had only dried buffalo grass and dogwood. He was about to give up when he spotted a hint of yellow in the brown grass about twenty yards down by a dogwood tree. He breathed hard as he snaked his way down, careful not to slip and fall on the wet grass. It was a rag. He took it back to the car.

"I've got to get this to Chief Parker, right away."

"But you promised we'd get my mother's ring."

Bucky grimaced. "Okay. But let's make it quick."

∞∞∞

VO lived in a neighborhood that smelled of oil. Oil money. Retirees secluded behind high walls and sweet-scented hedges that had outlived generations of gardeners.

VO recently graduated high school. Lanky, with a long nose and pimples, he had lettered in swimming and bragged about having his own heated pool. Hardly anyone had a pool. Even a cold one. He was one of those guys who boasted about all the girls he'd had. He'd strut into Gustafson's with his pals and a pair of handcuffs looped in his belt like a junior G-Man and sing out about having screwed this chick and that chick.

His father, Orville Overstreet, was currently running against the mayor. He bred racehorses, and, according to VO, raced them as far away as New York, even Mexico.

As Kindra drove toward VO's mansion, a lightning bolt ripped the sky. Seconds later, rain pounded the windshield like fists. Kindra leaned over the steering wheel, and the wipers slapped full speed. Two miles ahead, the road ended at a private gate. Like a castle, the Overstreet mansion had three tall spires and sat on a plateau.

Kindra rubbed her sleeve across the fogged windshield swarming with water and put her nose to the glass. "Dang, there're no lights on."

"Rich people don't waste electricity. I've seen lots of mansions back home." Bucky pointed ahead. "There's an intercom."

She rolled up to it and lowered her window. Buckets of rain hurtled in. She yelped, reached out, and pressed a button. "Hello! Hello!" She rolled up the window nearly all the way and put her ear to the opening.

After a minute, Bucky said, "Let's split."

"Darn!" She started to close the window when a voice with an English accent screeched from the speaker. "Overstreet residence. Who's calling?"

"Um, I'm outside your gate, and I need to see Vester." Long silence.

Bucky tapped her arm. "Say your name."

"I'm Kindra Gustafson—a friend."

"One moment, please." There was a long pause, and then the intercom squawked back to life. "Master Vester is out for the evening. Good night."

"Wait!" Kindra shrilled. "Are you there?" After long moments of silence, she rolled up her window that last inch, her left side drenched. "Gosh darn it! We'll wait for him to come back."

"He's already back, Kindra." Bucky explained impatiently. "He doesn't want to see you."

"Really?" She peered through the fogged windshield at the gate.

"Forget it. I'm not climbing over."

"You won't have to. I'll do it." She pointed. "There's a control box inside. We'll leave the car here."

He gaped through a curtain of rain and phalanx of ten-foot-tall iron bars—with spikes. Kindra jumped out and hurled herself over the gate like a monkey. It swung open, and he grudgingly rolled out of the car.

Rather than run along the looping driveway, they slogged straight toward the house, up the football field of grass cut even as carpeting. Kindra held her arms folded over her head. Seconds later, a piercing siren sounded, and harsh floodlights beamed down.

Kindra covered her ears, slipped and fell on the grass. Bucky helped her up and raised a hand to shield his eyes.

He had no idea how they'd activated the alarm. They were in no-man's land, caught between the house and car.

"Let's get out of here," Kindra yelled over the deafening siren.

Bucky grabbed her arm. "Hold it. Look, the downstairs window." A man inside wearing a black coat had picked up the phone. "He's calling the police. We've got to stop him." They sprinted for the house. At the front steps, the siren stopped and everything turned black. A porch light came on, and the door opened.

VO stared at them and sighed. "Everything's all right, Martin. Tell them it was a false alarm." He came onto the covered porch and shut the door. He had on pressed jeans, sneakers, and a Marlon Brando T-shirt. The snakeskin belt matched his piss-colored eyes. "What the fuck are you doing here?"

"Three guesses," Bucky said, "and the first two don't count."

"Screw off."

Bucky held out his palm. "Hand over the ring."

"Fuck you."

Kindra stepped forward. "I want to talk to Marybeth. We know she's hiding here."

"Get the hell off my property, or you're in trouble."

"No problem," Bucky said. "Come on, Kindra, we'll talk to Kansas."

VO grabbed Bucky's arm, his zitted jaw rigid as a horseshoe. Bucky prepared to duck VO's right cross and land a hard one to his gut, but VO's jaw loosened, then his grip. He moved back. "Come in and keep your mouths shut."

The servant laid a towel down inside the entrance and scurried away. He wouldn't want the precious rugs to get wet. Off the vestibule loomed a faintly lit staircase of carved mahogany as wide as a small road. It curved up into the darkness of a second floor. On the wall hung a life-size painting of a stuffy looking guy with a Roman nose and bushy white mustache. His black eyes followed Bucky as VO led them into a hallway lined with dozens of photographs—jockeys and horses and wreaths of roses. The same thin, wavy-haired man appeared in each picture. He had the identical high-bridge nose as the older figure in the portrait. Probably his father. Bucky stopped and examined a picture of two men. Next to the thin man stood a broad-shouldered fella resembling Bucky's landlord, Mr. Johnston, but with ink-black hair. Scribbled across the bottom: *A winning team. 1935.*

At the hallway's end, VO turned left. His parents had to be off somewhere, maybe racing horses. Another stairway appeared on the left, narrower than the first. Bucky imagined Marybeth in a tower, curled up on a bed of straw. VO padded past the stairs to a door. He unlocked it, and they slipped inside.

The room was large and painted purple except for the far wall covered with fuzzy red wallpaper. Equally interesting were the pool table and a bar straight out of *Gunsmoke.*

Posters hung everywhere: Elvis Presley singing, James Dean smoking, Mickey Mantle at bat.

VO led them across the room to a door decorated with a movie poster Bucky didn't recognize. *Reefer Madness. Women cry for it, men die for it.* Kindra darted a glance at a table near the door and raised her chin. Spread about were throwing knives and VO's best friend—a pair of handcuffs.

VO opened the door. "Come on out, Marybeth, you've got company." He snatched up the handcuffs and wandered toward the bar.

Marybeth appeared in the doorway and leaned against the jamb, staring down at her bare feet, one on top of the other, toes wiggling. She appeared flung together in a loose T-shirt and tight pedal pushers.

She looked at Kindra—a wet raccoon, claws ready. "You promised not to tell." She threw a sideways nod at Bucky. "And you shouldn't o' brung *him*."

Kindra fired back. "And you shouldn't have given *him*—" She jabbed a finger at VO lounging at the bar. "—my mother's ring."

Clickclickclickclickclick. VO ratcheted his handcuffs. As if summoned, Marybeth trotted over and hopped onto an adjacent stool. They leaned their backs against the bar.

Kindra marched up to them and thrust her open palm in VO's face. "Give it."

Clickclickclickclickclick. "Tell her, Marybeth."

"Tell me what?" Kindra snapped.

Marybeth stared at VO, her top teeth denting her bottom lip.

"Don't look at me." *Clickclickclickclickclick.* "Tell her."

Marybeth's chin quivered.

Hands on hips, Kindra hissed through clenched teeth, "I'm listening."

Marybeth's eyes turned into blue pools.

"Come on, you two." Bucky paced over to VO and snapped his fingers. "Cough it up."

VO spread his hands. "I don't have it."

Kindra folded her arms tightly. "I'm not leaving without it."

Clickclickclickclickclick.

Bucky was ready to knock VO on his ass when a horrible thought jumped in his mind. He turned to Marybeth. "Has something happened to the ring?"

She sprung off the stool and threw herself onto a black sofa. "I lost it, *okay?*"

Kindra started for her, fists clenched. Bucky wedged between them.

Clickclickclickclickclick.

Bucky whirled toward VO. "Put those down or you'll be wearing them around your neck." He turned back to Marybeth. "How'd you lose it?"

She shook her head. "I don't know."

"She said she lost it hitchhiking over here," VO piped up.

Kindra stomped to Marybeth on the sofa. "Tell me that's not true."

"It musta fallen outta my pocket."

Kindra turned to VO. "She said you had it and wouldn't give it back."

"That's obviously a lie," he said. "She probably still has it."

Marybeth sprang from the sofa. "I do not!"

"You're the biggest liar in the world," VO snarled. "I don't know why I even agreed to help you."

"I *hate* you!" Marybeth spat.

"Feeling's mutual." VO jerked his thumb toward the door. "All of you, take a hike. And I mean now!"

ᙇᙔᙇᙔ

The three rode through the night to the sound of rain pounding the car. Kindra stared through the windshield, kneading the steering wheel as if making a pastry twist. Bucky wondered why Marybeth wouldn't return the ring. Fell out of her pocket? Fish*ee*. He swung his arm over the backrest and turned to her. She stared into a pocket mirror, finger-combing her bangs and humming. She didn't look worried at all. Not the least bit afraid of returning to her father, the supposed child molester. Maybe Harman was full of crap.

"Where'd you lose it, Marybeth?" he asked, trying for a gentle tone.

She closed her eyes and took a deep breath like a skin diver going for the bottom. "I already said, in some guy's car."

"Don't get smart. Whose car?"

"How should I know? Hitchhiking. *Remember?*"

Her surly expression made Bucky want to slap that mirror out of her hand. He flashed back to his book's first rule. *Don't criticize, condemn, or complain.* He took a deep breath. "Okay, why'd you run away from home?"

"Had my reasons." She peered back in her mirror.

"What'll your father do to you?" he asked, though he had a pretty good guess he'd beat her. Could that be all?

She ran her tongue across her front teeth. "Nothin'."

Kindra shot a glance into the rearview mirror. Her mouth twitched like a small, injured thing. "I hope you realize the ring is the only thing I have to remember my mother." A tear trickled down her cheek.

"Nothin' I can do about that." Marybeth snapped her compact shut and dropped it into her purse. "Lemme out on the corner and forget you saw me."

Kindra screeched to the curb. Marybeth scurried into the rain like a swamp mouse.

Poor Kindra. She has to be devastated. There must be some way to get her mother's ring back. Too much rain now to show the chief where the rag was found. He'd do it tomorrow after Miss Iris's funeral.

CHAPTER 10

Alsop was late. He had been at the *Prairie Duster*'s office, complaining to Farnsworth, the paper's editor, about a disturbing front-page article, and he had just arrived at the First Methodist Church for Miss Iris's memorial service.

The early-morning light beamed through the stained glass windows, scattering a misty, diffused glow over the nave and pews, filled shoulder to shoulder with mourners. Alsop squeezed in among those standing in the rear. Evidently, Pastor Agnew had already finished his sermon, and Bucky was approaching the podium.

He coughed into his fist and began, "I've never given a eulogy before, and I've only been to two funerals, my mother's and my grandmother's. I was too young each time to get up and speak. But if I had, it would have been with the same love in my heart that I felt for Miss Iris. She was like a grandmother to me, always giving and never asking for anything in return. When I came to town two years ago, she got me my first job by recommending me to Mr. Gustafson. When I was sick with the flu, she fed me homemade soup, and when I was homesick for my daddy and little sister, she cheered me with her warm smile and hearty laugh.

"Although Miss Iris never expected anything in return, I did give her something. After finishing our Sunday suppers together at her place, she and I would sit on our back porch, and I'd teach her birdcalls, just like my daddy had taught me. And I'll tell you this, after only two weeks, Miss Iris could sing those calls as good as the birds themselves, if not better—but only after—" He raised a finger. "—after she removed her false teeth. Thank you."

The assemblage laughed and clapped as Bucky sat back down.

When the man standing before Alsop moved toward the podium, Alsop spotted Chief Parker sitting in the back row. He tapped him on the shoulder. "We need to talk. Now!"

The two went outside onto the steps. Alsop whipped out the newspaper from his back pocked and shook it. "Have you read this?" he spat.

"Don't get your horse feathers ruffled."

"Oh, yeah!" Alsop opened the paper. "'Indian burial site discovered under courthouse lawn.' My feathers are a hell of a lot more than ruffled. This bone thing is getting out of hand."

"Spreads like prairie fire, don't it? Come on, Cal, you know how these things go. Papers make a fuss over a fart in a whirlwind."

"You've seen the bone?"

"I've got it locked up until the archeologist arrives from OU."

"What's it look like?"

"I'm no expert, but it's definitely old. Maybe a leg bone. Tibia, femur. About a foot long, both ends broken."

"Looks human, huh?"

"Kind of. But you know how these things pop up every few years. Feathers ruffle. Turns out to be a horse or deer, and the show's over."

"When's this university fella arriving?"

"Tomorrow afternoon."

"*Tomorrow?*" The two stepped aside as a couple came out of the church. "We need him today—*Now.*"

"We're lucky it's not next week."

A rock formed in Alsop's chest. The delay would work in Johnston's favor. "Look, when the guy gets here, call me."

"Do me a favor. Inform the other council members what's going on. You're the second one to bug me about it this morning. I'm up to my eyeballs in crap over yesterday's bank robbery."

"I just read about it. Other than the money, what's the problem?"

"Should've caught the sons o' bitches, but…well, we didn't."

People began pouring out from the church.

"Here comes Bucky," the chief said.

"Who else asked about the bone?"

"Johnston."

Mad Dog Johnston. Dogs bury bones. The rock in Alsop's chest grew larger.

തതത

Bucky led the chief down the slope and through the grass to where he'd found the yellow rag. "It was here, by the dogwood tree."

The chief looked surprised. "Was it behind it? Because I looked down here earlier and didn't see it."

"No, but it was hard to see in the brown grass."

The chief leaned forward, put a hand on his knee, and looked around. "Okay, that's good." They climbed back up to the berm. "Hold up," the chief said. He hunched over and studied a deep indentation in the side of the berm.

"What's that, a gopher hole?" Bucky asked.

"Like hell. It's a toe imprint, and my experienced eye tells me it's fresh."

Bucky wondered if he had insulted the chief by finding a rag that he'd missed seeing. "The killer must've made it when he came back up."

The chief stared at Bucky's shoes. "It's not from you, is it?"

"No. See, mine are clean." He lifted one foot, then the other. "What about the tow truck operator?"

"No one would climb down here except whoever left the rag."

Unless somebody needed to take a leak, but he'd probably annoyed the chief enough already, so he kept the thought to himself. "Want me to take a picture of the hole?"

"Won't be necessary. I'll make a plaster impression and send it to Tulsa for a make on the footwear. Don't mention this to anyone." Chief Parker cast a stern look at him, and Bucky nodded.

Despite the chief's grumpiness and lack of enthusiasm, Bucky went home feeling charged. He had uncovered an important piece of evidence, which provided another solid lead. Nothing more to do, at least until the chief got a make on the footwear. Meanwhile, he'd get a make on Marybeth.

മൗ

With Tuesday's election less than a week away, Alsop spent the afternoon in Tulsa with the printer, inspecting ballots. Councilman Doc Little had planned to go with him, but he was tied up at the hospital, attending to one of the bank robbers that had been shot and captured in Kingfisher.

On his return home along 412, worries ran through Alsop's mind. For Defiance to become truly the *next great boomtown*, it needed the racetrack built in its own Garfield County. But Johnston and Overstreet had paid off enough state legislatures to back a bill awarding the contract to Tulsa County, where the two had invested heavily. Alsop's only chance of getting the racetrack constructed in Garfield County was for the governor to veto the bill. But he would only do that if Mayor Collins won reelection. The mayor was president of the powerful Cattlemen's Association, and if in office, would wield enough muscle to guarantee the governor's own reelection.

⁊⁊⁊

Alsop was about to leave work for home when the phone rang. He picked up. "Alsop Chrysler Plymouth Motors. Thi*sss* is Cal."

"Afraid I've got bad news," Chief Parker said.

A cold gust blew across Alsop's heart. "What?"

"An archeologist arrived this afternoon and took measurements of the bone. Said he's ninety-nine percent certain it's human. Claims to be an expert in this sort of thing and wants to run tests."

"He wasn't supposed to arrive until tomorrow."

"This was an Indian fella. Dressed up in a fancy suit and tie, except, you know, long hair. He talked Harman into letting him take a look at the bone, and he'd already made measurements before I got there."

"I hope to *hell* you didn't give him the bone."

"He tried like the dickens to get me to hand it over. I didn't care if he was from Harvard."

"*Harvard.* Holy Jesus. How do you know he's for real?"

"Gave me his card. Said he's visiting family here."

"His card, huh?" Alsop loosened his tie. "You believe him?"

"Doesn't matter. The bone's with me."

"What about the OU fella? He's still coming, right?"

"So far as I know."

Alsop sighed. "All right. But be sure you call me the second he arrives." *Harvard expert.* Smelled like bullshit—Johnston bullshit.

⌘

After stopping for a haircut that added bounce to his front curl, Bucky arrived home and turned on the heater. It did its usual clanging and banging while he heated a can of Campbell's chicken noodle soup on a hotplate. Sheila had taught him that trick back home. Saved lots of time. Bucky, like most other folks in Defiance, craved winter soup. The whole town was practically addicted to the stuff, and it didn't matter what kind. Bucky had eaten lots of soup back home on his daddy's shrimp boat. Gobbled up his gramma's spicy shrimp gumbo by the pot full.

The phone rang.

"Hi, Bucky, it's me, Kindra. What'd the chief say about your discovery?"

"Not much, but I think he was impressed with my sharp eye. We also found…well, the chief found a piece of evidence. I'm sworn to secrecy, but I think we're going to catch this guy."

"That's good, I guess."

"Don't kill yourself with enthusiasm. Anyway, I've been thinking about Marybeth, and her story doesn't jive."

"You think she still has my mother's ring?"

"When you gave it to her, did she seem to really like it?"

"She loved it."

"Then I'm right! She has it and wants to keep it. Pick me up tomorrow morning, eight o'clock. I've got an idea how to get it back."

"Where're we going?"

"Back to VO's."

⮰⮱

Jo-Dee placed her hand on Alsop's shoulder and removed the empty sherry glass from his lap. "Cal," she whispered, "there's a gentleman at the door for you."

Alsop opened his eyes and blinked. "Who'd you say?"

"He won't give his name and wouldn't come in. But I'm certain he's the young Indian from the Speedy Mart."

Alsop lumbered to the door, dreading more bad news. "Good evening, Tony. Come inside."

Tony stood away from the porch light, shoulders hunched in the cold. "I'd rather you come outside."

Now fearing the worst, Alsop grabbed his coat from the deer antlers and joined Tony. "Where's your car?"

"Parked at the bottom of the hill. Got a bad clutch." White vapor accompanied Tony's words. He'd probably heard about Will losing his brakes. They shuffled to the side of the house, away from the street.

"What is it?" Alsop asked.

Tony looked around and tugged the collar under his hair. "You can't say we talked. So don't tell anyone, including your city council friends, or I could get seriously hurt."

That's why Tony hadn't called on the phone. Party lines. No telling who could be listening in. "Okay, fine, you have my word."

"I found out about the bone."

"You mean from your grandfather?"

"From my little brother. It's kind of complicated."

"Let's hear it."

"He and his friends threw the bone into the hole when the tractor guy took a smoke break. You know, as a joke."

"Well, I'll be." Alsop could hardly believe the good news, though he wondered how Tony could get seriously hurt. "Where'd they get it?"

"From that abandoned excavation site at the end of Wheeler Road. Those guys from OU left a bunch lying around."

"The bone must not be human."

"Just some animal."

Alsop gripped Tony's shoulder. "I can't tell you how relieved I am."

"Um." Tony shot a nervous glance at the street. "There's more."

Alsop's pulse jumped into his throat.

"You know the Caddo people, right?"

"Down south. What about them?"

"They found out why the hole's being dug."

Alsop's pulse throbbed. "So?"

"They're mad about it."

"What the hell for?"

"You know how they feel about their land being taken. They plan to stop your celebration."

Alsop blew out a puff of air. "How? Put on war paint and dance?"

Tony stared down at his cowboy boots.

"Sorry, Tony. That was a stupid thing to say. But seriously, what can they do? Their phony archeologist didn't pan out. A real one's coming tomorrow and will tell everyone the bone isn't human."

"He wasn't phony. He's a real archeologist, and he knew the bone wasn't human."

"Well, there you go. Looks like their little game's over."

Tony shook his head. "Don't count on it."

"What do you mean?" By now Alsop wanted to shake the guy so he'd spill everything and not let the information trickle out in a rivulet.

"They're going to plant another bone either tonight or tomorrow night."

"*What?*" Alsop heard blood rushing in his ears. The Caddo protested Fourth of July events but had never tried a stunt like this.

Tony shot a glance at the street. "Later tonight someone's delivering a bone to the Caddo people. Real old, real human."

The rushing sound got louder. "And they're going to plant it in the hole?"

Tony nodded.

Alsop swallowed hard. "Who exactly?"

"That's all I know. I'm Cheyenne. I've never associated with Caddo people."

"Thanks, man." Alsop needed to put a stop to this, fast. He hurried back inside, grabbed the phone, and dialed. How did Tony know about the Caddo peoples' plans if he didn't associate with them? Didn't matter now. If this hoax business succeeded, the commemoration would not.

"Hello, Chief, do you have someone keeping those Indians company on the courthouse lawn?"

"Not any more. Why the hell would I?"

"Can't say over the phone, but you need to send someone over there right away."

"Not without good reason."

"There is good reason, I just can't tell you right now."

"I can't pull someone off patrol to sit around a hole and play tiddlywinks with a couple of Indians because you say so."

"Okay, forget it." Alsop hung up.

He gave Jo-Dee a quick account of what Tony had said and that they were sworn to secrecy. Then he went for his hat.

"Where are you going?"

"To the courthouse."

"What about your supper?"

He went to her and kissed her cheek. "Later. There's something I've got to take care of first."

CHAPTER 11

ucky woke up to sunshine slicing through the treetops and spilling across his bed. He dressed, ate breakfast, and opened the door to a frost-covered world so bright it made him blink. The *Prairie Duster* said a high today of forty-one degrees. He zipped his coat and trekked up the icy driveway to wait for Kindra. Cars with crusty-white windshields sat parked at the curb. He stood in the wintry silence and leaned against a barren elm. Across the street, a boy broke icicles off his roof with a stick.

The far-off drone of Kindra's Olds could be heard. The car technically belonged to her grandmother and was likely as ancient but in better shape. As it crested the hill, the whir grew louder and dropped in tone as the car glided to a stop. He climbed in.

"Sorry I'm late. I needed—" Kindra shot him a look. "Nice haircut." She reached over and touched his front curl.

He pulled his head away. "Hey, let's not muss the hair." He patted his curl.

"Touchy." She sniffed. "Is that Aqua Velva?"

Crap. Another one of those weird questions. "What were you going to say before?"

She tore away from the curb. "I needed to get gas."

"At least it's free at the store. Lucky you."

"Free, but I have to pump it. I also checked the oil and wheels—lug nuts, you know." She fell silent, gnawing her bottom lip. "That's how my parents died."

"Really?" Bucky hoped she might say more. He'd always been curious but too polite to ask.

"It was a freak accident. I was only three. My father was on leave from the Army. On the drive home with my mother from a weekend getaway in Tulsa, a wheel flew off an oncoming car on 412 and crashed through their windshield."

"*Geesh.*" Kindra lost her mother and father on a highway, and he lost his grandmother on the Tangipahoa River, and his mother after she gave birth to his sister Cassidy.

"Grandmother's been fanatical about lug nuts ever since. She's not exactly an astute car person. Anyway, tell me this plan of yours." She checked her teeth in the mirror, just like Marybeth. Must be a girl thing.

"Well, if she has the ring, and VO knows it, maybe I can bluff it out of him."

"How're you going to do that?"

"By working the father angle." Bucky glanced over his shoulder. "Better change lanes. His street's up ahead."

Minutes later, Kindra pulled up to VO's gate. "What do I say to the butler?"

"Press the intercom, I'll talk."

Then, the familiar English voice droned, "Overstreet residence. Who's calling?"

Bucky leaned over. "Inform *Master* Vester that Bucky is here to see him." He grinned at Kindra. "It's a matter of life and death."

"One moment, please."

Kindra laughed, and the gate opened. They parked

alongside six garages and trod over the icy redbrick walk lined with rosebushes. The lawn, so unwelcoming the night before with rain, sirens, and floodlights, was layered with glistening ice crystals. The servant, a wiry guy with a pea-size chin and yellow hair, stood outside the open doorway.

"The Limey is waiting for us," Bucky muttered in an English accent. They mounted the steps, and Bucky slipped and fell on his face.

"Careful," the butler said as Bucky scrambled upright. "Steps are icy."

"Thanks for the warning."

The butler allowed himself a razorblade of a smile and bowed. "After you."

The house was much brighter with sunlight streaming through the windows. Bucky stared at the portrait of the Roman-nosed man. Again, his black eyes followed him through the vestibule.

The servant stopped at VO's suite, knocked, and glided away. VO opened the door. "Look, my folks are coming home today. What's this bullshit about?"

Bucky scanned the room. A steaming pot of coffee sat on a hotplate near VO's trusty handcuffs. He pointed. "You can heat soup on that thing and eat right out of the can."

"If I ate soup."

Bucky started toward the open door that Marybeth had come through. "Is this your bedroom?"

VO shot past him and closed the door. "What do you want?"

Bucky and Kindra settled at the bar. "I want my mother's ring," she said.

"You heard Marybeth. She lost it. Take your life and death and shove it."

"Where's the baby?" Bucky asked, hoping to catch him off guard.

VO strolled to the table and picked up his handcuffs.

"Put those down," Bucky said, "and answer the question."

VO tossed them back with a clink. He leaned his back against the wall and crossed his arms tightly. "I don't know where it is."

"Something else you don't know," Bucky said. "I have a new job, and guess who my new best buddy is?"

"I should give a flying fuck?"

"Kansas Karradine. You two are related. You know, fathering his grandchild and all." Surely VO would return the ring in exchange for Bucky keeping quiet about that little nugget of truth.

"I didn't father any damn child." VO went back to the table and poured coffee into a mug with a pistol grip handle.

"Marybeth told me it was you," Kindra said.

VO took a swallow. "Like you can really believe her?"

Bucky sucked in air. Damn! His bluff wasn't working. "Okay, then who is the father?"

"Don't know, don't care. Look, I agreed to help Marybeth, but I never saw a ring, never saw a baby. If anybody's related to a baby around here, it's not me." He shot Kindra a side glance and sipped his coffee.

Bucky slid off the barstool and went to him. "But you and Marybeth took the baby away to be adopted."

"That's why she wanted the ring," Kindra added.

VO peered into his coffee for a long time. Finally, he said, "That didn't work out. Marybeth told me that the baby—"

"Master Vester," came a voice over the intercom, "your mother and father just arrived."

VO stomped his foot. "Shit!" He put down his cup.

Kindra groaned.

"Listen," VO said, scurrying to a glass door leading to the backyard, "if the ring's that important to you, find the baby and you'll find the ring. Now, split." He slid open the door. "And don't come back."

✂✁✂

Kindra dropped Bucky off at his rooming house, and he changed for work. Disappointed his threat hadn't panned out, he sat down to a bowl of cereal, wishing he had a banana. Idly shuffling through his photographs, he found Marybeth's and frowned as he once again saw the overexposed pet grave. He tossed the photo aside, vowing to make an improved print.

A moment later, it hit him.

Pets!

Kansas didn't have pets. That's what he told his buddies at the lunch table. Bucky grabbed a magnifying glass and studied the photo closely. Yes! The stuffed giraffe, the cross, the mound of dirt. Bucky's heart flew in his chest. Marybeth *did* have a baby—and buried it.

✂✁✂

At nine-forty-five a.m., Bucky parked his motorcycle behind the showroom and trotted inside to his desk. He was due in at ten, but he liked to arrive a few minutes early. It showed responsibility.

He couldn't get his mind off Marybeth and the baby. Everything fit together. Marybeth had a baby, the baby died, and she buried it. The poor thing was probably born dead. God, he hoped it was born dead. Hopefully she didn't—didn't kill it.

He thought about calling Kindra to tell her his new

theory, but she was working, and he didn't want to call the store and chance talking to Mr. Gustafson. Bucky hadn't spoken to him since he was fired. What an experience *that* was.

Gustafson didn't have the biggest grocery store in town but the only one with a neon sign. He offered fresh produce, fresh fruit, fresh meat. Feed lined one sidewall, magazines, toiletries, and notions the other. Canned goods stacked in back. Customers told Bucky what they wanted, and he rolled the cherry picker along a sawdust-covered floor, climbed up and got it down.

The shrewd storekeeper knew how to make a buck. The only thing free was his smile. Usually for the ladies—young ladies. He charged twenty cents a gallon for gasoline, two cents more for ethyl. Kindra did the pumping. You could buy lots of things for a dime: a novel, a cast iron toy, five jawbreakers—coke included. Caught short before payday? Credit was extended with that smile.

After Bucky told the old man that he'd be quitting soon, Gustafson rapped a sausage-like finger on Bucky's forehead like it was a screen door.

"Is this the thanks I get, is this how I'm repaid for hiring you—training you?" He carried on like that, calling Bucky a Louisiana foreigner, as if the place was still owned by France.

Bucky said he was sorry, *really* sorry. Would stay on until—Gustafson would hear none of it, shook that same fat finger toward the door, swiveled his dumpy bulk and waddled off.

Hard to believe, that was only a week ago. Bucky shook his head to clear it of the unpleasant memory. He'd wait and call Kindra at home that night.

CHAPTER 12

Bucky had read in the morning paper about a bank robbery and that the gang got away in a hotrod Mercury. They sped west out of town, guns blazing, police on their tail. When they reached Old Highway 64, the Merc torpedoed out of sight, leaving the cops wondering if the robbers had swung north into Kansas, south toward Texas, or shot straight into New Mexico.

Defiance's police drove ancient '48 Chevys that couldn't catch their own exhaust. They'd been shamed, and the *Prairie Duster* reported citizen outrage.

This was Bucky's opportunity. Defiance police needed new cars. Fast cars. He picked up the phone and dialed. "Hello, Mrs. Rheingold. This is Bucky." He couldn't risk asking for an appointment with the chief. She'd want to know why and take a message. He needed to pitch the chief directly and right away. Get him while he was still coughing up Mercury trail dust. "I have a photo of the chief and his daughter. I took it when he dropped her off at her girlfriend's sweet sixteen party. I'm sure the chief would love having it. Perfect for his desk. Think I could drop it by?"

"That would be wonderful."

"What time does he go to lunch? Hate to miss him."

"Let's see." He heard a page turn. "One o'clock. He meets with the bankers at two, so catch him in between."

"Great. He'll probably grab a soup and sandwich at Sally's."

"Oh, no. Woolworth's. Loves their chicken salad."

☙❧

Earlier that week, Kathy had presented Bucky with a new briefcase. On it was stenciled *Bucky Ontario. Alsop Chrysler Plymouth Motors.* She'd admitted it might be a little premature, but she had assured him that he'd be an official employee soon. At twelve-fifteen, Bucky crammed it with Fury brochures and raced home. He hoped he'd find that picture of the chief's daughter. He wasn't the most organized person in the world.

After rifling through his closet, he worried Kindra might have the only copy. He emptied the desk drawers onto the floor. *Crap!* He threw the bedspread up and clawed under the bed like a dog digging for a bone. Out came car magazines, his high school picture album, and a blue folder. Inside, pictures. On top, his kid sister in a new bathing suit that showed a little fat across her tummy. He flipped through the photos and found Kindra's.

After ten minutes of riding through cold, biting air, he reached Woolworth's just after one. He ran inside and slowed to catch his breath.

Searching the crowded lunch counter, he spotted two empty twirly stools by the wall. A *saved* sign perched in front of the stool nearest the wall. Bucky rushed to the seat beside it and plopped down, feeling lucky. A red-haired waitress with freckled arms came by. Bucky nodded to the saved stool. "For the chief, I'll bet."

"Not this time." She removed the sign. "What can I get you?"

Bucky gulped. "You mean he's not coming?"

She cocked her head toward a brown bag by the register. "His lunch is being picked up."

Bucky scurried off. The chief would probably eat at his desk, rehearsing excuses why the bank robbers got away. Damn! His strategy demanded he see the chief before he met with the bankers. He stopped and looked back at the lunch bag. A creamy-faced young waitress stood next to it. With the crowd, she might not have noticed him come in.

Before he could lose his nerve, he dashed to the register. "I'm here to pick up Chief Parker's lunch."

She handed him the bag, and Bucky dug into his pocket.

"It's on his tab," she said and turned away.

Bucky hightailed it the two blocks to police headquarters and dashed inside. The desk sergeant sat reading a newspaper and chewing gum like a cow. A cane rested across his lap. Panting, Bucky burst out, "Where's the chief's office?" He waved the bag. "His lunch."

Without glancing up, the sergeant pointed to the door beside him.

Bucky opened it and went in.

"Hey, hold up."

Bucky froze, and a sick feeling washed over him.

"Leave the lunch with me. I'll see the chief gets it."

"That's okay, he's expecting me." Bucky held up his briefcase. "Got some important papers to show him."

The sergeant nodded. Bucky scurried down the hall on wobbly legs, hoping Mrs. Rheingold was out and the chief in. He stood at the closed door, catching his breath, then entered an empty outer office. A nameplate on the desk said, *Mrs. Rheingold.* Nervous as a cricket on a crowded floor, he tiptoed the few steps to a partially open door and took a deep breath.

The chief sat hunched over his desk, writing. His blue uniform fit tight at the shoulders and across the chest. Rolled up sleeves exposed dark hairy forearms. Distaste showed in his face and in the set of his body.

"Lunch, sir."

"Put it here on the desk," the chief said, without looking up.

Bucky marched over, opened his briefcase, whipped out a brochure, and smacked it down.

The chief flinched, then glanced at the brochure's glossy cover. He shot Bucky a puzzled look. "You! What the blazes is Alsop up to?"

"Nothing, sir." Bucky tapped the pictured Fury. "But here's the solution to your problem."

"Solution to *what?*"

"If I could just have a minute. The town's riled up about your officers letting the bank robbers get away. Folks are asking for your head."

A blue vein throbbed in the chief's neck.

Bucky raised his palms. "I agree, sir. The perception of you heading a bumbling police force is outrageous. But you can change that by showing yourself as a chief who looks disaster in the eye and acts boldly."

The blue vein bulged.

Bucky snagged a chair and sat edgewise. "A fleet of these Furies is the ticket, sir." He nudged the brochure closer to the chief. Parker put down his pencil and leafed through. "Bank robbers will never again skedaddle scot-free out of your town. You'll have the nation's finest pursuit vehicles."

The chief turned a page. "Your minute's almost up."

"All right, listen." Bucky caught himself getting excited and talking loud. "I mean, every crook, thief, scoundrel, and would-be bank robber both sides of the Mississippi knows that Defiance's banks provide free withdrawals. Why? Because any souped-up jalopy can outrun your junk-heap Chevys. If you want to prevent that and remain chief, you'll convince the bankers waiting in your conference room that you're going to protect their money by purchasing a fleet of—" Bucky jabbed his finger at the brochure, "—those cars."

The chief tossed down the brochure, sat back, and locked his fingers across his chest. "What's so special about them?"

"In a nutshell—speed. Nothing touches a Fury. V-8 with dual quads. They blew Corvettes and T-Birds off Daytona Beach."

The chief hunched forward and picked up his pencil. "How much?"

Bucky turned to the last page of the brochure where he had penciled in the list price of $2,925. The chief scribbled the figure and did some arithmetic. He circled his answer and slid the paper to Bucky, then leaned back and tapped his pencil against his palm. "That's a lot of money, son."

The chief had written five cars and a figure of eleven thousand five hundred dollars. Bucky mentally did his own arithmetic. The chief was taking a twenty—twenty-one percent discount. Even with a five-car volume, Bucky couldn't sell at that price and make enough margin.

"Can't do it, Chief. The fact is, Furies are cheap at twenty-nine twenty-five. The closest car to a Fury costs a third more and is half as good. Tell you what, I'll knock off *fifteen* percent and sweeten the deal by including police lights and two-way radios at cost. Probably catch hell for this, but I'll throw in mounted shotgun racks." Bucky figured Chrysler would include those extras at fleet discount.

The chief scratched out more figures. Sat back and

didn't say anything, just clicked his thumbnail against a front tooth. Finally, he said, "Might be able to sell that."

"You have choice of colors. I suggest black and white. With gun racks, you'll have a squadron of screaming machines." Bucky looked at his watch. "I suggest you call the press and tell them you've found the answer to all your problems, a way to prevent robbers from ever messing with Defiance again. You can spread these around to everyone." Bucky pulled out more brochures. "Oh, and Chief, here's your lunch."

"Hello, gentlemen." It was Mrs. Rheingold. "Bucky, I see you've found the chief. Does he like the picture?"

"Oops, almost forgot." He grabbed the photo of the chief's daughter from his briefcase. "Here, Chief. This is for you." He handed it over and headed for the door. He had orders to write.

CHAPTER 13

Having given up on getting the chief to help, Alsop cruised the courthouse again on the second night, searching for a parking spot on the street with a view of the burial site. He would stand watch for someone planting the bone, although it started to take a toll. The short nap after lunch back home had helped somewhat.

He slid in between two cars outside a beer joint about sixty feet from the courthouse lawn. A generator whirled, and portable lights illuminated the hole. The same two Cheyennes sat guarding the site like junkyard dogs.

At ten-thirty, he finished his last cigarette and flicked the butt out the window. He'd been waiting two hours in the cold, running the heater on and off and wished he'd brought a thermos of hot soup.

A yellow pickup rumbled in and parked two cars over. It was the fourth vehicle to arrive; the others belonged to beer joint patrons.

He thought there were two people in the car, but it was dark, and he wasn't sure.

The driver's door opened, and a short-necked Indian with long hair and hunched shoulders slid out, carrying a brown shopping bag. He must be the Caddo Tony said would be delivering the human bone. He started up the courthouse lawn.

Alsop got out of his car and stood beside a phone booth by the beer joint. He watched as short-neck made his way up the brightly lit lawn, puffs of breath streaming around his head. He reached the ropes and stopped, glanced around and ducked under. Both guards rushed to him. Short-neck raised a hand. They talked a minute before the three disappeared a few yards behind an oak tree. The Caddo was probably paying off the Cheyenne guards. Another minute and the sentries reappeared and settled back into their chairs. Moments later, short-neck emerged from behind the tree holding something against his thigh. As he passed the hole, he flicked it in.

Alsop trotted onto the lawn and hollered, "You can stop right there, fella."

A second later something struck his head, and he plunged into an abyss.

❧❦❧

Alsop opened his eyes in an unfamiliar room. Jo-Dee, her eyelids shut, lay on a cot across from him. A Negro man wearing what looked like white pajamas stood by a machine making pinging sounds. Alsop pulled himself up.

Pajama-man noticed his movement, his eyes bulged, and he hurried from the room.

"Jo-Dee!" Alsop barked. "Wake up. Where are we?"

Her pool-blue eyes fluttered open. "Thank God!" She jumped up and dashed to his side, clutching his hand as tears flooded her eyes. "I was so worried! You're in a hospital. How do you feel?"

"Don't know. Kind of hungry, I guess. What day is it?"

"Sunday. Someone hit you on the head last night."

Pajama-man scurried back into the room, followed by a nurse with a white cap and reedy arms. She took Alsop's wrist, stared at her watch, and nudged his chest with her free hand. "You need to lie still until the doctor arrives."

"He's hungry," Jo-Dee said.

"When the doctor gets here."

The door flew open, and Dr. Carrington whisked in, white smock flaring, like Errol Flynn leaping from a balcony. Jet-black hair, pencil-thin mustache—everything but the sword. "Well, if it isn't my favorite car dealer back from the dead." He grinned as if posing for an eight-by-ten glossy. "I almost made it out the door for supper." He whipped out a flashlight from his breast pocket and shined it into Alsop's eyes. "How do you feel?"

"Head hurts a little." Alsop raised a hand to it.

"Follow my finger." He moved it left to right. "How's Bucky, that new car salesman working out?"

"Fine."

"I want you to get out of bed and stand on one foot. Bucky called me up. Said it was time for a new car. My Oldsmobile was due for an expensive valve job."

"How'd he know that?" The fella kept surprising him, though he rather wished the fog in his head would clear up.

The doctor helped Alsop sit on the bed's edge. "Didn't say. But he knew the year and guessed the correct mileage. Offered me a good deal on an Imperial."

"He must know you have good taste."

The doctor pulled out a little hammer from his coat pocket and tapped Alsop's knees. "What's the last thing you remember?"

"I yelled at a man. It was dark."

"Then what?"

"Then nothing. Two minutes ago, I woke up."

The doctor put away his hammer and asked Alsop to count backwards from eighty-five to seventy-five and state his date of birth.

"Is he all right?" Jo-Dee asked, hovering over her husband.

"He's had a concussion from a blow that didn't break the skin, and by all appearances he seems fine. But hey, I'm only a doctor." Carrington flashed that grin again and slapped Alsop's leg. "Looks like you're still in the car business."

"What the hell happened?" Alsop asked.

"Jo-Dee'll fill you in. I've got a hot date." He winked.

"Can I go home?"

The doctor made a sad face. "Sorry, you need to stick around overnight for observation. Don't worry, I'll probably free you in the morning." He headed for the door.

"Doc," Alsop said. "Are you going to buy it?"

He stopped and turned. "Huh?"

"The Imperial. You going to buy it?"

"Didn't you know? Bought it yesterday. Sweet dreams. I'll have someone order you a light supper and a meal for Jo-Dee."

The doctor fluttered out, and the nurse followed after.

Alsop turned to Jo-Dee. "Tell me what happened."

"When you hadn't returned by midnight, I drove to the courthouse and found your car. There were people everywhere, and someone told me a person got killed and taken away in an ambulance." She put a hand to her heart and took a deep breath, her voice failing her momentarily. "I rushed over and found you here with a concussion. A policeman told me you were lying unconscious on the courthouse lawn, and that a witness leaving the beer joint saw two Indians jump into a yellow pickup and take off. I insisted that Chief Parker be summoned at once. When he arrived, I was so upset I yelled at him for having you do his police work."

Alsop held back a proud smile.

"Don't worry," she said. "I didn't identify Tony, but I told the chief that Caddo people were scheming to plant a bone. He dashed right off."

She went on to say that Chief Parker had retrieved the bone and took the two Cheyenne guards into custody. They were interrogated and threatened with an attempted murder charge. They then admitted to accepting a hundred dollars from a Caddo who approached them with a bag containing a bone. The chief authorized Jessie to resume digging.

Alsop nodded. "There must've been a second Caddo in the pickup who clobbered me."

"And left you for dead. You know, Cal, the chief's going to ask about your informant, and you need to tell him. They've got to catch those hoodlums."

"Can't do it, Jo-Dee. I gave my word."

"I don't care about your word if you end up dead!" She burst into tears. "I was worried sick. I didn't know where you were or what had happened to you, and when I heard the report about someone getting killed—God. What if it had been true?"

"Shh, shh," Alsop murmured, pulling her into his arms. She buried her face in his shoulder. "I'm so sorry you had to go through this. I admit, trying to handle those Caddos by myself was stupid. It won't happen again."
Except if absolutely necessary.

CHAPTER 14

Bucky sat at the table eating chicken noodle soup and feeling mighty good about doubling his sales quota. Seven cars in one week. Including one to the boss's doctor. Not bad. That cinched the job. He thought about Marybeth's baby. And the more he thought about it, the more determined he was to find out if she really buried it. But there was a fly in the axle grease. Trespassing on Kansas's property posed a serious health risk. He got up and turned to his trusty Carnegie book: *The surest way to conquer fear is to do the thing you fear to do.*

He picked up the phone. Hopefully, Gustafson wouldn't answer.

"Hello."

Her voice sounded different. "Kindra, it's me. Are you all right?"

"I'm fine. We were at the hospital with Grandmother."

"What happened? Is she all right?"

"She fell, but she's okay."

"That's good, I mean, it's good she's okay. Can you come over? I've got a plan."

"Another one?"

Bucky knew the unspoken message: *Here we go again.* "You want your mother's ring, don't you?"

"Give me half an hour," she said, suddenly perking up.

"Wait. You've got a shovel, right?"

"In the shed. Why?"

"Bring it. And don't wear anything white."

☙❧

Dressed warmly in a turtleneck, chamois shirt, corduroy pants, coat, and gloves, Bucky waited outside his rooming house for Kindra. Thick clouds covered the partial moon like the crown of a skull. When she drove up, he jumped in and gave directions. She told him her crippled grandmother had broken a collarbone, and she didn't seem sad or anything. More excited about her cousin Abby coming up from Houston to help care for the poor woman.

After hearing about Bucky's big car sale, she asked, "Why the dark clothes and shovel?"

Bucky explained about the grave, and Kansas not having pets. "The baby must be buried."

"I don't know." Her shoulders shivered. "Digging up a baby doesn't feel right."

"VO said if we find the baby, we'll find the ring. Besides, aren't you curious about the baby? I am."

"It sounds creepy, but—if I'm going to become a nurse, I suppose I should get used to unpleasant sights."

At eight-forty, they arrived at the spot where Bucky had parked his motorcycle the day he took Marybeth's picture. Thick clouds now blocked the moon and stars. Perfect. No one could see them. Bucky had brought a flashlight to use, but he hoped it wouldn't be necessary. No point giving Kansas an easy target.

With Bucky carrying the shovel and leading the way,

they extended their arms to prevent crashing headlong into a tree. They inched down through thicket, shuffling their feet over leaves and twigs, around trees and rocks.

Bucky tripped, and Kindra tumbled into him. He whispered for her to hold onto his shoulders. She did, with her forearms pressed flat against his back. Whenever he stopped to change direction, she clipped his heels. He felt like telling her to stay back a little, but lumbered on instead.

They crept through depressions and over logs, and once got tangled in a thorny blackberry bush. Bucky's neck stung from scratches. A gust of air passed, silent as fog. Kindra yelped.

"Shh," he said.

"Wa—what was that?"

"Probably an owl. Their wings don't make noise."

They finally reached the clearing near the house. A dim light glowed inside. Bucky remembered roughly where the grave was. "We'll move left, then crawl toward the house, feeling for the mound of dirt."

They inched forward crab-like, the shovel cradled in Bucky's arms, commando style. "I think we missed it," he whispered, adding, "Let's spread apart and go back." Once there, Bucky turned and stared at the house. "We must've passed over the grave."

"I felt some soft dirt, but it wasn't a mound," Kindra said.

"I'll follow you back."

Once again, they dragged themselves across. "Here," she said, after going about ten feet.

Bucky felt around. "This is it. No mound, but the dirt's soft." They stood. "Move aside."

She grabbed his arm. "Wait! What if the baby's there?"

"What?"

"I mean, what do we do?"

"What do you think? We look for the ring."

"But—but then what?"

A chill raced down Bucky's back. He hadn't thought what to do with the baby. His mind spun for several seconds of stretched time. Leave it in the hole? That felt disrespectful. But where could they take it? What would they say?

"Look," he said, "if we take it anywhere, we're screwed. The newspapers—everyone will find out. Including Kansas. And I sure as hell don't want that. If we can't leave it here, we shouldn't do this." He heard her sniffle and felt for her hands. Found one and squeezed. "You okay?"

She sniffled again. "I guess."

"Does that mean dig? It's up to you."

She may have nodded, but he wasn't sure. "Well?"

"Go on."

The earth was soft and the digging easy. Down two feet and nothing. Maybe it wasn't a grave. Maybe—the blade hit hard dirt. He dropped to his knees and scooped out loose soil with his hands, then he stopped.

"What's wrong?"

"The baby's not there." He pulled the flashlight from his pocket. "Here, take this and keep your back to the house. Stick it into the hole and shield the light before you turn it on."

Bucky peered into the hole lit with slivers of light from between her fingers. He ran his hand around the bottom.

Something caught the light. "What's that?" Kindra said, a little too loud.

Bucky grabbed what appeared to be a large button.

A clank came from the house.

Bucky stuffed the button in his pocket. "Quick, let's fill the hole and split."

e∕ɔe∕ɔ

Bucky lay on his bed, absently rubbing the button between his fingers and staring at a spider web in the corner of the room. A black widow bit his girlfriend once. Right under her mop of red hair. Bucky had always thought a black widow bite killed people. But they just get really sick. He had ditched school to stay with her. Fed her chicken soup his gramma made. Read books to her, too. Tom Sawyer. Different ones. Those were the days.

He looked closely at the button. Quarter-size, brass and dome-shaped. A raised cluster of stars encircled the number seven. Where'd it come from? A shirt? Coat? Dress? Somebody had dug a hole there but what for? Certainly not to bury a button. Not even Kansas was that weird.

He put it on the nightstand and turned off the light. VO's voice looped in his head. *'Find the baby, find the ring.'*

CHAPTER 15

Bucky hurried into Alsop's office. "Take a look at this." He tossed a photograph onto the desk and slid into a chair.

Alsop shrugged. "I see Kansas scratching his ass."

"He's also about to go from your kitchen into the back yard." Bucky had been browsing through the party photos, and this one chilled his veins. "See, his left hand's reaching for the door knob." He stabbed a finger at the slightly blurred hand. "I took that picture about twenty minutes before I went outside and sat with you. How long had you been there before I came out?"

"Not more than five minutes, I'd say."

"That gave Kansas fifteen minutes to go out the door and sneak around the house to the street. He could've cut Will's brake line, then slipped back inside."

Alsop thought a moment, then reached for the phone. "I'll call the chief."

"Wait. Let's talk to Kansas ourselves. The chief won't do it until he's good and ready."

Alsop leaned back and rocked. "You've got a point. The man keeps to his own schedule." He reached over and pressed the intercom. "Kathy, tell Kansas to see me immediately."

Bucky scooted his chair to the side of the desk, leaving the other one facing Alsop, like a hot seat. "What's the deal with Kansas's limp, do you know?"

"An army wound. He was a sergeant in Korea. Motor Pool. That is, until he got wounded in the foot."

Kansas came in, wiping his hands on a rag. "They're done." He glared at Bucky like he was something sticking to the bottom of his shoe. Fine. Let him glare.

"Take a seat," Alsop said. "What's done?"

"The skids, o'course. I'll put those items you wanted in the car. Gasoline, postcards, beer—all of it. Then I'll wrap the car in plastic like a Christmas present. Guard it until Saturday when it gets buried."

"It's not the only thing that's going to get buried. Sit down."

Kansas stayed motionless, probably trying to read Alsop's mind.

"I told you to sit," Alsop barked. "Did you really think you'd get away with it?"

Kansas sat. "You talkin' about Will's murder?"

"I'm not talking about being late for work."

"Told you I didn't kill anybody."

Bucky thrust the picture onto Kansas's lap. "You told us you never left the house."

Kansas's jaw clenched. "I oughta stick that camera up your ass." He flung the picture onto the desk. "I left the house, not the premises. Was only in the backyard a couple minutes."

"Uh-huh," Bucky said. "Anybody see you?"

Kansas rubbed his elbow. "Hope not."

Alsop said, "What the hell's that supposed to mean?"

"I was taking a piss. All right?"

"A piss!" Alsop burst. "You have a problem using toilets?"

"My house has a cesspool and draining costs money. Habit, I suppose."

He really *is* weird. Bucky said, "So you pissed in the boss's bushes?"

"The jasmine, to be exact."

Bucky tried to calculate if Kansas had enough time to take a piss and cut the brake line. "How long were you outside?"

"I don't answer to you. But I'll tell you anyhow. Two minutes at the most. Told Hector I was gonna take a leak."

Alsop buzzed Kathy and asked her to send Hector in. "Kansas, wait in the lounge. When you see Hector come in, go back to work."

Kansas gave Bucky a cold stare, turned, and left.

"His story should hold water if Hector backs it," Alsop said.

Hector came in, head bowed, as though summoned by the principal. He scratched an ear with his hook and left a grease smudge. "Sit down, Hector," Alsop said. "You look agitated. What's the problem?"

Hector's eyes darted around like two scared finches seeking a safe perch. "I got no problem."

"You seem nervous."

"Not nerv—no, I'm fine."

A cold finger touched Bucky's heart. Hector? A murderer? "Hector, did you cut Will's brake line?"

He recoiled like he'd crossed jumper cables. "That what you guys think? *Jesus*, no! I talked to Chief Parker and accounted for every minute of that night."

But was he covering for Kansas? "Then who did?" Bucky asked.

Hector ran his hook through the back of his collar. "How the hell would I know?"

Alsop leaned close to him. "Look at me, Hector."

Hector's eyes flitted about.

"Hector, *look* at me."

His eyes slid over to Alsop.

"You're hiding something. Now talk!"

"Ka—Kansas said it was okay. Never done it before but had to."

Alsop squinted. "Never done what?"

"Left work early. And…and signed out normal quittin' time."

Alsop slumped in his chair. "Why'd you do that?"

"The school nurse called the house. Said my daughter had the curse." He flicked a glimpse at Bucky. "It was her first and musta scared her. So…you know…she had to be picked up. The wife called me 'cause she couldn't leave the house. Ate leftover fish chowder night before. Stomach churnin' and all. Luckily, I didn't have none."

"Jeez, Hector, you don't get docked for emergencies. That's not the way we operate."

"Only been here a few months. Thought maybe Kansas was being nice, stretchin' things."

Bucky blew out a quiet puff of air. It was just like Kansas to deliberately give Hector that impression.

"You're a good man, Hector," Alsop said. "You did nothing wrong. How are Millie and Suzie?"

"Suzie got fixed-up proper, and the wife's fine."

"Hector," Bucky said, "the night of the accident. What happened after you talked to Kansas in the kitchen?"

"Went into the living room, talked to Mrs. Alsop about her fine potato salad, then sat with the wife."

"What did Kansas do?"

"How should I know? Like I say, I went into the living room."

"But he did something," Bucky urged.

"What?"

"He was going to do something."

"I just told you—"

Alsop slapped the desk. "Hector, think! Did Kansas say he was going to do something?"

Hector blinked a bunch a times. "Take a piss. That whatcha mean?"

Bucky and Alsop exchanged glances.

"You can go back to work, Hector," Alsop said.

"Before you leave," Bucky said. "Did you see Kansas come back in after taking his piss?"

Hector puckered his lips and thought a moment. "Can't say I did." He got up and left.

"It's still possible Kansas cut the brake line, even if he did take a piss," Bucky said.

"Possible, but he has a good alibi."

Bucky nodded. Assuming Hector told the truth.

Alsop opened a drawer and pulled out a set of keys. "Here. They're to Peter Thomas's old roadster. Now that you're on the permanent roster, consider it a signing bonus. Besides, I'm tired of listening to that God-awful putt-putt of yours. By the way, what made you think to contact Doc Carrington?"

"Our records showed he bought his last car back in '54 and the one before that in '51. He was due."

"Cal." Kathy's voice came over the intercom. "Chief Parker just pulled onto the lot."

CHAPTER 16

Alsop grabbed his hat. It was a fair bet that Chief Parker wanted to know how he learned about the planted bone. To ease the chief's disappointment, Alsop took him out back for a stroll along the creek and maybe learn how the murder investigation was going. Although the chief was pretty good at keeping his cards close to his vest.

Alsop had fallen in love with the creek when he bought the property from Doc Little ten years ago and built his dealership. He enjoyed showing it to customers, especially with the dogwood in bloom. Put folks in a buying mood.

The sun peeked through patches of clouds, and the air felt nippy. After crossing a footbridge, the chief tucked a handkerchief under the back of his hat, covering his neck.

"That's a helluva coup you pulled with the bankers," Alsop said. "Everyone supports your plan to finally update the town's fleet of feeble cruisers."

"Works out nicely for you, wouldn't you say?"

"Not to bite the hand that signed the contract, but I've been after you to update for three years."

"Timing's everything. Back then, you didn't have anything to match the Fury. Our being friends didn't justify throwing the town's money into a fleet of new cars simply to please you. Besides, at the time you didn't have Bucky whatshisname. That boy's good. Now, about this business of you getting assaulted. Jo-Dee said someone tipped you off about the phony bone deal before you called me. Who was it?"

Alsop raised a blueberry branch for the chief to duck under. "If I told you, my informant would catch a lot more than hell from the Caddo people."

"Get serious, Cal. Someone tried to kill you."

"Sorry, Chief, I promised."

Parker stopped and glared at him, then shook his head. "At least tell me if it was a goddamn Indian."

Alsop nodded. "He also said the Caddo people are planning to demonstrate at the commemoration."

"They'll pour into town like grain in a hopper. Carry protest signs and chant their heads off. A waste of their time and my resources keeping them in line. They're crazy to think they'll ever get their land back. Maybe you'll spot the one who planted the bone."

"In case I don't, Bucky's taking pictures of every Indian male."

"That's good. Our photographer retired and hasn't been replaced. Bucky had better keep his camera dry."

"Hopefully, the storm won't hit until the car's in the ground and covered."

"I got word the governor's not coming."

Alsop puffed his cheeks and blew out. "Then we're screwed. The mayor needs his support to win the election. If he loses, Johnston and Overstreet will get the racetrack they've been angling for."

"It'll make Tulsa County folks happy as drunken Shriners." The chief picked up a small stone, studied it, and then dropped it. "You didn't take me out here for fresh air. I assume you have something on your mind."

"Have any leads on Will and Miss Iris's killer?"

"I might. You driving at something?"

"You've talked to Kansas?"

"He came into the station on his own."

"He tell you about his wanting Will's job as foreman?"

"That's why he came in. Figured that would make him a suspect. Offered to go to Tulsa and take a lie detector test."

Now that was interesting. "Did he?"

"No, but I'm not counting it out."

"Any other leads?"

The chief picked up another stone and studied it carefully. He planted his feet and skipped it across the still stream. It left rings on the surface like a series of plates. "As a kid we used to skip stones across Lake Hento. Search hours for the right stones. The best ones were silver dollar size, smooth and flat. A boy learns a lot about patience searching for stones."

Alsop hadn't the faintest idea of the chief's point.

"I found a partial foot impression in the berm near where Will parked his car. Only the toe area, but clear as a fresh-minted gold piece. Nobody knows except you and Bucky. Neither of you are to say a peep to anyone. I'm ass-deep with this commemoration whoop-de-do and haven't had a chance to follow up.

They returned up the creek in silence. Alsop considered the foot impression a big break, but wondered if the chief was holding something back.

Back in his office, Alsop found a *while you were out message* on his desk. It was marked urgent. *Tony called. Must see you ASAP.*

CHAPTER 17

Satan Wants YOU!

That's what the sign said in front of the same First Methodist Church that held Miss Iris's memorial. Now that Bucky's station in life had advanced from store clerk to successful car salesman, folks expected church attendance. Certainly for businessmen—and aspiring statesman.

The wooden structure was old, but it had a good feeling. Like being in someone's home. Bucky sat near the back waiting for the pastor to begin and listened to the cool breeze whisper through the open doorway. He thought of his mamma.

She had been religious, but she didn't talk much about it. His daddy said his religion was to do good and judge people by what they did. Some things are good, some aren't. That's all a man could say.

Pastor Agnew's deep voice snapped Bucky back to the present. A slender man in his early fifties, the pastor's narrow eyes sat close together like those of a falcon preparing for flight. He was a pretty good speaker, especially when he got riled up about supporting the church or resisting the devil.

Kindra and her grandfather sat a few rows up. Mr.

Gustafson's head looked polished on top, and scraggly catfish-like hairs stuck out from his ears.

Bucky wanted to make peace with his ex-boss and councilman. After all, if he wanted to eventually be seated on the council and then become mayor, he'd want allies, not enemies.

While the pastor droned on about sin and Satan, Bucky mentally leafed through his Carnegie book for something on disgruntled ex-employers. Couldn't remember anything, so he'd just smile and offer a friendly greeting.

Following the service, he lingered on the patio, amazed at how cheerful everybody seemed after listening to all the horrible things that might happen to them because of their sins. The pastor emphasized three: dishonesty, deceit, and devilment.

Bucky said hello to old friends from the store and introduced himself to new acquaintances. He fixed each person with a smile like a searchlight, as if thrilled to bits just talking with them. And he mustered all his positive thinking trying to feel it. Didn't want to be a phony.

He spotted Kindra and her grandfather talking to Pastor Agnew. Mr. Gustafson was probably gushing about the inspiring sermon. Bucky hadn't noticed Marybeth in church, but there she was, standing in the hot chocolate line.

When Kindra and her grandfather came down the steps, Bucky smiled and padded up to them. "Good morning, Mr. Gustafson. It's good to see you." He nodded to Kindra and wondered how she felt about their grave-digging excursion two nights earlier. All they had to show for their effort was a crummy button.

"Good to see you, too, Bucky." Gustafson extended his hand. He didn't smile but wasn't unfriendly either.

Bucky shook his hand and tossed a nod toward the refreshment table. "Can I get you two some soup or hot chocolate?"

Gustafson waved his hand, as if at a fly on his nose. "None for me, thanks. That was a beautiful tribute you gave to Miss Iris the other day, Bucky. And, well…I'm happy for you having garnered that job at Alsop's. Appreciate you stopping to say hello."

"Thank you, Mr. Gustafson. That means a lot to me."

Kindra piped up, "I'll take that hot chocolate. Grandfather, maybe Bucky can help me put up the posters, and you won't have to."

Gustafson waved his hand again. "Thank you, dear, but Bucky might be busy."

"What posters?"

"Advertising next Saturday's fiftieth anniversary," Kindra explained.

"Sure, I'll help."

Gustafson glanced at his watch. "Doc Little had invited me to go fishing with him this afternoon. So if you'll excuse me, I'll say hello to some friends and then run along." He shuffled off and started talking to Marybeth at the hot chocolate table.

Kindra stared at her with clenched fists. "Forget the hot chocolate. Let's go."

✷✷✷

Bucky drove Kindra home in his new roaster to pick up her posters. She thought the car was pretty neat, but told Bucky he should hang big fuzzy dice from the mirror. Like in her favorite movie, *Rebel Without a Cause*.

Along the way, Bucky asked, "How far's Tulsa?" He'd been thinking about the foot impression the chief had sent there for analysis.

"Seventy miles or so. Why?"

"Just wondering. I think Chief Parker might have a lead."

"You should just drop that whole thing. There's nothing anybody can do about it now."

"You can drop it, but I'm not going to. If it's all the same to you, I'd like to know who killed Will and Miss Iris, and why."

"That's what we have policemen for."

"Then maybe you should have them find your mother's ring."

"Oh, sure. And have Grandfather find out. He'd kill me."

"I doubt Chief Parker would get around to doing anything, anyway." It had been five days since they discovered the foot impression, and Bucky hadn't heard diddlysquat from the chief.

After picking up the posters, Bucky stopped at his house to grab his camera and a photo he wanted to surprise Kindra with later.

They started at the south of town and worked north, stopping at major thoroughfares. Bucky nailed posters to signs and telephone poles. Kindra taped them to store windows and a Third Street bus bench advertising Fromm Mortuary with the slogan *Proper Burials Save Souls*. Bucky took a picture of her plastering a poster over Lamar Fromm's solemn face.

COME CELEBRATE OUR STATE'S FIFTIETH ANNIVERSARY WITH THE BURIAL OF A TIME CAPSULE. COURTHOUSE LAWN, NEXT SATURDAY, ONE O'CLOCK.

They had yet to do Main Street, but hunger prompted a stop at Sally's, the only café open Sundays. They served large portions and had a screen door that *kerboinged* and *bammed*, making every entrance an occasion. Bucky ate many of his meals there, but never on

Mondays when they served liver. Couldn't stand to even smell the stuff.

They parked in the café lot next to a pickup full of chickens clucking their heads off and tramped inside to the sharp smell of coffee. A lazy fan, always on to clear out cigarette smoke, twirled above the entrance. Most of the church crowd had cleared out. An elderly couple in blue bib overalls, probably the chicken ranchers, sat at the counter gabbing it up with the cook. Above the kitchen door behind him hung a fly strip that looked pretty full. On the back wall was a pay phone with a sign—*Whites only.*

Bucky grabbed his favorite booth near the front window. From there he had photographed Doc Little getting a ticket for making an illegal left turn. That same day, he photographed a funeral service at Greenhill Negro Cemetery. Two colored workers dropped a casket, and the corpse slid into the grave like an at-sea burial. The photo showed a pair of legs sticking up and Lamar Fromm dashing to the rescue.

Kindra got in first and patted the seat. "Sit here."

Bucky plopped down across. "That's okay. More room over here." He liked having space.

Jolene, a long-faced waitress, stopped by. She had loose-fitting skin, like those dogs with coats several sizes too large. She wiped the table with a gray rag, emptied the ashtray into it and wiped the ashtray clean. Jolene wasn't the type to talk much, nor worry about crumbs landing in Bucky's lap.

He brushed what seemed like piecrust from his pants and got a hankering for peach pie.

Jolene grabbed a pad and pencil from her apron and touched the pencil tip to her tongue. "What'll it be?"

Kindra said, "Hamburger, fries, and a vanilla shake."

"And you?"

"The same, but make my shake chocolate. You got peach pie?"

Jolene swallowed and her Adam's apple did a little dance. "When have you seen peach pie in November?"

"Okay, forget it."

She left, and Bucky griped, "Damn, I was counting on that. Next time I'll order popcorn crawfish. That'll get her."

"She's creepy looking, don't you think?" Kindra whispered.

"She has an Adam's apple."

Kindra made a face. "Yuck."

"Girls don't have one. She's probably a man but doesn't know it."

"*Stop.*"

"That can really happen. I'm not kidding. Read about it in a magazine."

"*Surrre*. Tell me another one."

"You probably never heard of Christine Jorgensen. He was a man who changed into a woman."

"I've *heard* of her. So?"

"If a man thinks he's a woman, he's got to have a reason. You know, he might like girl things, sewing and cleaning house. Looking at it in reverse, her Adam's apple probably means she's a man, but if she never heard of Christine Jorgensen, it never occurred to her. I probably didn't say that very well, but I'll bet there's thousands of them around. Lotsa folks would puke if they knew. I don't mind. Live and let live, that's my philosophy."

Kindra wrinkled her forehead. "What about...you know?"

"Can't remember. Pretty sure they chopped it off."

Kindra leaned in. "Do you think Marybeth—"

Jolene swept by and dropped off two overflowing glasses of ice water.

Kindra tried again. "Do you really think Marybeth buried her baby?"

Bucky chewed on an ice cube. "Makes sense if she didn't want anybody to know about it."

"But it wasn't there anymore. Why would she dig it back up?"

"She knew I saw her kneeling at the grave and was afraid I might tell someone." That was the only explanation he could think of, and it took him a long time to think of it.

Kindra took a sip of water. "Why do you think the baby died?"

"Complications. No doctor, maybe Marybeth didn't know to spank it. Maybe the cord got around its neck a buncha times. That happens. Tell you something else. I'll bet she has a coat that's missing a button. Maybe got snagged by the shovel."

"She came in the store yesterday and talked to Grandfather. You know how she is with him, all friendly like. Anyway, I gave her a dirty look. I know I should feel sorry for her for losing her baby, and I guess I do. But I'm still mad at her and want my mother's ring back."

Jolene plopped down their orders. Bucky reached for the ketchup. "Want some?"

"No thanks."

He shook the bottle over his fries. Nothing. "Crap, I hate these things." He struck the bottom with his palm. Still nothing. "Now watch, it'll shoot all over the place." A hard strike and ketchup drenched his fries.

Jolene appeared with a cigarette between her creased red lips. "Everything all right?"

"We're fine," Bucky said.

She started to leave, but Kindra touched her arm. "Wait a minute. Bucky, her pin." Jolene wore a pin showing a milkshake surrounded by stars. "Don't the stars look familiar?"

"Lemmmeesse," Bucky said, trying to manage a mouthful of hamburger and speak at the same time. He swallowed and looked close, then fished out the button from his pocket.

Jolene peered at it through a haze of smoke. "It's a button."

"We know that," Bucky said. "But what do the stars mean?"

Jolene removed the cigarette from her lips and puckered them. "Probably nothing. The number seven's gotta mean something though."

Bucky felt suddenly hopeful. "Like what?"

Jolene tugged her saggy throat and sank into thought. "My son had a button with the number four."

"What'd it mean?" Kindra asked.

"Cub Scout troop number." Jolene toddled off.

Bucky smiled. "You think Marybeth was in troop seven?"

Kindra's eyes were moist. She lowered her head and pulled a hankie from her purse. She dabbed a tear.

"Golly, I was only joking."

"It's not right. Shouldn't the baby be baptized, or christened, or something?"

"I don't know. Maybe." Bucky didn't want to think about that. What was the point? There was nothing he could do about it. Besides, he didn't even know if the baby was dead. A hole in the ground didn't mean anything. Yet, *find the baby, find the ring.*

⌘

Bucky nailed the last poster to a power pole. "That's it. Let's stop by the dealership. It's closed, but I have a key. I want to take pictures of the Belvedere while it's still above ground."

He pulled into the agency lot, parked, and they went inside. There were four bays, each with a grease gun and air hose hanging above. Kansas's skids leaned against a wall in the tire-changing area. The device consisted of a steel frame with parallel trays where the car's wheels would sit. Bucky attached a flash to his camera and got a shot.

"Is this the car?" Kindra called from the back bay.

Bucky joined her. "That's it."

"It's beautiful. A shame to bury it."

"In fifty years it'll still be beautiful." He pulled out a small photo from his pocket and showed it to Kindra. He'd seen it the other day among her sweet sixteen pictures and retrieved it when he fetched his camera.

"I *love* that picture." She jumped up and down. "It's my favorite sweet sixteen picture." It showed Bucky with his arm across her shoulder, making a face for the camera. Eyes real big.

Bucky opened the passenger door and slipped the photo under the visor. "In fifty years you can show it to your grandchildren."

He closed the door and realized it would be better to shoot the car in sunlight. The key was in the ignition, so he moved the Belvedere outside under the dogwood trees. They weren't in bloom, but the late afternoon sun bathed the car in warm light, and the chrome sparkled.

He patted the front fender. "Hop up, Kindra."

"Oh, Bucky, I don't—"

"Come on, pretend you're Debbie Reynolds."

Kindra grinned and bounded onto the fender. Bucky posed her. "This leg up. Arms back." He looked through the camera. She really did look like Debbie Reynolds. "Tilt your head up and smile. Perfect." He got the shot.

"Now get in and wave." Giggling, she climbed inside. Bucky raised his camera. The crunching sound of tires on gravel drowned out its click. A black pickup yawed and bounced in their direction. It skidded to a stop.

Kansas.

Kindra jumped from the car.

"Don't worry," Bucky said smoothly. "We haven't done anything wrong."

Kansas vaulted from his truck and hobbled toward them in a firm stride, his face red. "Lucky I don't have my shotgun."

"Just taking pictures," Bucky said calmly.

"You got no business touching this car."

"Nothing to get your drawers in a bunch about. We're not hurting it."

"Don't matter, I'm in charge of this here automobile." Kansas ran a hand and critical eye over the hood. "Always pokin' around where ya got no mind to. You'll fry in hell someday." He glanced inside, then wiped his hands on a rag. "Ya didn't open the trunk, did ya? Important stuff in there."

"No need to be touchy about it. Besides, it's kind of hard since you have the trunk key." Bucky knew about all the stashed items. Including the postcards. The person closest to guessing Defiance's 2007 population would get the car.

"We just took pictures is all," Kindra whimpered, drifting closer to Bucky.

Kansas glared at her, then Bucky, his face redder than ever. "Don't ever touch my car again. Now get your asses outta here."

"It's not *your* car," Bucky shot back. "It's Cal's. And why are you so jumpy anyway?"

"Why, you son of a—" Kansas lurched forward, fist raised.

"Now look here!" Bucky stood his ground.

"Stop it!" Kindra burst, tugging on Bucky's sleeve. "Let's just go."

Bucky scowled, but Kindra was right. No point making things worse. They left, with Bucky wondering why Kansas was so protective of the car.

CHAPTER 18

Tony's urgent message could only mean bad news. Alsop hurried to the Speedy Mart and strode inside to the smell of spicy oxtail soup. Tony stood behind the counter, caught Alsop's eye, and shrugged. Too many customers. Alsop would wait outside for the place to clear out.

At the door, he grabbed a copy of *The Oklahoman* and sat on a stack of empty Coke cases under a dark gray sky and lit a cigarette. A small headline in section two caught his eye. *Double Murder Casts Pall Over State's Fiftieth Anniversary.* It was a follow-up story that described the circumstances of Will and Miss Iris's death. Alsop stiffened at the last sentence. *Defiance Police Chief Parker is following a lead and is confident he'll catch the killer.*

Alsop looked up from the paper. Did the chief tell Thomas about the foot impression? Even if he hadn't, he shouldn't have mentioned having leads. The killer might guess he left a footprint and dump his shoes.

A white pickup caked with red dirt bounced into the lot and skidded to a stop. The driver, an Indian, maybe eighteen, let out a high-pitched laugh. He sat hooting it up with a can of Schlitz beer and a fellow Indian passenger. He wore a patch on his shoulder, a square pattern of four tomahawks. Alsop knew the number four was sacred to the Caddo people, but the tomahawks were new.

Alsop took a deep drag of his cigarette and thought about how the Caddo people—among other nations—were driven from their homelands and marched into Oklahoma, forced to drag along only what they could carry, and that many had died along the way. He flipped his cigarette into the parking lot and wondered if the young Caddos were acting out generations of resentment. He went back inside and was pleased to see Tony was alone.

"Thank you, Councilman Alsop," Tony said.

"What's to thank me for?"

"Not giving me up to the cops. Heard you got knocked out. But, um…" His eyes flitted to the door. "Caddo people aren't finished yet."

Alsop tensed. "Finished with *what?*"

"Tomorrow, at your celebration, they're going to demonstrate. Couple hundred. Maybe more."

"Chief Parker will handle them."

"There's something else." A bell jingled, and Tony flinched. An old white male shuffled through the door.

"That's okay," Alsop said. "He's going to the back."

Tony opened his mouth when the bell jingled again. A teenage girl came in humming.

Alsop grabbed Tony's arm. "What is it?"

Tony leaned close. "A bomb."

The word slammed Alsop's chest like a fist.

Tony yanked his arm free. "Tomorrow. That's all I know."

Alsop took a pack of Juicy Fruit gum from a box and threw down a twenty. "Keep the change."

"That's okay. I just don't want to see anyone getting hurt." Tony slid the bill back.

Alsop stuffed it into Tony's shirt pocket, then side-stepped the girl near the door, opened it, and held it open for the two Indians from the parking lot. One bellowed, "Hey, Tony, my man!"

Alsop drove away, swiping sweat off his neck. What the hell kind of bomb? Gasoline? Dynamite? Maybe a time bomb under the grandstand—Or inside his Plymouth Belvedere.

CHAPTER 19

ucky, you don't have to call me twice a day," the chief said over the phone. "When I have more information, I'll let you know."

"But what about the toe print?"

"I'm leaving for Tulsa to check on it," he said sharply and hung up.

That's good that he's doing something. But once he gets a make on the shoe, how's he going to find the foot that goes in it?

Bucky got up from his desk and drifted to the Coke machine beside Alsop's office. Dug into his pocket for a nickel, but pulled out the dome-shape button. As he looked at it, sadness washed over him like ice water. *Button, button, who's got the button?* That was a game he played with sister Cassidy and gramma the day before she died.

She lived in a wood-frame house along the banks of the Tangipahoa River, and every day after school, she took care of him and three-year-old Cassidy until daddy picked them up. On this day, when the bell rang, he ran the three miles to her house, excited to show off his straight-A report card.

Gramma, rough-born and Southern-bred, hugged him

with her spindly arms and gnarled hands and stuffed him with his favorite homemade peach pie. To celebrate his grades, they left Cassidy with a neighbor, climbed into her rowboat, and headed up the river among the herons, gators, and mosquitoes, determined to catch that big striped bass that had broken Bucky's line days earlier.

Forty minutes of Bucky's hard rowing had brought them to the right spot. The low sun streamed through the swamp oaks, and the water sparkled like Gramma's blue eyes. She tossed over the anchor and smiled at Bucky with her wrinkled face and red-button cheeks. "Toss out your line, Bucky."

She pulled a camera from her bag, clutched her lower back and stood. Her braided hair hung over her shoulder like silk ropes. Unsteady on her stilt-like legs, she lifted the camera to her eye. "Smile."

The shutter clicked as a speedboat roared around a bend and zoomed past. The rowboat rocked in its wake. Gramma dropped the camera, her arms flailing, and tumbled over the side. Bucky grabbed for her, missed, and hit the water. Gramma thrashed and screamed while he heaved himself back into the boat and grabbed an oar. A seven-hundred-pound gator battered the water that sprayed red, its jaws locked onto Gramma's leg. It flung her about as if she hadn't a bone in her hundred-pound body. An instant later she was thrown over the boat. The gator arched high out of the water, its underbelly shiny as marble, twisted and swam off with her leg.

Bucky heaved a rugged breath and chased away the horrific images swirling in his mind.

"Oh, this door!" came a female voice from across the showroom floor.

A knockout blonde, thirtyish, had pushed open the heavy plate-glass door and squirmed into the dealership. She made a few short steps, stopped, and bent to straighten her low-cut red dress. Placing a hand on a well-rounded hip, she jutted her chin out, as if the door had been a major inconvenience aimed just at her.

Had he seen her in movies? She looked that good. Had the kind of figure that make a guy step back. He rolled his tongue up and tucked it back into his mouth and gripped the handkerchief in his right pocket. Women sometimes shook hands, so he wanted his dry.

He padded over to her, flashed his best smile, and snapped a card from his breast pocket. "Good afternoon, ma'am. Bucky Ontario, at your service." Her plump red lips and lavender eyes made his lips tingle.

"Do you have water?" she asked, placing red fingertips to her throat like she was really thirsty.

She said "worter," so he pegged her for a Noo Yawker.

"Yes, ma'am, water fountain's yonder." He pointed. "I'd be happy to fetch you a Coca-Cola."

"Maybe later." She started for the drinking fountain, tweaking her head for him to follow.

Heck *yeah*. She could've led him naked and draped with pork chops into a pack of salivating pit bulls.

"Willow!" A fleshy man with wavy dark hair and a sharp suit pushed through the door and headed their way, arms swinging.

The woman turned, and Bucky's eyes darted to her half-exposed breasts, jiggling like bobbers in a rough sea.

"Chamberlain scored fifty-two points," the man boomed. "*Murdered* North Carolina."

"La-di-da," she murmured, after taking a drink from the fountain. "Is the battery worn down again?"

He pinched her cheek with furry fingers. "If so, you push."

She smacked his hand away, while Bucky extended his. "Bucky Ontario. You're a Kansas fan?" Bucky wasn't big into sports, but as a salesman he knew to keep abreast.

"Bart D'Amato." He took Bucky's hand. "A New York man, but since Chamberlain plays for Kansas, I guess you could say I'm a Kansas man, too." His accent was more pronounced than the woman's. He leaned close to Bucky, smelling of Old Spice. "I'd give my left nut for the Knicks to snatch up Chamberlain in the draft. He'll score a hundred points someday." He gave a humorless bark, and his mismatched colored eyes widened. "You a basketball fan?"

"You bet." Bucky bent close. Old Spice met Aqua Velva. "Oklahoma. But don't tell anyone, my heart's with Louisiana, who murdered North Carolina last week."

Bart gave Bucky a friendly punch to the shoulder. "We're gonna look around."

Bucky slipped outside to check out the man's car. Dark blue '55 Cadillac Coupe de Ville, New York plates. He cupped his hands to the window and saw an ashtray crammed with cigar butts, and blueprints spread out on the seat.

He went back inside, figuring that Bart, like a lot of Caddy owners of two years, planned to trade in. But if he was just passing through, he might be comparison-shopping with plans to buy in New York.

Willow tagged along with Bart while he wandered from car to car. They lingered at a New Yorker. She checked out her reflection, and Bart checked out the grille.

Bucky sidled up to him. "Chrysler's ranked number one car maker of the year."

"You don't say?" Bart brushed his hand across the sleek hood.

"Motor Trend magazine says. Watch, in two years Cadillac will have this same look." Bucky couldn't think of a smooth way to add that it wouldn't be as good.

"What are we talkin' horse power here?" Bart strolled round to the car's side.

"Three-two-five." Bucky tried to sound like a seasoned pro. "Chrysler engines are ranked best in the world."

"My depth perception's crap since I lost my eye. Willow drives. For her it's about comfort and show."

Bucky had noticed his mismatched eyes. "Car accident?"

"Army jeep. Got drunk and slammed it into a ditch. Lost the eye. They never found it."

Bucky examined Bart's eyes, back-and-forth. "Incredible. Is it real?"

"Fuck no. Told you they couldn't find it. It's glass. People can't look me in the eye. Freaks 'em out 'cause the colors don't match perfectly."

Perfectly? Bucky squinted. One was black, the other light blue. "Looks real, anyhow. The dark one's glass, right?"

"No, the other one."

Bucky nodded. "You folks live here in Defiance?"

Bart jerked his thumb toward the car. "When this thing flies. I'm here on business."

Bucky remembered the blueprints in his car. "I'm guessing you're an architect."

Deep creases shot along both ridges of Bart's flat nose. "Now why would you guess that?"

"I don't know." Bucky shuffled his feet, afraid he'd offended the man. "All those tall New York buildings, I guess. Must be lots of architects."

"I hire architects." Bart and Old Spice leaned in. "And my business is confidential."

Bucky gulped. He'd guessed right.

Bart brushed the back of his hand down Bucky's tie and tugged his plaid lapels. "I'll be around awhile."

Bucky cursed himself for being so clumsy, but now he wanted to work on Willow. "Sir, you mentioned comfort." He opened the New Yorker's door. "Slip inside, nice and cushy."

While Bart did so, Bucky hurried to his desk and dialed. "Kathy, have someone bring the Chrysler 300 up front." He hurried to the Coke machine and caught Alsop watching him from his office. He got a Coke and searched for Willow.

She leaned against a yellow pillar, her rounded rear cocked to one side. Bucky breathed deeply, and oxygen screamed through his veins. She ambled over to a Fury, while he stared at her gorgeous Yankee figure. He didn't think he had ever seen a woman so perfect. She *could* be a movie star.

He edged up and handed her the frosty Coke. "This car isn't for you."

She gave a provocative giggle that made him want to smother her in his arms. "Is that so, Bucky?"

Nice, she remembered his name. "Don't get me wrong, it's a fine car. They sell like Aunt Jemima's. But—"

"What, I don't look the sporty type?"

"On the contrary. I see you in something more…more you." She'd like the Fury, but she'd *love* the Chrysler 300. It had both the Fury's sportiness and the New Yorker's elegance. She put her glossy red lips to the Coke bottle and threw back a long gulp. Her breasts rose and Bucky caught a fruity fragrance.

"If you're pitching Southern charm," she said, "I'm not catching it."

"Come with me." If she liked what he had in mind, maybe she'd get Bart to spring for it.

He led her outside, where she seemed to be lit by a personal cinematographer. "This is the car for you." He stepped back to let the magic happen. Like Willow, the car had gorgeous curves and screamed to be looked at. Not something you'd roll out of granny's garage. Sexy enough to make folks tingle in shameful ways and shield children's eyes.

Willow's lashes fluttered. "A *red* convertible."

"Chrysler 300. Luxurious, and it'll get you there on time. Six-way power seats. Power everything."

She sauntered around the car with the lubricated hip movement of a ship rolling in gentle waves. Her fingers brushed along the first ever leather upholstery.

"There you are!" Bart called from the door. He tramped over, puckered his lips, and whistled. "Not bad. Never saw four headlights before."

"Came in this morning," Bucky said. "Limited edition. Be gone in two days."

Willow slid in behind the wheel. She adjusted the mirror and snapped on the ignition. It caught at once with a heavy growl. Her eyes went wild.

"She'll blast off zero to sixty in under seven seconds," Bucky said, as if describing a Goddard rocket.

"Jump in, Bart," Willow said. "Let's find out."

Bart climbed in, and Bucky's stomach sent a worrying signal. "It's…it's not broken in, so don't—"

Her head jerked back, and the 300 shot off in a booming roar.

Bucky slogged back inside to find Alsop waiting. "I didn't see a check on your desk, so they sure as hell better bring that car back."

"They will. Their Caddy's here."

"Who is that guy? Dresses like a sharpie."

"His name's Bart."

"Just Bart?"

Bucky couldn't remember his last name. "Gosh, I don't—"

Alsop snapped his fingers. "Let's see what you've got."

"Um…nothing."

"*Nothing?* No license information?"

"Guess I forgot."

Alsop glared at him with a look hard enough to split rocks. "Remember when I told you to save your regrets for things important? Well, this is one of them. Bart and that sex-bomb you fell all over yourself for took off with a five-thousand-dollar car in exchange for what might be a hot Caddy."

"You don't think they—"

"Don't ask questions. Go check that Cad. If it's unlocked, look at the registration. On second thought, stay right here."

Alsop marched outside and returned two minutes later. He reached across Bucky's desk and pressed the intercom. "Kathy, a man came in with blueprints for a racetrack here in Garfield County. Call around and see if anything's up with that."

"I'll start with Mrs. Rheingold. We just hung up. I told her you needed to speak to the chief, but she said he's in Tulsa on business."

"I'll talk to him later." He turned to Bucky. "Give those characters ten more minutes, then call the cops." He stormed off, adding, "You'd better pray nothing happens to that car."

CHAPTER 20

Bucky spun the wheel and roared west out of town. Smacked the dashboard with his palm. How could he have been so stupid? Willow saw him and thought, *There's a sucker. I'll just wiggle my ass and wrap that hick around my little finger.* Lots of luck getting on the council now.

Bitch!

He sped through Enid, then swung south onto Eighty-One. In open prairie now, he leaned on the accelerator, and his roadster's speedometer nipped eighty. The police said the crash occurred just north of Kingfisher. He gunned it past Hennessey and through a wide valley with streams of light through fluffy clouds, and grazing cattle. Fence posts flicked past in a blur.

Five miles farther, the road jogged. Coming out of it, he slammed on the brakes. Ahead, the road veered sharply left in front of a cliff. A tow truck backed up against its edge. The door said *Kingfisher Towing.* Willow and Bart stood peering down.

Bucky's car dipped forward on its springs in a screeching stop, and he jumped out. The tow truck's winch growled, and a cable strained to pull the Chrysler up from the ditch. Bucky stood beside the two people he hated most in the world. A miracle the car stayed upright. Must've spun a one-eighty. The front grille had weeds jutting out like cat whiskers.

"I thought we were goners," Willow said in a flat voice.

Bucky glared at her. The car eased over the crest. More weeds and dirt filled the underside. Once on flat land, the tow truck driver lowered the car's front end to the ground.

Bucky surveyed the damage. Thick shrubs had scraped the driver's side and may have kept the car from rolling over. The front quarter panel appeared dented. Difficult to tell for sure since red dirt caked both the convertible's inside and out. A hard hand smacked his back. "Sorry 'bout that, pal. Rotten luck."

Bucky whirled around to Bart. His heart pounded so hard it hurt. "Asshole!" He pointed at Willow. "And *you*. You've ruined my life." Bucky wanted his voice flat, intimidating, but it jumped an octave or three.

"What was that?" Bart put his hand behind his ear, like a deaf guy. "What am I?"

Sweat trickled down Bucky's left temple. He let it go.

Bart dropped his hand. "Wasn't her fault."

"Right. It was the road's fault. Or the car's."

Bart sniffed the air. "I believe I'm smelling sarcasm. I was driving, so don't go accusing my wife of ruining your life."

"You can't drive. You've only got one eye."

"Had to try it out myself, pal. Nothin' around but fuckin' cows. They should've had signs and shit. Curve came at me like a horseshoe."

"I yelled to slow down, you jerk." Willow spat either blood or red dirt. "You almost got us killed, and you ruined Bucky's life."

Bucky couldn't tell if she was mocking him or really did feel bad.

"And look at this." She shook her head, and red powder flew from her hair like blackboard eraser dust.

"Another thing, numb-nuts," Bart said, his voice showing a restrained, under-the-surface aggression. "You need to learn to speak with respect around a lady. And since I happened to forget my driver's license, Willow was driving. That's what we told the cops. Got that?"

Bucky looked around. "What cops?"

"I gave a statement and they pissed off. Can't believe you reported the car stolen."

Bucky's anger swelled again. "They should've arrested you."

Bart grinned. "A well-respected man like me?"

The driver of the tow truck waddled up, holding a clipboard. His mesh shirt gave his chest hairs enough room to curl through. He asked, no one in particular, "You gonna try to start it? 'Cuz if it don't run, you'll need it towed."

Bart glared at Bucky. "Key's in the car, dip-shit."

Bucky yanked the handle, but the door wouldn't budge.

Bart yelled, "The panel's jammed against it. Climb over."

The inside smelled of sagebrush. Bucky gunned the engine—*Varooooom!* He pulled the car up a few feet to be sure the wheels were clear of debris. He twirled the key off.

"Guessin' you won't need me no more," the tow truck driver drawled. "That'll be fifteen dollars." No one reached for a wallet. "Cash."

Bucky waited and listened to the driver wheezing.

Bart turned to him. "You gonna sit there with your dick in your ear or pay the man?"

With clenched teeth, Bucky yanked out his billfold and peered in. "I only have twelve dollars."

"*All* cash," the driver said.

Nobody spoke. Only a meadowlark from a fence post. "Oh, for goodness' sake," Willow snapped. She rummaged through her purse and came up with three dollars. "*Here!*" She flicked her arm out to the driver and waved the bills.

The trio climbed into the 300, and Bucky switched on the engine. He didn't trust those crazies to drive the car back to Defiance.

❦❧❦

"Kindra," Bucky said, over the phone. "I'm at work and need a lift to my car out near Kingfisher."

"Kingfisher? I—I guess."

"Thanks. I'll be out front." He trudged to the curb and gazed absently across the highway. The sun hung just over the horizon; the sky the color of flamingo feathers. Swifts, catching insects from the air, cut sharp curls above the buffalo grass that rippled in the meadow, as if waving goodbye. He felt ashamed letting Alsop down after so few days on the job.

Kindra pulled up. "Head toward Kingfisher," he said and climbed in.

"First we need to make a stop," she said.

Bucky slouched with his head against the backrest and told Kindra about Willow and Bart. "When I first met him, I thought, what a wuss. Boy, was I wrong. On the ride back to the dealership, the guy talks like we're poker pals. Said he'd offer to pay for repairs, but that's what insurance companies are for. He's the friendliest guy in the world until you piss him off. Then you hope he doesn't kill you. Might as well say it, I'll probably lose not only my job, but my future in this town."

"Oh, Bucky."

"I screwed up."

She tugged his sleeve. "Anybody could've made that mistake. Mr. Alsop is lucky to have you as a salesman. Why, I'll bet he's never in his whole life had someone sell a car on his very first day. And look at all those you sold to Chief Parker. What, four?"

He allowed a tiny smile. "Five. No, actually six. He ordered another one."

She grinned. "*See.*"

"Cal might not fire me right away. He wants me to photograph the celebration tomorrow." He stared out his window at a ragged row of eucalyptus trees stutter past like propped up coffins against a graying sky.

Kindra turned off the highway into Potter Park and pulled in across from the library under a canopy of trees. A stiff breeze in the willows sounded like an enormous silk dress. "Why are we stopping here?" Bucky asked.

She turned off the engine and scooted around to face him. "Listen. I was pumping gas for this Army guy and noticed a jacket hanging in his back seat with big mound-shaped buttons like the one we found in the grave. Except his buttons had an eagle, not a number seven like ours. I remembered Jolene saying numbers meant something."

"Yeah, like a troop number."

"The guy said if our button was army, the number could mean Seventh Medical Battalion, Seventh Military Police Company…and other stuff I forgot."

"Cal told me Kansas was in the army and had a foot injured in Korea."

"That's it!" she said, suddenly excited. "Let's go inside and check."

Bucky reached for his door. Finally, something to feel good about. "I think you're on to something."

They went into the brightly lit library. Nouveau colonial brick, picture windows, and beech-wood shelves. The two hurried past a large portrait of former President Calvin Coolidge and stopped at the card catalogue. They searched through encyclopedias and several books listed under Korea U.S. military. In one thick book titled *Korea: Companies and Divisions*, they scanned pages with headings like 7th Ordnance Company, 7th QM Company, 7th Ranger Infantry Company, Airborne.

Finally, Bucky spotted the Seventh Motor Transport. "That's it! Alsop said Kansas was in the motor pool."

"See. The button *does* belong to Kansas, and he lost it burying the baby." Kindra's eyes grew wild, like Willow's when she fired up the 300, and she slapped the book closed and jumped up. "Let's get out of here."

Bucky sensed an idea growing in her head that he wouldn't like. "And go where?"

"To see Kansas. Force him to make Marybeth give me the ring, or we'll tell about him burying the baby."

"Tell who?"

"The police."

"Forget that. At least for now." Chief Parker had a double murder to solve and didn't need more distractions.

"It was your idea, remember?"

"Well, it was a bad one. Besides, your grandfather will find out. *Remember?*"

Kindra glared at him and stomped off. He followed her into the car. She slammed it into gear and spun the wheels before turning on the lights. Her tiny mouth pressed into a thin line.

"Kindra, we'll think of something else. Kansas would blow a fuse. Also, if you recall, he did say he'd shoot me if I set foot on his property again."

She kept her gaze straight out the windshield.

"Goddamnit, Kindra, you know what he's like."

"Don't shout." That was very funny, because he wasn't even shouting. She went on, "Why did we go to the library and investigate if you're going to chicken out?" She hauled the wheel over, and they swung into the next lane.

Bucky turned his head this way and that, checking traffic.

"You said you'd help get my mother's ring back. Go ahead, quit. I'll do it myself."

A muscle or something in the middle of Bucky's body grabbed hold. Quit? He had never quit anything in his life. Even his insides knew. "Okay," he said. "Let's go."

Kindra's face beamed like that of a girl stepping onto a carnival ride. She whipped a sudden U-turn, then cut across traffic and made a left through a red light. Someone honked and she honked back.

"It'll be interesting," Bucky said, now starting to feel revved, "to see if Marybeth sticks to her hitchhiking story in front of Kansas."

Kindra glanced at him, eyes sparkling. "This'll be fun."

"You don't have to face me when you talk." Bucky's eyes had locked onto traffic, watching for the moment he might have to seize the wheel.

They took the route down Valley Spring Lane, then continued three miles before turning onto a dirt road that led to Kansas's house. Kindra rolled the car down the drive and stopped in a clearing not far from the abandoned baby grave. Kansas's car was gone and the house dark.

"Dang!" Kindra whined. "No one's home."

Bucky got out of the car, and a screech owl called in the blackness. It sat perched in a tree above, silhouetted against a crescent moon. Bucky hopped up the steps to the door and tried the knob. Locked. He slid around back to search for a way in. They'd find the ring themselves. He checked two windows; the third gave to his pressure.

"Kindra," he called in a loud whisper. "Come here."

She crept around the corner, shoulders hunched as if one false step would trip a landmine. "What are you do- ing?"

"Get over here and I'll boost you up."

She looked around. "Isn't this called breaking and en- tering?"

"It's called getting your mother's ring. If we find it, we won't need to talk to Kansas. And while we're here, let's check for a Swiss Army knife with brake fluid on it. That'll prove he's the murderer."

Bucky helped her up and followed her inside. He found a light switch and flipped it on. No point worrying about being caught by Kansas. He'd see their car anyway.

This must be Marybeth's bedroom. It was small, and, except for an arrangement of orange poppies in a vase on the chiffonier, the place looked ransacked: clothes strewn about, drawers open, unmade bed, corners crammed with magazines.

Kindra searched through drawers, while Bucky slipped into the living room. Nothing fancy. A coatrack and a pair of snow boots by the door, a wooden couch covered with bearskin, two oak chairs, and a coffee table with a history book on it. It showed an Indian in a feath- ered headdress on a horse. A mounted buck's head above the mantel, along with a rifle that may have belonged to Davy Crockett. A narrow wooden stairway led up to what looked like a loft. The place seemed more cabin than house.

Bucky opened a closet door to search for a coat with buttons matching the one in his pocket. Two rifles leaned upright in a corner by a carpet sweeper. A rod held coats, but none with brass buttons. On the floor sat rubber boots and a toolbox. His heart skipped. He bent down, opened it, and checked for a Swiss Army knife. Darn!

On his way to Kansas's room, he found Kindra sitting on Marybeth's bed reading a small spiral notebook. "Psst, aren't you supposed to be looking for something?"

She waved him away and turned a page.

Kansas's room was totally different than Marybeth's. Bed made tight with military corners, and nothing out of place. Bucky opened a drawer. Socks rolled tight, underwear folded. Probably learned this stuff in the Army. In the closet, shirts and trousers hung on hangers evenly spaced about two finger widths apart. In the corner hung a dark blue coat. He pulled back the lapel and his heart hammered. The buttons!

"EEEEEE!" screamed Kindra.

Bucky ran into the hallway and nearly crashed into Kansas and Marybeth. They must've entered through the front door. Kansas had a rifle trained on Kindra. Marybeth stretched on her tiptoes, looking over his shoulder. "What are you doin' in my room?" she yelled.

"Shut up, Marybeth," Kansas barked. He swung his rifle on Bucky. "*You*, into the living room." He leveled the rifle back at Kindra. "You, too. Marybeth, get in there and close the door."

Kansas herded the intruders into the living room. "How'd you two get in here?"

"Through my window," Marybeth shouted through her door. "And thanks for leaving it open and freezing me to death."

"Look," Kindra said to Kansas, sounding surprisingly composed, considering she had a shotgun pointed at her. "I just want my mother's ring back. I lent it to Marybeth, but she says she doesn't have it. I don't believe her."

Marybeth opened her door and shouted, "I told you a thousand times I lost it. And I don't appreciate you snooping through my stuff." The door slammed, and something crashed to the floor. Possibly the vase of orange poppies. Marybeth let out a wail.

Kansas, his eyes hard, hissed, "You think you can break into my house and—"

"Where's the baby?" Kindra burst.

Kansas's fuzzy eyebrows shot up. "What are you talkin' about?"

Bucky whipped out the button from his pocket and thrust it in Kansas's face. "Do you deny this is yours?"

Kansas lowered his rifle and snatched the button. "Where'd you get this?"

"Right where you lost it," Kindra said, pointing out the window. "In that poor baby's grave."

Kansas turned to Bucky, his mouth twisted. "Harman's behind this, admit it! Got you to break into my house and swipe a button off a coat I haven't worn in years. That son of a bitch is tryin' to frame me for Will's murder. Baby's grave, my ass." Kansas pocketed the button and leaned in close to Bucky. His nose had tiny red veins, and he smelled rabbity. "I oughta blow your stupid brains out for bustin' into my house." He backed up a step and raised his shotgun to give Bucky a good look down both barrels. An all too familiar view. Bucky froze. "You come here again, there won't be parts of you big enough to bury."

Bucky's heart felt like it wanted to bang its way through his chest and out the door.

Kansas waved his rifle. "Both of you. Get!"

They hotfooted to the car, and Kindra drove toward Kingfisher to retrieve Bucky's roadster while he struggled to keep his legs from shaking. "Do me a favor," he said. "Don't ask me to go over there again. That maniac is obviously capable of murder."

"Think he killed Will and Miss Iris?"

"I sure as hell do now. Let's face it, he wanted Will's job and knows how to cut brake lines." Bucky's pulse finally crept south of the two hundred range. "Do you believe what he said about Harman?"

"*Surrre,* our deputy chief's out to frame him."

Damn! The Button. He'd screwed up by giving it to Kansas. It happened so quickly he didn't think. He gave up proof of…of probably something. Kindra stared at the road ahead, plucking her lower lip with her thumb and finger. Bucky asked, "Do you think Kansas was pretending he didn't know about the baby?"

"Hard to tell. Maybe."

"What about the ring? Did you check all of Marybeth's drawers?"

"She probably doesn't have it."

"What was that notebook you were reading?"

"Her diary. She wrote in code, but I know Pig Latin."

"What'd it say?"

"Nothing much."

He turned to her. "What's that supposed to mean?"

"Just girl stuff. That's all."

He tugged her sleeve. "Come on, tell me."

She yanked her arm free. "Stop being so annoying."

"You're the annoying one." *Screw it.* He turned and peered out his window. He had other things to mull over. Such as returning to Louisiana to face his daddy and Uncle Rupert like a worthless mongrel, if Alsop didn't have insurance for the damaged car. Or maybe, even if he did.

CHAPTER 21

It wasn't until Alsop got home that evening after seeing Tony that he reached the chief and told him of the bomb.

"Same source as last time?" the chief asked.

"That's right," Alsop said, grateful he wasn't asked for a name. "And remember, he was right about the bone."

The chief remained quiet. Alsop smelled chicken cooking while he wondered if he'd be pressed for a name.

"Is it already planted, or are they bringing it with them tomorrow?"

"The person didn't know."

"You should've pushed for it. Now I'm going to have to search the courthouse area immediately. And that car of yours."

Good. He's moving quickly. "I'll send Kansas over to remove the plastic covering."

Alsop hung up and phoned Kansas, then told Jo-Dee he had to leave, wolfed down a chicken leg, and headed for the door.

Jo-Dee took his arm. "Darling, please be careful."

He kissed her hand. "I will. Promise."

ა᠍ა

By the time he arrived at the lot, the bay door stood ajar and lights were blazing. The chief's men removed the car's backseat. Kansas stood leaning against a stack of old tires. "Did you take out all the memorabilia," Alsop asked him, "the gasoline, and everything?"

Kansas's eyes stayed glued to the car. "Glove compartment and trunk are cleared out."

"Kansas!" The chief jerked a thumb up. "Hoist it onto the lift."

Marybeth sat in Kansas's pickup, leaning forward, looking in the mirror, and plucking her eyebrows. Alsop paced over to the Chrysler 300 to inspect the damage. He stared at the car and shook his head. *Je*sus key*rist*. He reached in and wiped what looked like red flour off the odometer. Forty-nine miles spent in a tornado. Dirt and weeds inside and out.

The search team finished, and the chief stood talking on his car radio, Harman at his side, flipping a Zippo lighter open and closed. Alsop moseyed over and lit a cigarette, waiting to talk to the chief.

"What's the status at the courthouse?" the chief said into his mic.

"No bombs, Chief," came a voice through the speaker.

"I'm sending Harman over to position men at every corner of the courthouse. They're to maintain security throughout the night." He hung up and turned to Harman. "I hear you've been harassing Kansas."

"Is that what he—"

"Shut up. He says you pulled him over without cause and accused him of killing Will."

"Just rattling him is all. We know the pervert did it to get his job."

"Stop calling him a pervert. Fathers live with their daughters all the time. Now get over to the courthouse."

Alsop dropped his cigarette and ground it with his foot. "Got time to come in for a short one, Chief?"

"Doesn't have to be short." The chief's radio crackled. "Give me a minute, and I'll meet you inside."

Alsop yelled for Kansas to button up the Belvedere. As he started for the office, Bucky rolled onto the lot.

CHAPTER 22

After picking up his car in Kingfisher, Bucky dropped by the dealership to take another look at the 300. Maybe it wasn't as banged up as he feared.

He pulled onto the lot to see two police cars parked outside the repair shop, and Alsop looking straight at him, stone-faced.

Bucky's stomach did a flip-flop. He got out and trekked over to him. "Hi, Cal," he said, trying not to sound cheerful and phony, and at the same time not show how jittery he felt inside.

"I'm glad you're here," Alsop said.

"I want you to know I take full responsibility for screwing up and will pay for fixing the car." He had no idea how, but he would.

"Won't have to. Kathy told me what happened. Insurance will cover it."

"Gee…well, thanks." *That's a relief!*

Chief Parker strode up. "Okay, Cal. You say you've got a drink with my name on it?"

"You betcha. Bucky will join us. We need to discuss tomorrow."

Bucky couldn't believe his good luck. Not only was he

off the hook for the car, but he'd also be in on tomorrow's planning.

They trooped through the showroom and into Alsop's office. He pulled a bottle from a drawer and filled three shot glasses of Jack Daniels to the brim. "To a successful celebration." They clinked glasses and threw down their drinks.

"That call I just got," the chief said, frowning, "was about another Peeping Tom report. Someone's looking through bathroom windows. I advised them to get a dog."

"They caught a guy doing that once back home," Bucky said. "The judge made him wear a fluorescent jacket every time he went outside after dark."

The chief nudged his glass toward Alsop. "What's this I hear about the racetrack coming here?"

Alsop's eyebrows shot up. "What exactly did you hear?" He refilled the chief's glass. Bucky held his thumb and finger a half-inch apart. He didn't want to get soused to the eyeballs.

"That's all I heard," the chief said, picking up his glass. "Whole town's talking about it."

"Where'd they hear it from?" Alsop refilled his own glass.

"Your girl Kathy's been calling around. Maybe from her."

"Oh, for God's sake. All she knows is that this guy Bart had blueprints in his car that said Garfield County Racetrack. She's been trying to find answers." They tapped glasses and gulped their shots.

The chief ran a knuckle across his mouth. "You mean no one knows what this Bart guy's up to?"

"Guess not. But his blueprints could be a ruse. We've already had phony bone relics to worry about."

The chief held his empty glass to the light and watched an amber droplet dribble down the inside. "Jack

Daniels never sold his whiskey to Indians. Believed it caused them to act crazy." He set the glass down.

"Speaking of Indians," Alsop said, "are you going to search their cars?"

"The mayor thinks it's impractical, and I agree. A bunch of Caddo people are already here. Might've already brought a bomb."

"A bomb?" Bucky said.

"That's why I wanted you here," Alsop said. "We'll need pictures. Chief, how's this going to work tomorrow?"

"Everyone enters the area at Wilbur and Main near the bank. Caddo people can keep their protest signs, but every male will be searched."

"Only males?" Bucky asked.

"Caddo women abhor violence. Won't even swat mosquitoes."

"They can still raise hell," Alsop said. "Chant their lungs out."

"I've asked Chief Trigger to give us a hand. He and his officers will come up from Edmond to deal with general disturbances. My men will be on the lookout for would-be bombers."

Alsop frowned. "What if the Caddo people get confrontational?"

"Trigger's handled them before down in Oklahoma City. He's bringing two German Shepherds trained in Korea during the war."

"Trained to do what?" Bucky asked.

"Ensure the peace. He says they can tear a man's arm off and rip out his throat."

Alsop winced. "For God's sake, don't let the Caddo people drink."

"They'll receive free soup and hot chocolate." The chief chuckled. "Maybe spiked with tranquilizers."

"You've organized things well in a short time," Alsop said.

"Some things demand speed."

"Speaking of speed," Bucky said, "what's happening with that toe impression?"

"Nothing much yet. But don't worry, the killer's not going anywhere."

"Why in the world," Alsop broke in, "did you tell that out-of-town reporter, Peter Thomas, about it?"

"Where'd you get that crazy idea?"

"He wrote in his newspaper that you had a lead."

"That's different. He's talking about tinsnips."

Bucky's heart skipped. A new lead. "Tinsnips?" he said.

"Heavy-duty scissors." The chief tapped the rim of his empty glass. "Someone slipped a typed note under Thomas's motel door. One word, *Tinsnips*."

Alsop poured. Bucky put a hand over his glass and said, "The guy who wrote the note must know who cut Will's brake line."

Chief Parker threw back his drink. "Maybe. But if he's wacko, it could mean nothing."

"That's a weird way of conveying that, don't you think?" Bucky said.

"Anonymity's not unusual in these cases. Someone sees something—knows something—but is afraid to get involved. Won't identify the perpetrator for fear of reprisals. So he gives a clue."

"Did the note have fingerprints?" Alsop asked.

"Only Thomas's. We made a deal. He's not to mention tinsnips, and I keep him abreast of the investigation."

"How are you going to find them?" Bucky said. "Search everyone's toolshed and car that was at the party?"

"When a chicken flies the coop, you don't catch it by waving your arms."

"But again," Bucky said, still wondering about the toe impression, "knowing nothing much means something, right? What have they found out in Tulsa?"

The chief leaned back, and his chair squeaked. "The impression was made from a special shoe. Most have a standard sole depth. This one's much thicker. In a day or two I'll know the size and make. That will confirm my suspicions. Then I'll make my arrest."

"Who's the suspect?" Bucky asked, gripping his armchair.

The chief's eyes twinkled. "All in good time." He slid his empty glass toward Alsop. "Suppose you pour us one for the road?"

Before the cap left the bottle, Alsop's phone rang. He answered and handed it to the chief.

"Yeah, what is it?" The chief's eyes widened. "I'll be right there." He hung up and reached for his hat. "They've found the bomb."

CHAPTER 23

Bucky followed Alsop and the chief to the courthouse in his roadster. Both cars skidded around the corner and came to a burning halt beneath a street lamp. Everyone jumped out. "This way!" Harman hollered from the lawn.

They raced up the grassy knoll to a long table set up for tomorrow's dignitaries. On top sat a blue cardboard container with a peaked roof, the size of a twin Twinkies package. It said *DO NOT OPEN. Grasshopper trap. Agriculture Research Service.*

"What the hell's this?" the chief spit out, panting as if he'd climbed Mount Everest.

Harman, standing among several officers, said, "It's a government trap to monitor the locust population."

Bucky had worked one summer for the Agriculture Research Service back home, and he knew that was no trap. The service's traps were a different size, shape, and color.

"Don't get too close, people." A beefy man with a gruff voice and a bullet-shaped head came forward. He wore a thick orange vest that looked heavy as concrete. He hefted a red steel box, roughly two feet square, onto the table. It said, *Property of Tulsa Police Department Bomb Squad.*

"Is there a bomb in that box?" the chief asked.

"There is now. I removed it from that bug trap. A six-inch galvanized pipe with steel caps screwed on at both ends. Powerful enough to stop a tank."

"Show me," the chief said. Several officers stepped back.

"No can do, Chief. The filler is highly explosive TNT. I removed the fuse—" He pointed to it on the table. "—but even without it, a spark, or the slightest friction, could blow us all halfway to Tulsa."

The chief backed up. "Get that bomb out of here." He turned to Harman. "Where'd you find it?"

"In that tree, the other side." The deputy chief pointed to a large oak behind the grandstand.

"Why'd it take so long to find?" the chief snapped.

"Well, um, we didn't exactly find it," Harman said, shuffling his feet. "You see, the fella in charge of inspecting the grandstand did. Said it was a standard government trap that he sees all the time. Except this one had a fuse coming out the bottom."

The chief picked up the fuse. "Put this back in the box the bomb was in, then put the box back in the tree. We'll catch the son of a bitch when he tries to light it tomorrow." He turned to his officers. "Okay men, listen up. We'll proceed with the plan as I've laid it out. Everyone except those on guard duty can go home and get some rest. See you all in the morning, and be ready for trouble."

The officers dispersed. Alsop said to Bucky and the chief, "The two Cheyenne guards and the short-necked Caddo slipped behind that same oak tree just before I got knocked out. The Caddo must've planted the bomb in the tree before tossing the bone in the hole."

Alsop and the chief left, but Bucky stayed behind to examine the trap while Harman talked to the bomb guy. The trap was homemade, and without the usual government markings on the bottom. "Say, Deputy Chief, who was that grandstand inspector that found this?"

"How the fuck do I know? And put that thing down."

Asshole. Bucky laid it down and paced over to the grandstand. He found a stenciled phone number and name. *Rent All Company.* He was heading across the lawn toward the phone booth by the beer joint when Peter Thomas approached, whistling and swinging his arms. "The chief called from his car," he offered. "Said they found the bomb. Where was it?"

Bucky pointed to Harman. "That officer can fill you in. See you tomorrow." He dropped a nickel in the payphone and dialed the Tulsa number. Routed to an answering service, he identified himself as a Defiance official and insisted on speaking to someone in charge. He left his number and waited.

Three minutes later the *Rent All Company* president Desmond Chilling told him no one was assigned to check out the grandstand. Furthermore, the company had no inspectors.

Just what he thought! Bucky hung up and returned to his car. Someone must've known about the bomb and wanted it found. He'd notify the chief when he got home.

CHAPTER 24

Bucky's alarm clock jiggled and clanged. It was an hour before sunrise on the morning of the commemoration, He got up and checked the newspaper. The storm would arrive before nightfall. Forty minutes later, he clomped outside under a gloomy sky, dumped a couple quarts of oil in his car, and took off.

Peter's old roadster needed an expensive ring job, verified by the blue smoke belching from its exhaust. Bucky found it cheaper to just add oil when it got real low. If he forgot for a couple days, the engine started sounding funny.

He was feeling more philosophical about Willow and Bart. Maybe they'd been fated to screw him over. Of course, he also screwed himself over, being more interested in Willow's breasts than Bart's credit. His book said, *If you're wrong, admit it quickly and emphatically.*

Mentally, he ran though his photographic agenda. The crowd, the speakers, Indian males. And of course, the Belvedere sinking into a half century of hibernation.

He turned left onto Main. Two blocks up, the redbrick courthouse stood tall against a dark-clouded sky. Sawhorses draped with red ribbon blocked the road at Wilbur Avenue. Lots of Edmond police milled around. One officer sporting muttonchops and wearing calf-length black boots directed Bucky to turn right. He parked on the nearly empty street and approached an officer with a round nose and stomach that swelled over his gun belt.

"Mornin', Officer," he said cheerfully. "You fellas helping out today?"

The cop pointed a gloved finger up the street. "Cross over at Main and enter by the bank."

"That's okay." Bucky raised his camera. "I'm the official photographer."

"That's nice. Now do as you're told."

Bucky snapped a picture right in his face, knowing there wasn't enough sunlight to properly expose his 120 film but wanting to piss off the asshole anyway. He hoofed it around the block to the entrance. More Nazi-type goons had cordoned off a two-block perimeter around the courthouse.

Figuring it would be another hour before he could take pictures, he dallied up Main Street to get coffee. Kansas lounged on the courthouse steps, leaning on an elbow, legs stretched. He could strut lying down. Still, he looked more like an elf rolled in a blanket than a child molester—or a killer. To show he wasn't intimidated, Bucky said, friendly like, "Howdy, Kansas. You're up mighty early."

Kansas's head swiveled to Bucky as if he'd never heard his own name before. He pointed to the car hovering from a crane high above the skyline. "Keepin' watch on things."

He had probably camped there all night. Bucky threw him a salute. "Don't let anyone steal the hubcaps."

"Not steal 'em, bomb 'em. Check out those Caddos." He jabbed a finger toward a bunch gathering at the bank. "Before long they'll be whoopin' and hollerin' like banshees. We shoulda killed them and left the buffalos."

Bucky resumed walking. In addition to all his other charming traits, Kansas was a jerk. Too bad about that blanket covering his feet. The chief said one of the killer's shoes was thicker than normal, and Bucky had noticed when he dropped a coin between Kansas's feet at the food truck that one shoe seemed especially thick. He'd have liked to double-check that.

It seemed crazy that Caddo people would want to bomb everybody to death. Bucky knew some of them resented their land being taken, but as a people, they were gentle and warm hearted.

He bought a coffee to go at Sally's and made his way to the corner of Third Street. Rustling trees and thick air signaled the storm's approach. He climbed onto the back of the bus bench with Kindra's poster plastered over Fromm's face, sat down with his feet on the seat, and looked around for her. She'd offered to assist him. He still wanted to know what she read in Marybeth's diary. She'd been so focused on those pages, instead of looking for the ring, she must be holding something back.

Across the street by the bank, the police were setting up a soup and hot chocolate stand. A van marked *Edmond Police Canine Corps* pulled up and parked near a vendor filling balloons with helium. A mustached man with thick lips and a chief's hat wriggled from the vehicle, tugging on his red suspenders. He opened the back, and out jumped two German shepherd dogs. Restrained by leashes, they nosed the ground in clouds of white breath. One of them used the vendor's chair as a fire hydrant.

"Mornin', Bucky." Alsop climbed onto the bench, clutching a cup of steaming coffee, just as Peter drifted over from across the street, whistling.

"Hello, gents," Peter called out. "Just got back from a drive up the bluff overlooking the Sixty-Four. The sky's so dark in the east it's hard to distinguish it from the trees. There's also a caravan of cars, fender to fender, coming from Caddo County. So thick, the asphalt disappeared." He tipped his hat. "You boys have a good day."

Peter sauntered off, and Bucky turned to Alsop. "Have the Caddo people always been violent?"

"Only this new breed." Alsop pulled out a pack of gum and unwrapped the last piece. "Share?"

Bucky shook his head.

"They act like children who weren't invited to the party and want to spoil it for those who were. Caddo youngsters are the first generation exposed to television. Day and night, they watch images of white men driving long cars and living in wide houses. Of Indians, slow-witted and savage. As teenagers, they're exposed to the same people, same mange-eaten dogs and rust-eaten cars, until numbed by monotony. Then they drink. If one actually graduates high school and considers college, he's putting himself above the others. They're like crabs in a bucket. Whoever tries to get out is yanked back down."

Someday, as a respected public servant, Bucky would try to improve their situation. He told Alsop about the fake inspector and his theory that the person knew about the bomb and wanted it found. "Whoever it was probably didn't want anyone to know it was him." Like Chief Parker said about the guy who wrote the tinsnips note. He may have wanted to stay anonymous.

Alsop cupped the coffee in his hands and stared at his feet. Moments later, his head snapped back up. "My God! Johnston. It was Johnston!"

"*He* was the inspector?"

"Not personally. But he and a certain Indian worked me like a second-rate Chevy salesman." Alsop checked his watch. "It's nine o'clock. Let's take a drive. We won't be long."

❦

Alsop spun his wheels into a U-turn and headed to the Speedy Mart. "A clerk named Tony has been dealing from the bottom of the deck and is about to get his hands smacked." He rolled down the window and spit out his gum. "It would be just like Johnston to get Tony to tell me that the Caddo people were planting a bomb. A perfect way to torpedo the ceremony and knife me at the same time."

"Knife you?" Bucky blurted. "How come?"

"By forcing me to sabotage my own project. Johnston knew I'd have to tell Chief Parker about a non-existent bomb. But his plan backfired."

"Wait a minute." Bucky questioned Alsop's sanity. "The bomb was real. We saw it."

"It only became real when the Caddos planted it." Alsop turned into the Speedy Mart lot. A lone Nash was parked at the far end, dented, rusted, and minus a rear fender. They marched inside. Bucky didn't see anyone around, only the clerk behind the counter preparing soup. Alsop hung the closed sign on the door and flipped the lock.

The clerk glanced up, saw Alsop, and his shoulders twitched. "Councilman Alsop. Surprised to see you so early."

"That makes us even in the surprise department," Alsop said, approaching the counter.

"I—I don't understand." Tony got busy straightening the candy and gum display.

Alsop grabbed his wrist. "Truth or dare?"

"Tr—truth wha—"

"Truth. Good choice." Alsop dropped the man's wrist. "Who told you to tell me there was a bomb planted?"

Tony jerked his head toward Bucky. "Who's he, a cop?"

"He's documenting the anniversary."

"I'm not talking in front of a reporter."

"Sure you will. The truth will set you free."

Tony's eyes flitted around nervously. He ran a hand through his straight black hair. "A big guy—never said his name—comes in and lays down a C-note. Wants me to tell you that Caddo people are gonna set off a bomb. You know, a joke. Claimed you were his friend."

"Some joke. What'd he look like?"

Tony rolled his shoulders. "Old, kinda rugged."

"Craggy face, talks like he has mush in his mouth?"

"Yeah, that's him. Who is he?"

Alsop's mouth curled into a smile that held little amusement. "Someone who never intended there to be a real bomb. Who'd you tell about this little joke?"

Tony nibbled at a hangnail and spit it out. "Maybe a couple friends. It was funny, you know, the joke."

"Friends, like the two Caddo people I saw come in the last time I was here? Caddo people you said you didn't associate with because you're Cheyenne?"

Tony raised his chin and scratched his neck with a thumbnail. "Maybe."

"A few days ago, as a prank, your kid brother and his buddies tossed an animal bone into a hole in front of the courthouse. Then some Caddo people got the bright idea to follow suit with a human bone. And now, *maybe*, you broke into your crisp hundred dollar bill, bought a case of beer to share with your Caddo blood brothers, and decided my friend's *joke* would be even funnier if it was real." Alsop banged the counter. "*You* planted the fucking bomb!"

"Not me! I had nothing to do with it."

"Then your Caddo pals did. And afterward, Mr. C-note returned to make sure you told me about his bomb joke. That's when you told him about the real bomb. Isn't that right?"

Tony stared at the floor. "You might say that."

Alsop fished five cents from his pocket, tossed it on the counter, and grabbed a pack of Juicy Fruit. Bucky followed him to the door.

"Hey," Tony cried, "that reporter's not going to get me in trouble, is he?"

Alsop waved over his shoulder.

"Don't say my name!"

Alsop sped from the lot and back to the courthouse.

"Looks like my landlord's a big tipper," Bucky said, admiring Alsop's interrogation skills.

"Mr. C-note wants to show the mayor the door. He and Overstreet bet the barn on the governor signing the racetrack bill, but he'll veto it if the mayor wins reelection. If so, our own Garfield County gets its name on the contract."

"It must've frosted Johnston to learn the Caddos actually planted a bomb."

"He's ruthless, but not enough to blow people to kingdom come."

"How'd he know you'd get the message from Tony?"

"I pass news about Indian affairs to the council. Johnston knows Tony's my contact."

They arrived back at the courthouse. "Remember," Alsop said, before getting out of the car, "the bomb's fuse is still in the tree. If you see anyone there so much as light a cigarette, I want a picture."

CHAPTER 25

Two hours before the noon ceremony began, Bucky stood with one foot on the bus bench overlooking the growing crowd and reloaded his camera. Music had kicked in over the loudspeakers, and vendors were already selling balloons, hot dogs, cotton candy, hot chocolate, and soup. A real carnival atmosphere, in spite of the cold air blowing in from the east, accompanied by soft rolls of thunder.

Chief Parker strode up and leaned in close to Bucky's ear. "I want you to keep an eye out for—Hey! What the—" Two dogs lurched with speared teeth at the chief. He fell back against a balloon stand, arms flailing.

"Back, you two," Edmond Police Chief Trigger shouted, yanking the leashes with all he had.

"What the hell got into them?" the chief cried.

Bucky helped him up. "Sorry Chief. Must be your kerchief."

The chief had a white handkerchief draped from the back of his hat, covering his neck. "What about it?"

"Nothin, Jerry, it's jus' these dogs been trained to attack enemy Koreans wearing kerchiefs like yours. You know, part of their chink uniform."

"Well, it's part of mine when I'm outside, so keep

your damn dogs under control. They're supposed to intimidate, not kill, for Christ's sake." He waved Trigger off and turned to Bucky. "Fuckin' skin cancer. Doc Little insists I keep my neck covered when I'm outside." His eyes darted left and right before he leaned in close. "I wouldn't put it past those Caddo sneaks to smuggle in another bomb, so stay alert for anyone suspicious."

Kindra and Harman strolled up, laughing. Kindra wore a pink cap and matching mittens, and her cheeks were flushed from the chill. Bucky noticed how close Harman stood next to her, and he didn't like it.

The chief frowned at Harman. "Aren't you supposed to be watching that tree?"

"No sweat, Chief. Sparks and Murphy have it covered."

"Get your butt over there. I'll join you as soon as I make a call."

After Harman was out of earshot, Bucky turned to Kindra. "Why are you hanging around with him? I thought you were going to assist me."

"We weren't hanging around. Besides, I'm here, aren't I?"

"You acted awfully chummy," Bucky said, slipping into protective big brother mode.

"Don't be silly," she said with a fake laugh. "We just met. Officially, I mean. He gave a talk once to our civics class."

"On what, flirting with underage girls?"

She swiped his arm. "Bucky Ontario! It was on civic responsibility and the law. In case you've forgotten, I'm almost eighteen. And by the way, my birthday's coming up." *Hint, hint.* "Besides," she said, "Officer Harman's kind of—"

"Yeah, right. Since you're so mature and everything, tell me what was in Marybeth's diary."

She stared at her saddle shoes.

"Come on, I won't tell anyone if you don't want me to."

She glanced around, then whispered. "She's been having sex since she was ten."

"*Ten!* No kidding?"

"That's why I didn't want to talk about it."

"She actually said that in her diary?"

"In Pig Latin. Xseay means sex and nteay means ten."

"Was it with VO?"

She shook her head. "It didn't say. But she's been doing it for six years."

"Harman said her father molested her." At least he implied that.

"Then why doesn't he arrest him?"

"Said he's going to. Maybe he's still gathering proof. Anyhow, let's get to work."

The smell of rain filled the air as they snaked through the growing crowd, Bucky taking pictures. Mrs. McCoy came up and greeted him. She had been one of Bucky's favorite customers at Gustafson's, and when she greeted you, you stayed greeted. She kissed and hugged as if you were a long lost friend.

They shared something they pretended was a secret. She had inquired about what to take for her irregularity, and Bucky told her his gramma drank four ounces of prune juice every morning. After that, Mrs. McCoy bought a bottle every week, and they'd wink at each other.

Bucky and Kindra moseyed over to the bank, and Bucky took pictures of Caddo people getting patted down. They behaved orderly in spite of their signs with varying sentiments of *Unjust Statehood* and *Return Our Stolen Land*.

Working their way back toward the bus bench, Bucky

elbowed Kindra. "Look, couple of the year. The misfits are back to being friends."

VO handed Marybeth a cone of pink cotton candy from a vendor. Kindra pursed her lips. "I still want my mother's ring back."

They sat on the back of the bench, where Bucky had an unobstructed view of the tree, the street crowd, the podium, dignitaries, and the car. Peter came by and said hello. Bucky intended to introduce him to Kindra, but she smiled. "Nice to see you again, Peter."

"Ah, right." His face turned red. "Good to see you, too," he added and took off.

Kindra turned to Bucky but had trouble meeting his eye. "Peter came into the store the other day when I was serving soup samples. You told me he was your first customer, so I called him over and we yakked."

"What was his favorite?"

"Huh?"

"Soup. Which one did he like best?"

She shook her head. "He didn't want any. Oh, Bucky look." She pointed and jumped from the bench. "You've got to take a picture." A mother had her baby propped up in a pram. Bucky moved his lens in close. The infant looked as gleaming white as if she'd been squeezed from a toothpaste tube. She wore a pink bib that said *I'll be back in fifty years*.

Bucky caught a glimpse of Willow weaving through the crowd, coming his way. His heart did a little giddy-up. Man, no way could he stay mad at her. She held a green balloon, and under her black leather jacket, a red sweater hugged her large breasts. Yellow pedal pushers showed off a pair of shapely legs. Marilyn Monroe never looked hotter.

Kindra caught him staring. "What are you looking at?"

"The woman in yellow pants. Willow. She almost cost me my job."

"That's Willow? You never said she looked like…like *that*."

Willow passed within ten feet. Kindra grabbed Bucky's arm. "I know that woman! I saw her in the motel, but she looked different. Her hair was short and brown."

"What motel? When?"

"The other day, when I was picking up my cousin. Remember, I told you Abby came to take care of Grandmother?"

"Then why was she at a motel?"

Kindra's eyes fluttered. "Just one night. Her bus got in late. But listen, as I, I mean as we were leaving the motel, I saw that woman through her window. She saw me looking and quickly closed the drapes."

"Yeah, well, I guess she wears a wig sometimes." He didn't know why such a hot blonde would change her perfect looks.

"But, Bucky, there was a gun on the table."

A loud commotion erupted behind them. A Caddo with a blue headband yelled at an Edmond cop holding a hard-bitten expression. A busted sign lay at their feet. Bucky leaped from the bench and clicked off photos. A second officer arrived. They handcuffed the Indian and dragged him to a paddy wagon.

Bucky got it all, then weaved his way back to the bus bench to find Kindra talking to Peter again. "I don't like the tension around here," Bucky said to her. "You should go sit with your grandfather in the stands."

"I don't want to sit with him. I'd rather stay with you."

"No, go on. We'll catch up later."

"Bucky's right," Peter said. "I'll walk you over."

She handed Bucky his camera bag, and she and Peter

roamed off, whispering to each other. What was it with her interest in older men? First Harman, now Peter.

Alsop climbed onto the bench, and Bucky told him about the Caddo getting arrested.

"If these Edmond boys get hard-assed," Alsop said, "we could end up with another Wounded Knee disaster."

"Look," Bucky said. "An Edmond cop on the roof."

"What the—Where the hell's the chief?"

Bucky spotted him in the crowd and pointed. "Over there."

Alsop whistled through his teeth, piercing, with a loop on the end. He motioned the chief over. "What's that Edmond officer doing on the roof with a rifle?"

"Tear gas. Trigger says it's only a precaution."

Alsop shook his head. "I've got a bad feeling about it. Anything on the bomb front?"

"Not yet."

The chanting started. "Way-la-bey-ley, ya-hey-oh-bay-la-hey…"

Alsop turned his head in all directions. "It's coming from where the band is gathering on Wilber Street."

"There's more Caddos yet to arrive," the chief said. "Hopefully, they're getting the chanting out of their systems."

Alsop said he would go investigate, and Bucky reloaded his camera. Glancing up, he saw Peter leaning against a tree, staring at the chief, his lips puckered like he was whistling. When Peter caught Bucky's gaze, he turned away. Probably uncomfortable about whatever he and Kindra had cooking.

"I just made a call that confirmed what I thought about who's responsible for the death of Will and Miss Iris," the chief said quietly.

Bucky's heart surged. "You know who it is?"

"Be behind bars before the day's out."

"Come on, who is it?"

The chief gave a cunning smile.

"At least tell me if he's here."

The chief glanced around, then leaned in close. "The murderer's no more than a stone's throw from where we're sitting."

CHAPTER 26

The American flag blew above the courthouse in a stiff breeze under a sky the color of black ink. Minutes earlier, slate-colored mountains had been the color of lavender and plum.

While the mayor led in the Pledge of Allegiance, Bucky sat perched on the bus bench and scanned the crowd. He estimated the crowd to be around a hundred-fifty Cheyenne and probably double that number in Caddos, all wearing Tomahawk arm patches.

A Caddo cried out, "You're all hypocrites!" Two swift-moving Edmond officers whisked him off his feet. His sign, *Liberty and Justice for All Is a Lie*, lay trampled beneath a herd of shoes and boots.

As the cold air mixed with the air of anticipation, Alsop approached the microphone dressed in a topcoat, dark two-piece suit with wool tweed jacket, and a splashy red, white, and blue tie. He flashed a warm smile at the crowd and the CBS News cameras.

"Governor Wishbone." Alsop tipped his hat. "Thank you for coming. And to everyone, Mayor Collins, members of the City Council, distinguished guests, and all you wonderful citizens of Defiance, I wish you a hearty welcome to this historic event."

Bucky swung his camera around and fired off shots of the thunderous crowd, then hopped off the bench for close-ups: hand clappers, flag wavers, whistle blowers, and a frail white man dressed like Father Time, whose sign read, *The End Is Near.*

While Alsop continued his speech, Bucky scanned the grandstand and caught Bart sitting behind the governor, whispering in his ear. A minute later, someone tugged Bucky's sleeve. *Willow.* Her face, luscious as whipped cream, caused a hotspot near his spine. Her eyelashes flashed a come-hither wave, and she sauntered off, crooking a finger behind her back. He glanced around, then hopped from the bench and sidled up to her.

She continued strolling, as if in a park, until they were on the fringes of the crowd, then stopped and turned to him. People shuffled around them. "There's something I want you to know." She rummaged inside her purse and came up with a cigarette, which she brought to her lips, and a lighter, which she handed to Bucky.

As he lit her cigarette, he caught sight of an Indian woman in front of Seaborne's drugstore across the street. She stood bent over with a gray shawl across her heavy shoulders. His gaze fixed on the woman. "What do you want me to know?" Something about the woman wasn't right.

"I want to talk to you about the damaged car. Bart—" Willow followed Bucky's stare. "What are you looking at?"

"Nothing. What about the car?" Something definitely wasn't right.

"What's so interesting about that woman?"

"Notice how she's holding her cigarette."

Willow looked again. "Okay. What about it?"

"Now check out how you're holding yours."

Willow peered down at the cigarette she held between

her first and second finger, then glimpsed back at the woman.

"See what I mean? She's cupping it like a man does, between her thumb and first finger."

"You think she's a man?"

The woman glanced at her watch, then flicked her cigarette halfway across the street. The chief had said to keep an eye out for suspicious people. And she was definitely suspicious. "I've gotta get going. Nice seeing you."

"Wait." Willow grabbed his arm. "I wanted to tell you that Bart talked to your boss. He's going to pay for the damaged car."

"That's great. Uh-oh."

The woman was on the move.

"And now, ladies and gentleman," came Alsop's voice booming over the loudspeaker, "the moment we've all been waiting for." Right on cue, the band kicked in, church bells rang, and the crowd beat their hands together. Ten thousand volts of wild energy.

The Indian woman moved swiftly toward the grandstand. Bucky kept even with her—or him—from across the street. He got a shot before the high school marching band blocked his view. Then his suspect was gone.

He darted through the crowd, hoping to spot her before she reached the grandstand and got completely lost in the mob. He angled across the street, his pulse pounding in his ears, eyes searching. Shit! Where'd she go? Maybe up the grassy knoll to light the fuse in the tree.

The crane holding the car high in the sky growled to life, and Alsop's voice continued over the loudspeaker. "It gives me great pleasure..."

Bucky made it onto the grass but got tangled in the crowd. "We can't see past your filthy signs," screeched a blue-haired woman poking her umbrella into a Caddo's back.

The teenager whirled and grabbed the umbrella. "I should run this through your throat, granny." He snapped the umbrella over his knee like a spear, and the woman screamed.

Bucky couldn't break clear from the uneven waves of shoving. *The woman! There she is, going into an outhouse.* Something sharp slammed into his back, and he hit the frigid ground. A boot scraped across his forehead. Ignoring the blood and searing pain, he scrambled to his feet and spotted Chief Parker talking to Chief Trigger. His dogs growled with bared teeth and tugged at their leashes.

A muffled gunshot from a rooftop. White smoke. Bucky's eyes burned from sputtering tear gas. What was going on?

People scattered. Children cried. A woman wailed, "Lucy, where are you?"

Bucky's world spun. He wiped blood from his eyes. A gunshot rang out—then another. Through the tear gas he made out Chief Trigger's broad back and red suspenders. He held a gun at his side. Smoke oozed from its barrel.

At the chief's feet lay one of his dogs, its head half gone. The other dog, red flesh hanging from its mouth, had collapsed on top of a lifeless Chief Parker.

CHAPTER 27

Thunderclaps crashed, and lightning blazed in sheets. Raindrops the size of quarters splattered the ground knee-high.

Chaos generated by smoke and gunshots leapt across the street like a spark.

Alsop stopped his speech and jumped from the podium.

Radical young Caddos gripped their signs like axes and stood toe to toe with seething whites. The rain pounded, while Indians shouted, "Thieves! Liars! Murderers!"

A tear gas canister coming from a roof bounced in front of the bank. Alsop dashed over and covered it with a trashcan. He looked up at the Belvedere and gasped.

The automobile—that proud symbol of national greatness and Defiance's ticket to fame—was descending into its resting place with Indian boys standing on the skids. They reached into imaginary quivers on their backs, loaded their make-believe bows, and shot invisible arrows at the dazed dignitaries and Chief Trigger's blood-lusting cavalry. Jessie yelled for his crane operator to stop, and more young warriors clambered aboard.

What a disaster! Alsop charged through the crowd to

see youthful phantom-fighters riding the car like a swing. The rain hammered, and the boys' glistening wet hair bounced in their gleeful faces with each crash of the skids into the flaking concrete crypt.

Alsop cupped his hands. "Jessie, raise it out of there!"

Jessie pointed to the crane. An Indian sat at the controls. Holy shit! He could shake the kids off and then hoist the car up thirty feet and let it crash to the street. Alsop looked at the CBS cameras. He wanted national coverage of a car burial, not a riot.

One of Chief Parker's men yelled for the Indian to get down. The cop had a good strong voice and a bullhorn to help it along. Whipping out a long-barreled six-shooter, an Edmond policeman snarled, "I'll fix the son of a bitch!"

Alsop knocked the policeman's arm down. "No shooting!"

Beside a demolished balloon stand stood the drenched and crinkle-faced music teacher, her fingers locked in prayer. Alsop rushed over and grabbed her shoulders. "Miss Smits, get the band playing." As an afterthought, he added, "Make it the National Anthem."

Jo-Dee dashed up to Alsop, holding her umbrella. "Cal, this is madness."

"Honey, go home. This could get a lot worse."

∽∾∽

Bucky stood up on the knoll, weak-kneed and dizzy, a handkerchief pressed to his bleeding forehead. Doc Little charged up, rain-soaked and wheezing. "Move aside," he gasped, falling to his knees beside Chief Parker. The doc reached for a wrist, shook his head, and mumbled, "He's gone."

Nausea lurched in Bucky's stomach, and he turned

away from the gruesome sight. Chief Trigger stood beside him, staring blankly, his gun still held limply at his side. With Chief Parker dead, he should be taking charge. Bucky yanked his arm. "Chief, in the outhouse, a—"

"Hold it right there!" shouted Deputy Chief Harman, charging over. "Trigger, put your gun away." Harman knelt and unclasped Chief Parker's badge. He pinned it to his own jacket and turned to Bucky. "I'm in charge now."

Bucky pointed to the outhouse. "There's an Indian in there dressed as a woman. A Caddo, I guess, with a bomb."

"You think there's a Caddo fixin' to blow himself up in a shitter?" Harman said, with a stifled laugh.

"Not himself. *Us.*"

Harman seemed to think for a moment, then swiped rain from his eyes and yelled to his men, "You heard him. Check it out."

With the tear gas mostly dissipated, several lawmen charged across the grass for the outhouse as the National Anthem began. Citizens, those who hadn't fled, ignored the downpour and placed their hats over their hearts.

Bucky followed the officers.

"Not so fast, piston puss," Harman barked, passing him from behind. "*You* stay outta the way."

So full of himself. Bucky took a picture of his bowed legs and trailed after him.

Officer Sparks reached for the outhouse door as it burst open. Out jumped a short-necked Indian, sporting a fancy headdress of red, green, and blue feathers. Armbands showed red tomahawks. His colorful makeup was smeared, like he'd rushed to put it on. If the Indian's dress and face paint didn't convince everyone he meant business, the hand grenade held above his head did. The cops stumbled back.

"Stand your ground," Harman ordered. The officers fidgeted.

A staccato of loud pops erupted over the sound system. Everyone except Bucky, Harman, and the Indian hit the ground. The music stopped. A voice came over the loudspeaker. "Attention, please."

Bucky couldn't see the stage and didn't recognize the voice.

"Brother Long Feather is holding a grenade. Allow him to join me, and no one will die."

The officers, now on their feet, their guns aimed at the Indian, glanced at their new leader. Harman hesitated only a moment before nodding.

Brother Long Feather trotted down to the podium, and the crowd followed.

"Hey, Bucky!" Kansas yelled from behind. He hobbled to him and pointed to his forehead. "What the *hell* happened to you?"

"Nothing." Bucky wished he could sit down.

"That grenade's a bluff. Harmless as a water balloon. Saw thousands of 'em in Korea. Fragmentation type, killing radius about ten yards. But o'course not that one."

Bucky stopped walking. "How do you know that?"

"Ain't got a pin. Could tell a mile away."

"But he was holding it, I saw."

Kansas shook his head. "He's fakin'."

Bucky pointed down the hill. "For shit's sake, go tell Harman."

"I oughtta knock you on your ass."

"Wa—what?"

Kansas's deep-sunk eyes turned to cold iron. "For you and him tryin' to frame me for Will's murder by stealing my button. Now get over there and tell 'em before those prairie niggers fuck up my car."

His car? Asshole!

Bucky hurried down the slope in search of Harman. At the street, he stopped short in front of the grandstand and saw Bart holding the courthouse door open for the governor and Willow to go inside. He didn't stay long to gawk—he had to find Harman. But as he frantically scanned the crown for the officer, another horrible thought struck him—What if Chief Parker hadn't told anyone who the killer was?

CHAPTER 28

The Caddo swung the crane's cab in fits and starts, trying to prevent Alsop from climbing aboard. Alsop had to stop the maniac, or people could be killed. When the machine stopped to change direction, Alsop grabbed the handrails and jumped on, straddling the cab's open entrance. The Indian swiveled in his chair and kicked Alsop's chest. A hand tore free, and he swung around, crashing his backside against the outer cab.

Ouch! That bastard! He rocked back, and regained his hold. A foot shot past his shoulder like an arrow. Alsop grabbed the Indian's leg, and both men fell onto the cab's steel floor, Alsop on top. His knees gripped the Indian's foot like a vise. A sharp body twist, and the Indian's kneecap snapped. He howled.

The crane operator jumped into the cab. "Alsop, you're one tough son of a bitch." A succession of loud pops burst over the loudspeaker, and the music stopped.

What now?

A young Indian, no more than twenty, in a buffalo headdress and wrapped in a red blanket, stood on stage in a haze of smoke. A spent package of firecrackers lay at his feet. The kiddy warriors had abandoned their wrecking swing.

"Quick, lower the car into the hole," Alsop yelled to the crane operator and struggled out of the cab. Pain shot through his back.

Those up on the knoll behind the grandstand had fled. The dignitaries—governor, mayor, council members—had also melted away in the rain. Undaunted, the CBS news cameramen remained at their post, cameras whirling. Police and Caddo also held their ground, gripping their respective guns and signs.

Alsop ran to the bus bench for a better view. A second Indian joined Buffalo-Boy on stage. He held a grenade above his feathered war bonnet. Son of a bitch! It was Short-neck, the bone-thrower who had also planted the bomb in the oak tree.

The two Indians faced two dozen revolvers and several shotguns, all held by nervous officers. "If I die, we all die," Buffalo-Boy shouted and turned to the feathered short-necked Indian, who grunted and shook his grenade like dice. "You have 'til the count of three," Buffalo-Boy continued, "to drop or holster your weapons. Otherwise, journey to the great unknown. One…two." He looked at his feathered brother and nodded. "Three."

All weapons disappeared from sight. Relief battled with anger inside Alsop. What were those idiots up to? Buffalo-Boy strutted across the stage, hands stuffed inside his blanket, hard-eyeing the police. "You celebrate statehood, but statehood is a falsehood. You steal our land and call it a state."

Alsop, scanning the thinned-out crowd for Chief Parker, spotted Bucky up front among the officers.

"You are a nation of thieves," Buffalo-Boy said, "who stole everything you have. I spit on your *national greatness*." And he spat. "How smooth is your language that can make right look wrong and wrong look right."

Alsop edged up to Bucky and Deputy Chief Har—

What? He tapped Harman's badge hard with his finger. "What's this?"

Harman's mouth twisted. "Parker's dead." His eyes stayed on Buffalo-Boy.

"*Dead?*" Alsop ran a hand through his hair. Could things get any worse?

"Like these injuns gonna be." Shifting sides of his mouth, Harman whispered to his nearest officer, "Pass the word. When I take out grenade-man, it's open season on the other asshole."

Alsop started to object, insist Harman not do it, but Buffalo-Boy locked eyes with him. "*You*, you talk of American ingenuity. I see only America's nightmare. You attempt to civilize us because we're *un*civilized, but it is *you* who are *un*civilized." His eyes shifted to the crowd of mostly Indians and officers. "The Great Spirit gave us land and game. You came here, killed off our game and stole our land."

Harman inched his hand to his gun. Before Alsop could react, Bucky grabbed Harman's wrist. "Hold it! Kansas said the grenade's harmless."

"Get your fuckin' hand off me and don't interfere."

"It'd be murder if—"

Buffalo-Boy's eyes now locked on Bucky. "Nobody *gives* you freedom. Nobody *gives* you equality or justice. If you're a man, you *take* it." The Indians cheered and whistled.

Buffalo-Boy turned away, and Bucky pushed toward the platform. Harman drew his gun. Bucky leaped onto the platform. "Don't shoot!" He spun around, arms spread to face Harman and his men. "The grenade's not—"

Harman fired and Short-Neck's face exploded. A deafening rain of bullets perforated Buffalo-Boy. His legs unhinged and he crumpled to the ground like a puppet with broken strings. Bucky remained on his feet.

While onlookers, mostly Indians, stood in frozen silence, Harman jumped onto the platform and sneered at the two bodies, then turned to Bucky and snarled, "I warned you not to interfere." Motioning to Officer Sparks, standing in a rising cloud of smoke, he said, "Arrest this man."

CHAPTER 29

Alsop called the meeting to order. With the exception of Gustafson, tending to his wife suffering from bedsores, the entire city council convened with the mayor in his office to settle on a plan.

Lamar Fromm took a fierce drag from his cigarette and then bared his teeth as if enduring pain. "What do we say to the press?"

"What *can* we say?" City Manager Horning asked. "Facts speak for themselves."

"Facts don't speak, people do." The mayor pulled a cigarette from his coat. "I just hung up talking with Edward R. Murrow and agreed to an interview." He shoved back his cuff and checked his watch. "In three hours."

Doc Little's paper-white eyebrows flung up. "He's coming *here?*"

"We're meeting at the CBS affiliate station in Oklahoma City."

Horning fiddled with his cufflink anxiously. "What will you say?"

"The truth, of course. It's all on film. Tonight's news will open with Murrow showing clips of the events, then I'll take over." The Mayor lit a cigarette and took in a lungful.

Alsop thought the mayor was done for. Just like Chief Trigger. He might as well go back to cow punching.

Johnston's shoulders shook as he stifled a laugh. The mayor gave him a hard glare and spit a piece of tobacco off his tongue. "Believe me," he said, "when I'm through, the country will salute our policemen for their bravery and dedication."

"Bravery?" burst out wide-eyed *Prairie Duster* editor Farnsworth. "Bucky told Harman the grenade was inert, yet his men murdered two unarmed Indians."

The mayor donned his hat. "The police knew nothing of the kind. I'm leaving to prepare my presentation. Good day, gentlemen." The mayor turned and treaded out the door. Alsop would have liked discussing strategy for his interview with Murrow. Defending the police actions would be a hard sell, especially if news footage depicted Caddo people as peacefully exercising their right of free speech and the police as jackbooted thugs. Unimaginable to think that the mayor could win over a nationally televised audience.

"This is a fine kettle of fish," Lamar Fromm lamented. "What'll we do now?"

"In case anyone forgot," Johnston growled, "I stood against this whole business from the beginning. But what's done is done. We need to draft an immediate press release. Explain that errors in judgment were made all the way around."

Alsop needed to stop this hooey before it caught fire. "Hold on. It's a little early to fall on our sword. There's no need to do something that might undermine the mayor's efforts. We need to sit tight until tomorrow. In the meantime, let's address the need for a new police chief and the unwarranted arrest of Bucky Ontario."

"We have a quorum," Johnston said. "I say we vote now and make Chief Harman's status permanent."

Alsop couldn't think of a worse police chief. Harman was the kind of rotten cop that gave rotten cops a bad name. Chief Parker only appointed his nephew deputy chief because older veterans had retired and he knew he could keep an eye on him.

Doc Little shook his head. "He's too young. Still wet behind the ears."

"Dry enough to handle those two Caddo," Johnston shot back.

"In times like these we need a chief who can act boldly," Horning said. "Not to sound disrespectful of the dead, but Chief Parker was too soft on criminals. There, I said it."

"Let's compromise," Alsop said, knowing he and Doc Little were about to lose this battle. "If the mayor succeeds in justifying the killing of the two Caddo men, we'll appoint Harman permanent chief. If not, he's dismissed from the force and we find a suitable replacement. That way we show the nation that the people of Defiance will not tolerate misconduct from its officials."

"That's sensible," Farnsworth said. "I suggest we retire to watch the news and convene tomorrow at nine o'clock."

Chairs squealed back, and everyone stood.

"Hold on!" Alsop said. The group froze. "Regardless of how we handle the Caddo shooting, Harman was wrong to jail Bucky Ontario. He risked his life trying to prevent what became butchery. I'm going to the jail now and insist on his release, but I need everyone's support. All in favor raise your hand."

Everyone's hand went up except Johnston's. Alsop's eyes narrowed. "Maynard, I said everyone."

"What difference does it make? When Judge Thompson—"

"Oh, Maynard," Doc Little snapped. "Shut up and raise your hand."

CHAPTER 30

The first thing Bucky did in jail was heave his guts into the toilet.

After that, he felt much worse. Trembling hands, jumpy stomach. Too much thinking about how he could have—should have—been dead. He touched his bloody forehead, which felt sticky, like wet airplane glue, then wiped his hands on his cold wet pants. He gazed out the barred window, hoping his headache would hurry up and go away.

His eyes still stung from tear gas, and all he could see was a steamy brick wall with a shadow of a crow on a wire.

His legs felt rubbery, so he lay on his cot and stared at the ceiling. He pictured Chief Parker with his throat torn out. What a way to die. Hopefully, he'd told Deputy Chief Harman who murdered Will and Miss Iris.

He shuddered. A million bullets had whizzed by him within the width of a feather. He thought of his gramma and the gator. He should've tried to save her, dove back in the water, but he didn't. So he told himself—promised himself—the next time someone's life was in danger, he'd do something to help.

He turned onto his side and pulled his knees up. They

say it's better to be a live coward than a dead hero. He added under his breath, "What about a live fool?"

"If you're askin' me," came a voice from somewhere, "I couldn't tell ya."

Bucky bolted upright. A man with his arm in a sling stood in the cell across from him. Late twenties. Lean and bony, hair yellow as corn and thick enough he could do okay combing it with his fingers. A piece of cheatgrass dangled from his lips.

"Geesh!" Bucky said. "You scared the hell out of me. Didn't know you were there."

"That's 'cause I didn't want you to know. Part of my trade, ya might say. Besides, I enjoyed watching you puke and fret like a pregnant nun. Was you out fightin' injuns?"

"Not exactly." Bucky touched his forehead.

"Heard a couple Caddos had a date with the undertaker." The man patted his vest, then the pockets of his jeans, stiff and shiny with dirt. "You got a cigarette?"

Though Bucky didn't smoke, he slapped his trouser pockets. "Afraid not."

The man cupped both hands to his mouth. "Hey, Sparks!" He gripped the bars. "*Sparrrrks!*"

Bucky gazed around for the first time. Four cells made up the Defiance City Jail, two pairs against opposite walls. The one next to him was empty, but someone slept in the cell diagonally across.

A door opened at the end of the corridor, and Officer Sparks stomped in, his hair cut military style and brushed up stiffly on the sides.

"Damn, Sparks," the man said. "Hope I didn't interrupt your jackin' off."

"What do you want now, Tyburn?" the man said.

"Now, Sparks," Tyburn cooed, "is that any way to talk in front of a distinguished guest?"

Sparks turned to Bucky. "Don't pay any attention to that one. Even his old man calls him a scoundrel. Oughta hear him tell."

"Don't go badmouthing me, Sparks. I got shit on you that's pret*ty*—"

"All right, Tyburn, that's enough. Whadaya want?"

Tyburn yanked the cheatgrass from his mouth. "A goddamn smoke."

Sparks pulled a Marlboro from his breast pocket and waved it slowly in front of Tyburn. Tyburn grabbed for it through the bars, but Sparks pulled it back. "What's the magic word?"

"Stop the bullshit and hand it over."

"Bucky, would you like this fine cigarette?"

"Give me the fucking thing." Tyburn snapped his fingers. "*Please.*"

Sparks handed it over but didn't offer a light.

Tyburn frowned. "Expect me to chew the fucker?"

Sparks pulled out a Zippo lighter and lit it through the bars. Tyburn gripped Sparks' wrist steady, lit up, and kept his grip. Sparks gave a hard yank and broke free. "Asshole!"

"Just messin' with ya, Sparks. You always were a pussy."

"I'll tell you somethin', *mister* hotshot. You're up shit creek this time. No more butt whacks for stealing jawbreakers, or a stint in reform school for cracking Gustafson's safe. No sir." He tugged on shirtsleeves that had ridden up into his jacket. "Even Mr. Overstreet can't get you out of this one. That bullet hole in your arm ain't nothin'." Sparks put his face close to the bars. "'You'll be doin' nigger-dick time with extra Sunday sausage, and I'll laugh and lau—"

Tyburn shot his arm through the bars and sizzled Sparks' cheek with his cigarette. Sparks flew back and grabbed his seared face. "Son of a *bitch!* You almost got my eye."

"That's where I was aimin'."

"I'll kill you for that!" Sparks snarled then turned and stomped out.

"Like I'm really scared. Fuck you!" Tyburn hollered after him, then glanced at Bucky and grinned.

Listening to all this uproar had improved Bucky's health. Eyes and stomach felt fine, his head hurt only a little. Might as well strike up a conversation to pass the time. "Tyburn's an interesting name. Never heard it before."

"I didn't pick it. But hey, Tyburn Newgate's the name, crime's the game." He put a finger to his lips. "Keep that under your hat."

Bucky stepped up to the bars. "Bucky Ontario. Cars, new and used."

Tyburn grinned. "I know who you are." He shook his finger. "You're the guy who sold the cops those Furies, ain'tcha?"

Bucky saluted. "Guilty as charged."

"Well, *Lordy*. You owe me a debt of gratitude, friend. It was me who robbed the bank—with a couple of associates, that is."

Wow. A real bank robber. "How'd they catch you?"

"One of my dumb-ass associates blabbed his ass off in a Laredo bar. Said he was smarter than Willie Sutton. Well, shit, everybody knows Willie Sutton robbed banks. So the bar owner puts two and two together and here I am."

"How come it's you and not your, er, associates?"

"'Cause I passed out at the bar and the two of 'em hauled ass across the border for snatch. Hope they got crabs."

"Officer Sparks said you used to steal jawbreakers at

Gustafson's. Just so you know, you screwed it up for future generations. Gustafson now keeps the jar behind the counter."

"Mr. Magoo, that's what we called him, used to live above the store until his wife got crippled. He knows how to get his way with the younger female gender. I could tell stories about him that would curdle your toothpaste. I seen him twist kids' ears till they squealed. He crapped a litter of lizards when he caught me stealing one of his chickens."

"Chickens? You poor or something?"

"Fuck no, not poor. Lived inna biggest house in town. Wanted to cut off its head an' see if it'd run around like they say." Tyburn picked up his crushed cigarette from the floor, straightened it, and tucked it behind his ear.

Tyburn knows the town pretty well. Maybe he'd know if Harman was right about Kansas molesting Marybeth. "Do you know a guy named Kansas Karradine?"

"You kiddin'? I popped his daughter's cherry. Least that's what she said, the lyin' bitch. Don't go tellin', she was a mite underage."

My God, another one who molested Marybeth. Now Bucky really felt sorry for her. Bucky hated to pry, but he was curious. "Why'd you call her a lying bitch?"

"Tol' me she was pregnant just to scare me. She's smart, I'll give her that. She'd get old man Gustafson to let her read magazines and eat ice cream while her old man shopped."

"She has a boyfriend. Least I think so. Name's VO."

"I know him. He was our lookout when we played revzies over at Harvey's used car lot on Central. We'd start 'em up and rev 'em until they screamed. If anyone got caught, it was VO. Sparks, Harman, and me would always make him—"

"Did you say Harman?"

"Sorta funny, ain't it? Him being your new police chief and all. Hell, we go back to before having hair on our balls. Talk about poppin' cherries, you think I was bad? Harman was a million times worse. We useta get drunk and bull whores at the wigwam house on the reservation. Harman was never particular. He'd fuck a cat with a broken back. He should give Marybeth a ride. She'd go for him in his fancy uniform. But I'll tell ya this, I wouldn't want to be in his moccasins right now."

A cough echoed off the walls. A stringy-haired Indian in the cell next to Tyburn sat up from his cot, heaved up phlegm and spit it on the floor, then scratched his belly with all ten fingernails. "That's the only intelligent statement that asshole's made all day. Your chief will be tied to a stake and baked in the sun. His tongue will swell, and ants will gorge upon his flesh."

The door down the hall opened. Officer Sparks stomped in, his cheek bandaged. "Social's over, Mr. Ontario. You're outta here."

"Bucky," Tyburn said, with a salacious grin. "Do me a favor. Tell Marybeth to come visit. For old time's sake."

CHAPTER 31

Alsop sat stiffly in a straight-back chair by the water cooler, smelling the fragrance of disinfectant. Behind him, the slap of a wet mop hit the floor. He tried to rotate his head, but the muscles were too jammed up. Defiance's oldest policeman, Sergeant Tom Hazelwood, sat at a gray desk with a cane across his lap and gum in his mouth. He was lame from a motorcycle encounter with an armadillo. To his side, a doorway led down to the jail.

For fifteen minutes, Alsop had listened to the sergeant field phone calls from the press with the same message. "Mayor Collins will explain everything on national television this evening."

Bucky jaunted into the room, fastening his wristwatch, a camera bag slung over his shoulder. He felt surprisingly calm, considering how close he'd come to being riddled to death. Alsop stood and yanked a paper cup from a water cooler's dispenser and filled it for Bucky.

Bucky downed it and had another. "Didn't know I was so thirsty. Thanks for bailing me out."

"Didn't have to. You had no business being there." Alsop put an arm across Bucky's shoulder. "Let's get out of here."

They pulled out from the lot in Alsop's Chrysler Imperial. "I want Doc Little to examine your head."

Bucky felt his forehead. "It's okay."

"Don't argue. You may need stitches." Alsop gave Bucky a sharp stare. "That wasn't very smart."

"What, trying to prevent murder or disobeying Harman's orders?"

"Jumping onto the stage. If Harman remains chief, he could make it rough for you in this town."

"What could he do? I don't make a habit of breaking laws like longtime citizen Tyburn Newgate."

"He's always shaking hands with trouble. You two got chummy, did you?"

"Said he grew up in the biggest house in town."

"In *back* of the biggest house. His father is Orville Overstreet's butler."

"We've met."

"I'm not surprised. He's glad-handed everyone in town and will probably be mayor in three days."

"I meant the butler." Bucky put a hand to his forehead. "How rough can Harman make it for me?"

Alsop snorted. "You don't want to find out."

CHAPTER 32

Doc Little was a wee scrap of a man, just over five and a half feet with his toupee. He arrived in Defiance more than twenty years ago from Chicago, but was tight-lipped about his past. He soon became the largest landholder in Garfield County—four times that of runner up, Maynard Johnston. He had a white stubbled face, tooled around town in a '34 cream-colored Duesenberg, and possessed nothing that demanded feeding—wives included. Refused Social Security, it being socialistic. He always said eight to ten thousand a year of honest income was enough, but never let on how he got so rich.

The doc sat perched on a stool and dabbed Bucky's forehead with a damp cloth. "I've got a bad feeling," he said wearily.

I've got that and a bad back, Alsop thought, standing in the corner by a picture of the human digestive system. "The mayor's televised defense may assuage our nation, but not the Caddo people. They saw what happened."

"We may need the national guard," the doc said. "I hope the governor realizes that."

Bucky's gaze flicked to Alsop. "A Caddo guy in the jail said Chief Harman will get tied to a stake and eaten by ants."

"Hold still," Doc said.

"The Caddo people have gone home," Alsop said, pressing a hand to his back and arching it. "At least for now."

"I saw the governor talking to Bart," Bucky continued. His eyes shifted up to Doc's spiky white whiskers. "That's the guy who ran off with the car."

The doc glanced at Alsop. "The one with the blueprints showing the racetrack in Garfield County?"

"That's right." Alsop made his way toward a straight back chair in the corner. "When was this, Bucky?"

"Just before all hell broke loose. Then Bart, Willow, and the governor ducked into the courthouse together. *Ouch.* That stings."

"It's iodine. Won't kill you," Doc said. "What do we know about these jokers?"

"Bart and Willow?" Alsop eased into the chair. "Nothing. But we need to find out what those blueprints mean. If Johnston's connected with them, they'll mean trouble."

"Willow has a gun," Bucky said. "Kindra saw it on a table in her motel room. She also had short brown hair. I've only seen her with long blonde hair."

Doc pursed his lips. "Blueprints, guns, disguises. And now the governor." He slapped a Band-Aid on Bucky's forehead. "I don't like it."

"The governor wasn't going to come," Alsop said. "Something changed his mind, and I'd like to know what." He stood slowly. "If you're done with your patient, we'll run along. I was going to take the missus out for a steak dinner, but it looks like instead I'll be watching our mayor on TV either hang himself—and us—or pull a Nixonesque Checkers speech. Let's hope the mayor's lucky spurs hold out."

⌘⌘

Huddled against a cold breeze, Bucky and Alsop hurried across the dirt drive to the big Chrysler. A thin blade of moon hung low in the western sky, and the long cloudy Milky Way trailed overhead.

Gliding across the bumpy gravel road toward Johnston's boardinghouse, Bucky made two mental notes. One, to take Kindra out for a steak dinner for her birthday, and second, remember to talk up the car's smooth ride to potential buyers. He turned to Alsop. "Before Chief Parker was killed, he told me he knew who cut Will and Miss Iris's brake line. I wonder if he told Harman. I'd ask him, but I know he wouldn't tell me. Maybe you could talk to him."

"Good idea. I'll do that." Alsop turned onto Bucky's street. "How many photos did you take?"

"Over a hundred."

"Did you get a picture of the Indian with the hand grenade?"

"Several, why?"

"He planted the bomb in the oak tree. My identification will prove he had intended to kill. Considering that and the grenade, we should have a strong enough case to—"

"But the grenade was inert."

"The bomb wasn't. Look, don't get me wrong. I'm not condoning the actions of Harman and Chief Trigger. They acted irresponsibly right down the line, and Trigger was rightfully forced to retire. But we can't afford to let Defiance's reputation get further tarnished by two idiots. Especially now that we have a shot at getting the racetrack and possibly hosting the County Fair."

Bucky's face grew hot. "I get it. Sweep it under the rug." He hated that everybody seemed so indifferent to the Caddo killings. Even Alsop. When and if Bucky got into office, he'd do things differently.

Alsop pulled up to Bucky's building. "You live in the back, right?"

"That's okay, here's fine." Bucky wanted to get away before he said something he'd regret.

"You've got integrity, Bucky. It's an admirable quality, but in politics you've got to make judgments. Nourishment for one fella may be poison for another."

"Right." Bucky reached for the door.

Alsop held his arm. "Don't forget to bring the pictures tomorrow. First thing."

CHAPTER 33

I'm in here, dear," Jo-Dee called from the den as Alsop hung his jacket in the foyer. She sat on the couch in front of a soft fire, sipping a glass of Squirt and darning the heels of his socks, a mending basket at her side. A nineteen-inch television console warmed up in the corner, while a log crackled and shifted in the hot coals. Alsop bent to kiss her, and pain soared through his back. He braced it and straightened.

"What's wrong, dear?"

"Just a little spasm," he said, not wanting to give her something else to worry about. "Bumped into something." He settled into his leather wingback. "I see the nursery delivered your winter flowers."

"I'll plant them tomorrow." She put the back of her hand to her forehead. "I'm just *sick* about what happened today. Such a tragedy with Chief Parker. And *shame* on every one of those policemen who shot those poor Indians. And their families. I can't bear to think about it."

"I know, sweetheart, I know."

Alsop had little hope of surviving this nightmare. CBS had pictures, and pictures spoke louder than anything silver-tongued Mayor Collins could say.

People would flock to Defiance, not to the site of his

precious buried car, but to that of an Indian slaughter.

He made it to his feet and poured a glass of sherry. "I think I've disappointed Bucky. I must say, I feel a little ashamed."

She squeezed his hand as he walked back. "Oh, darling, why?"

He settled back into his chair. "He jumped onto that stage and risked his life to save those Indians, and I downplayed everything. Told him it was more important to save the town's image. I'm sure I look pretty small in his eyes."

Edward R. Murrow appeared on the TV. "And now, a special report."

Alsop held his breath.

"*This*...is Defiance, Oklahoma," Murrow said in his matter-of-fact baritone voice. He sat in a chair—black jacket, gray tie, white shirt—a cigarette between his fingers. "Tragedy struck today with the death of two Indians and a police chief. It happened here, seventy miles north of Oklahoma City. As a gimmick to celebrate fifty years of statehood and gain notoriety for the town, a new automobile was buried in front of the courthouse, intended to remain until the state's centennial, fifty years hence."

"A *gimmick?*" Alsop spat.

"The combined police forces of Defiance and nearby town of Edmond brutalized, tormented, and eventually shot and killed two Caddo people. Indians, whose crime was nothing more than peacefully expressing their constitutional right for a redress of grievances, claimed the state had usurped their land. Our CBS cameras were at the scene."

With growing dread, Alsop watched himself make the opening speech, intercut with shots of a cheering crowd. The governor and mayor beamed with delight, and the Belvedere hovered in a tar-black sky. Then the rain, and clips of chaos—police pushing Indians, kicking Indians, close-ups of Indians and police yelling. The two Caddo stood on stage, with the feathered one holding his arms high, but no grenade in sight. Bucky jumped onto the stage. Explosive gunshots, Indians collapsing in a heap.

Jo-Dee turned away. "I can't watch."

Alsop pounded the arms of his chair and hollered, "The grenade! Mention the goddamn grenade!"

Murrow came back on. "We have with us in the studio an eyewitness to today's events, the mayor of Defiance, Jimmy Collins."

The camera cut to a long shot of the mayor looking grave as he sat behind a desk. He wore a dark jacket, bolo tie, and white shirt fresh out of the box. American and Oklahoman flags framed the set.

"Good evening, fellow Americans." The mayor removed his pearl-gray Stetson, laid it on the desk and folded his hands atop a tan folder. "Today, a terrible tragedy has befallen our great country." The camera started a slow move in. "On behalf of all Defiance citizens, I wish to extend our deepest sympathies to the family of our beloved police chief, and to the families of the fallen Caddo people. We in Defiance love Caddos as brothers and sisters. We love all Indians. Sadly, events occurred behind the grandstand that the CBS cameras failed to show: smoke bombs and dogs, vicious dogs trained by Caddo Indians, brutally mauling white citizens and ripping out the throat of our cherished police chief."

Alsop gasped. "Did you hear that?"

"In an oak tree sat a bomb—a time bomb. A bomb discovered only moments before it was set to explode. A bomb capable of slaughtering hundreds of innocent men, women, and children. A bomb put there by deranged Caddos. It's unfortunate that some find lawful treaties no longer to their liking. However, no God-fearing white community could reasonably be expected to stand by while a small band of willful renegades commit horrendous, unspeakable violence." He picked up the tan folder. "I have here photographs showing dastardly deeds committed by Caddo people, courageously taken by Buck Bentario, himself a victim of vicious assaults."

Alsop could barely think, he was so angry.

"Ladies and gentlemen, we citizens of Defiance grieve the loss of human life—all human life. I hope that your prayers are with us tonight and that God, in His infinite wisdom, will help us heal and move past this terrible ordeal. Thank you, and good night."

Murrow's voice came from off screen, "Mr. Mayor, please show the viewers the photographs."

The mayor closed his eyes and shook his head. "I'm afraid, Mr. Murrow, they're much too graphic for television."

Murrow came back on screen. "That's our report from Defiance, Oklahoma. Good night, and good luck."

Jo-Dee turned to Alsop. "Ye gods and little fishes! Where'd he get the pictures?"

"From his imagination. Along with everything he said." Alsop unfolded himself from his chair. "Do you think folks bought that snake-oil pitch?"

"I certainly wouldn't," Jo-Dee said.

"We know the Caddo people won't. Frankly, what he said sickens me. Politics is one thing, but maligning innocent Caddos is going too far."

CHAPTER 34

Chief Harman used Sunday morning to organize his new office. He'd already read the good news in the *Prairie Duster* and the *Oklahoma City Free Press* about the country falling for the mayor's speech. He'd stopped earlier at Seaborne's drugstore and bought a leather-bound pocket notebook. As chief, he wanted to keep accurate notes.

He stared out his window onto a parking lot with puddles of gasoline rainbows, thinking he should have a better view. He checked out his chair. Nice. Swiveled and rocked. He fiddled with a side lever. The chair rose, then lowered, then rose some more. About right.

He opened his desk drawer. Nothing but paperclips and a few cigars.

Mrs. Rheingold was off today, so he told Sergeant Hazelwood to box all the useless books. *The Roots of Justice: Crime and Punishment in Tulsa County; Taming the System: The Control of Discretion in Criminal Justice.*

"Ray—I mean Chief," Hazelwood said. "What about this one, *Black Gun, Silver Star: The Life and Legend of Frontier Marshal Bass Reeves?*"

"Sounds good. Keep it and the one about lone star justice. When you're done, put that picture of me on my motorcycle up on the wall and order me some lights and a siren. Gonna make the bike official."

The door swung open, and Maynard Johnston swept into the room. "Howdy, gents."

Johnston gazed around with a promise of trouble. He swayed up to Harman's desk, jiggling coins in his pocket, and eyed him. He leaned back like he was studying a picture on the wall, unsure if he liked it, then turned to Sergeant Hazelwood, probing his teeth with his tongue. "What do you think of our new Chief of Nottingham, Tom? Up to protecting our town and its fair maidens?"

Harman straightened his shoulders. What was that crap about? Councilman or not, the sleazebag should show a little more respect.

"I'm sure he'll do fine, Mr. Johnston," Hazelwood replied.

"Let's hope so." Unsmiling, Johnston removed his hat and settled into a leather couch. "Tom, Harman and I have business to discuss. Why don't you hobble off and get yourself some coffee."

Hazelwood threw him a sharp stare and left the room.

Hobble off? Hazelwood suffered a motorcycle accident, and the asshole insults him. Not to mention his refusing to address Harman as Chief Harman. What a prick. "What's on your mind, Maynard? You don't mind I call you Maynard?"

"Familiarity is fine so long as it doesn't breed contempt." Johnston patted the chair in front of him. "Why don't you come over here? I'm not used to talking up to people."

Staying cordial, Harman strutted over and sat down.

"Ever been in trouble with the law?"

"What are you talkin' about? I am the law."

"Not so many years back, you palled around with the man who's now locked up downstairs."

"That don't mean nothin'."

"Old habits die hard. Being a policeman, maybe you happened to know about the silver in the bank vault. Maybe you whispered in his ear."

"You out of your mind? I didn't know about any silver." Why would anyone tell him what's in a bank safe?

"Nonetheless, you're going to be investigated, maybe even for murdering two Indians, and you'd better be clean as a bar of soap. Any dirty secrets that Uncle Parker buried to protect you, I need to know now."

"I didn't mur—" Harman shook his head like a wet dog. "No, no secrets. Jesus Christ!" His mind raced back through vaults of time. Revzies in Harvey's car lot, swipin' stuff at Gustafson's, bustin' into his safe.

Shit! That girl in Fort Sill. Wait, those charges were dropped.

"There's more at stake here than just your ass," Johnston cautioned. "Our town's good name rests on legally justifying those killings. Favorable press doesn't count. You've got enemies that can put you down so fast your ears will whistle."

"Caddo don't scare me. Who else?"

"Ever hear of the feds? They're required by law to give a shit about Indians' rights, and I don't want to be blindsided trying to protect you."

"There's nothing to blindside. You were there. They tried to bomb us, and when that didn't work, tried to fucking grenade us. We saved lives by killin' those injun bastards."

"I admire a man who doesn't back down, but the fact is, you're no more the police chief than the dog catcher."

"Bullshit! Deputy chief is like vice president. Takes over."

Johnston raised his hands. "Fine." He peeked at his watch. "In ten minutes, we on the council will vote to either keep you in office or kick your ass out." He shook his head doubtfully. "Frankly, it doesn't look good."

Kick him out? What a joke! "The fucking papers said I was a savior. Did you read that?"

"Relax, Jesus. I didn't say your situation was hopeless, but to be brutally honest, the council thinks you're immature and won't take the job seriously."

Harman jabbed his finger at him. "That's a load of crap! I took those Caddos seriously."

"I agree, and I'll try to convince them. Can't promise, but I'll do my best. Here's what you can do to help yourself." He handed Harman a hundred dollar bill.

Suspicious, he stared at the money, trying to guess the strings attached. "What's this for?"

"Your new wardrobe. Order one from a police catalog. It'll show you're serious about being chief."

"I'll check it out," he agreed, although it smelled fishy.

Johnston grabbed his hat and strode to the door.

"Maynard." He stopped and turned.

Harman snapped the bill. "You can call me Ray, but if you forget, I'll answer to Chief or Chief Harman."

CHAPTER 35

An hour later, Alsop volunteered to give Harman the news. The police station was quiet. No one got out of jail on Sundays.

"Howdy Tom," Alsop said to Sergeant Hazelwood. "Your new boss in?"

Hazelwood had a police equipment catalog open on his desk. "He's in. He told me to order a siren and lights for his motorcycle. And look what else he wants." Hazelwood turned a page. "He gave me a hundred dollars to purchase collar pins, gold stars, eagles, and two blue gabardine uniforms to go with this." He pointed to a picture of a powdery-white Stetson.

"Let's hope the uniform makes the man."

Harman's door stood ajar, and Alsop went inside. On the desk rested a cheap pen and pencil set, a blotter, and Harman's foot. He was peering out the window, probably imagining himself the new Wyatt Earp.

"Sorry to bother you, Chief," Alsop said and paced over to him. "I wanted to be the first to congratulate you. You've been officially appointed Defiance Chief of Police. Judge Thomson will administer the oath at noon today."

Harman burst from his chair, as if he'd been launched,

and grabbed Alsop's hand. "Thanks, Cal. Say, here's something I got special." He opened his desk drawer and handed Alsop a cigar.

Alsop ran it under his nose. "Very nice, thank you. Chief Parker appreciated the same brand."

Hazelwood knocked at the open door. "Cal, your wife's on the line. Says it's important."

"I'll take it here."

Harman handed him the phone.

"Jo-Dee?" Alsop said into the phone.

"Cal, I was planting flowers and found a strange footprint outside our bathroom window."

Alsop glanced at Harman. "Don't touch it. I'll be right there." He hung up. "Grab your hat, Chief. You may have a lead on that Peeping Tom case."

⁓⊰⊱⁓

They drove to Alsop's house in Harman's squad car, barreling along under a blue sky that stretched to the horizon, siren screaming until Alsop suggested it was unnecessary. He asked Harman, "Did Chief Parker tell you he knew who cut Will's brake line?"

Harman frowned and shook his head.

Alsop explained about the foot impression, the yellow rag found down the slope from where the car was parked, and that Chief Parker believed the perpetrator lived in the area and was at the commemoration. "I suggest you check Chief Parker's notebook for more information."

"Already know who the perpetrator is. Matter of fact, the person knows I know."

"Great." Maybe Wyatt Earp did have something on the ball. "Who is it?"

"Uh-uh, not so fast. A bit more police work to do."

The squad car squealed to a stop, and Jo-Dee scurried

down from the front porch. "On the side." She led them around the house, past bags of mulch and flats of witch hazels and giant snowdrops. She pointed to a footprint in the damp soil before a covered doorstep leading into the house.

Alsop squatted to inspect it, but Harman grabbed his shoulder. "Don't touch anything. Lemme see." He bent to examine the lone footprint facing the door, then straightened and hovered his shoe over the print. "I'm a size nine-and-a-half, and this appears almost the same." He looked at the door's window, covered with a blue curtain.

Jo-Dee said, "Inside's the bathroom, but we don't use this outside door."

"Why's that?" Harman stood on his tiptoes and tried to look in.

"We just don't, that's all," she said huffily.

The chief moved away and asked Alsop to look in. "You see above the curtain, don't you?"

"Yeah."

"I'm five-eight and couldn't reach. You're what, six-foot?"

"Close enough."

Harman whipped out a leather-bound notebook from his breast pocket. "Our Peeping Tom wears a size nine-to-ten shoe and stands at least five-eleven. Our first good lead." He scribbled a few notes and tucked his book away. "Stay clear of this area until my officer comes out and takes an impression. Ma'am, I appreciate you exercising your civic responsibility by bringing this to my attention."

Harman strutted off with his head in the air like a gander. Alsop gave Jo-Dee a comforting hug. "I'll put up a nightlight and install a larger curtain over the window." He brushed her cheek with his finger, then tramped inside and called Kathy to find out if she'd learned anything about those confounded blueprints in Bart's car.

"Cal, I'm sorry. The whole town's heard about them, but no one knows what they mean. By the way, what did you think of the mayor's speech last night?"

"That was a performance, not a speech. Cecil B. DeMille and Joe McCarthy rolled into one. He'd do well in Washington."

"Or Hollywood. While I've got you, Bucky stayed up all night printing his photographs, and he brought them in this morning. I told him to take the day off."

"That's fine. I'll see them later."

"Bucky wants you to see the top picture. He blew it up, said it's important."

"You have it there? Look at it and tell me."

"Let's see…it just shows people going into the courthouse. Hmm, looks like the governor followed by that Willow woman. Her companion's holding the door open."

"That's it? Nothing else?"

"Wait a minute! Now I see."

"What, what is it?"

"It's kind of fuzzy. But just inside the door, a man is shaking the governor's hand. His jacket says FBI."

CHAPTER 36

Tom," Harman barked into his cruiser's radio, "I'm leaving Alsop's house. Get a hold of Mr. Death and tell him to get his butt over to his funeral home, pronto. I'll meet him there."

"It's Sunday, Chief."

"Drag him out of church if you have to. Police business. He's got Chief Parker's notebook that was on his person when he died, and I need it."

It was lunchtime, and Harman stopped at Sally's. Fromm could wait. Harman munched a turkey sandwich and thought of Chief Parker—son of a bitch—confiding in Alsop but not his own nephew. Don't matter, his notes were gonna prove Kansas was the killer. He slurped the last of his malt and settled his account, laid a toothpick on his tongue and sauntered out feeling mighty pleased with himself. Two days on the job, and he was about to put away a murderer.

❦

An hour after meeting with the undertaker, Harman threw Chief Parker's notebook across the length of his office. There was no proof of shit. He tapped his jaw like a drum, running through the list of clues. Yellow rag in bush, foot impression in berm, Swiss Army knife, tinsnips. Nothin' but meaningless words.

He thought of something, stomped over, and snatched up the notebook. Here. *Call Grady about foot impression.* Harman stared blankly across the room at his motorcycle picture. Grady who? He tromped down the hall to the evidence locker but found only a rag and an unsigned note with the word *tinsnips*—probably an anonymous tip—and no foot impression. A double homicide and hardly any hard evidence. Maybe this Grady person had the impression and determined the footwear belonged to Kansas.

He should visit the son of a bitch, maybe scare him into slipping up. At least leave knives turning in his chest.

Twenty minutes later, he rumbled down Kansas's gravel driveway, spun a doughnut and cut the Fury's throaty engine. He got out in a cloud of dust and listened to the tinkle of the engine, which sounded like a family of mice living underneath the hood. Midday, no rustling trees or chirping birds. A puffy white cloud blocked the sun, making the house and grounds gray and eerie. He leaned against his front fender, feet and arms crossed as if he was fixin' to stay awhile. Let Kansas peek through the window and sweat going to jail.

After two minutes, he'd grown impatient. "Hey Kansas, get the fuck out here."

The front door opened, and Marybeth appeared.

"Well, lookie here!"

She let a shoulder fall against the jamb. "He ain't back from church yet."

She stood with one foot caressing the back of her leg. A bud of a mouth, cute and ripe, like a tomato, and a natural spot of red on each cheek. Her sweatshirt said American Bandstand and pictured dancers. He wondered about her titty size. Hard to tell in that getup. He liked 'em firm and perky. Couldn't remember what Tyburn had said about hers. Jus' that she was a virgin 'til he cured her.

He put on a friendly grin and ambled her way with a sloping gate and casual correction of his gun belt. "Howdy doody, Marybeth. Like to dance, do you?"

She fingered the silver cross hanging from her neck. "Sometimes, if it's fast."

"Betcha'd enjoy dancin' with Elvis." He wiggled his hips. "All that *gyration*."

"I heard you's the new chief."

He stepped onto the porch, groin tingling. "Good news spreads fast, don't it?"

"Saw you shoot that Indian yesterday."

"Did ya?" He grinned as wide as he could. Took a step nearer and jutted his chin up close. "It *scare ya?*"

Without flinching, she said, "If you'd a used a 44 Magnum Blackhawk, you coulda blowed his head clean off."

He bent back at the hips. "You some kinda *mu*nitions expert?"

"Seen it in a magazine is all."

"Tell ya a secret." He hitched up his pants. "Already got one of 'em ordered, along with a new uniform and a siren for my motorcycle."

Her large pupils got larger. "Super! Get a red light, a flashin' one."

He pointed at her with his first finger, thumb up, and clucked his tongue. "Read your mind." He squinted into the house. "Why ain't you at church with your daddy?"

"Was gonna, but had cramps."

That's right, filly is old enough for red river. "Your old boyfriend Tyburn's been asking for you."

Tomato-face turned a shade brighter and stared at her red toenails.

He raised her chin with his knuckle. "Might wanna wait 'till your cramps is done with."

An old black pickup rumbled into the drive. Harman turned to see Kansas. Just the man he was hoping for.

Kansas jumped out, hollering, "The devil's gonna get you, Harman. You got no business harassing my daughter. I reported you once. If you ain't gonna stew in jail, you'll roast in purgatory." He grabbed a shovel leaning against the porch. "Marybeth, get in the house."

Harman drew his gun. "Uh-uh-uh. Put that down, or catch a bullet where it hurts."

Kansas glared at him and threw the shovel to the ground. He yanked a rag from his pocket and wiped his hands.

Harman twirled his gun and took three jabs to holster it. "For a murderin' snake, you act awful high and mighty."

"Chief Parker knowed I didn't cut no damn brake line."

"That so? Well, you and him can ruminate about that in the spirit world, 'cause we found evidence. One of them rags like you're holdin'."

"Don't mean nothin'." Kansas stuffed the rag back in his pocket. "Why you gettin' those punk kids to steal my button to use as false evidence?"

What in hell's he talkin' about? "Don't need to plant nothin'. Got *new* evidence."

"New evidence, my ass. I got no reason to fear human judgment. And I'll do fine on the Lord's scale."

Harman continued his bluff. "Like I say, new *incontrovertible* evidence that'll put you in the state loveseat. An expert in Oklahoma City's been workin' on it, and by day's end, I'll be back with a search warrant and personally tear your house apart, plank by plank."

Kansas started to reach for his rag, but stopped himself. He glanced at the house, then to Harman, then the ground. He picked up a twig and began stripping its bark. "I um…I saw somethin' the night of the party, but didn't say."

Curious what shenanigan he'd try now, Harman took a step closer. "What somethin'?"

"A shadowy shape, a person, tall, didn't see his face."

Could Kansas actually be innocent? "Go on."

"I was takin' a piss out back of the Alsop house and seen him go inside through a side door. Don't recall much more."

Shadowy shape? Doesn't recall much more? "Next words outta your trap better be a name, or you'll taste gunpowder." That outta jar his memory.

Kansas looked down, found his memory in the dirt. "You didn't hear it from me, okay?"

"Spit it out."

"Hector. Was dark, but it was him. Had somethin' in his hand."

"What something in his hand?"

"I don't know. Maybe a tool."

Harman turned on his heels and strode to his squad car. Priding himself on his interrogation skills, he sat with one foot on the ground and called the station. "Tom, I just finished questioning Kansas and need to see that mechanic he works with, Hector. Look up his address. I'll wait."

❧❧

Harman pulled into a driveway behind another car with a couple getting out, probably returning from church. He got out and hollered, "You Hector?"

The man, tall and hunched over, sported dark trousers, blue coat, and no tie. The woman wore a green dress with pink flowers and no makeup. They looked at each other befuddled—or scared.

"I'm Hector." The man lumbered up to him.

Harman grabbed his bony arm and whirled him around. Jesus Christ! Forgot about that hook.

"Wa—whatcha doin'?" the man stammered.

Harman shoved his belly against the squad car. "Save your breath to cool your soup." He produced handcuffs and went to work, difficult with the hook.

"Let go of my husband!" the wife yelled, her face ragged as a cloud-torn sky. "You have no right!"

Harman pressed a hand against Hector's back and gave the screamer a shut-the-fuck-up look. She simmered down, but glowered at him with buckshot green eyes. Harman almost laughed. Poor thing. Mother bear whose cub had been snatched away. "Ma'am, if you want to help your husband, answer me one question."

"What question?" she snapped.

He nodded at Hector's shoes, black with a fresh spit shine. "Did your husband wear those shoes the night of Cal Alsop's party?"

She scrunched her eyes together, separated by a razor-thin nose. "They're his dress shoes, if that's what you want to know."

"I wanna *know* if it were them shoes he wore that night. Yes or no?"

She stared at Hector.

"Don't look at him," Harman ordered with steel in his voice. "Just answer the damn question."

She raised her chin. "Yes, I suppose they are."

He grabbed Hector's arm and hauled him to the squad car, opened the door and shoved him in. "You step out of this car, and I'll knock you right back in again." He turned to the woman. "Thank you, ma'am. I'm arresting your husband for the murder of Will and Miss Iris Chambers." That, he'd know for sure after comparing Hector's shoe to the impression outside Alsop's bathroom.

"This is ridiculous, you can't—Hector, don't say a word till I call my brother. Chief, you'll be hearing from our attorney."

After arresting Hector, and with a strong feeling Kansas had told the truth, Harman called Alsop and advised him to hire a new mechanic. "I've got Will's killer and the evidence to prove it. I'll be at your place in fifteen minutes."

CHAPTER 37

Alsop waited with Jo-Dee on their front porch when Harman and Sparks finally pulled up. They jumped out, and Harman grabbed a bag from his backseat. "Let's go round to the side."

Sparks, Jo-Dee, and Alsop watched as Harman bent before the footprint and took a shoe from his bag. He held it just above the impression and then exchanged it with the other shoe in the bag.

"I'd call that a perfect fit," he declared. "Sparks, get to work with your plaster."

Jo-Dee glanced at Alsop. "Cal, you said Chief Harman had proof Kansas killed Will. If that's Kansas's shoe print, that means he's a Peeping Tom, not a killer."

Harman grinned. "That ain't Kansas's shoe print, and he ain't no Peeping Tom. Or a killer." He held up the shoe. "This here shoe's still warm from Hector's foot."

Jo-Dee threw a hand to her mouth.

Alsop frowned. He couldn't imagine the always eager to please Hector peering into their bathroom.

"You ain't never had a Peeping Tom, ma'am," Harman said. "Just a killer. Kansas saw him go in through a side door the night of the party. And I'm betting, it was *that* side door." He pointed.

"That's impossible," Jo-Dee insisted. "It's always locked."

Gritting his teeth, Alsop realized the door could simply be opened from inside, but didn't correct his wife.

"We'll see about that," Harman said.

While Sparks made the shoe impression, Alsop led Harman through the back porch and into the bathroom. Jo-Dee followed and pointed to the clothes hamper before the door. "See, the door's blocked. Besides, it's bolted."

Harman slid the hamper aside, unlocked the deadbolt, and opened the door. He stood back and spread his arms, as if to accept applause.

Alsop rubbed the underside of his chin. As he feared, Hector could've left through the door, performed the deed, and returned. But why would he want to kill Will and Miss Iris?

The phone rang, and Jo-Dee left to answer it.

"Have to admit," Harman said, "I thought Kansas had done it, but by thoroughly interrogating him, I caught an inconsistency in his story and got him to give up his friend."

Jo-Dee returned. "Chief, Sergeant Hazelwood's on the line for you."

They followed her into the den. Harman picked up the phone. "Chief here." He listened for a minute, then laughed. "That supposed to make me rattle? I don't care if he's Clarence fucking Darrow." He glanced over at Jo-Dee. "Sorry, ma'am." Back to the phone he said, "Missed that, Jefferson who?…Davis. Never heard of 'im, but if he calls back, tell 'im I'll keep his client safe from vigilantes who might want to string him up." Harman hung up, chuckling. "Hector's hired some Mississippi lawyer who'll be up tomorrow."

When Harman and Sparks left, Alsop settled in the den with Jo-Dee. He couldn't get his head around the idea of Hector killing Will and his sister. Jo-Dee sat knitting, deep in thought. Alsop spoke up, "You thinking what I'm thinking?"

She glanced up. "Kansas planted Hector's shoe print."

"Sometime after the party he visits his *friend* Hector and somehow manages to get away with a pair of his shoes. Makes the impression, then returns them." At least that seemed far more plausible than Hector killing for no reason at all.

"Poor Millie. Imagine how she must feel."

"Would be interesting to see Hector's famous attorney."

"He's got a fancy name. Any relation to *the* Jefferson Davis?" She chuckled. "Of course, Harman would never have heard of him."

"Great grandson, Jefferson Davis the fourth. Hector's brother-in-law. One of the top defense lawyers in the country. Quick and cutting. He's a cheetah who tears into prosecutors like they're limping gazelles. Harman's in for the surprise of his life." And the fool deserved it.

CHAPTER 38

Harman decided he'd go and have himself a sixteen-ounce porterhouse steak at Cattlemen's Steakhouse, where cuts were the size of catcher's mitts, thick as a fist and rare enough to run out the door. It wasn't every day that a man put away a murderer.

He slid into a booth and signaled the waitress over. She was a puffy woman with a permanent scowl etched into her face. An old horse that should've been turned out to pasture after long service. He ordered beer and steak. A cowboy band played *Home on the Range* in the bar. Spears and rifles and buffalo heads covered the walls. The place had a good feeling. He drank the beer, and, when his steak arrived, with a crisp tap of his fingertip, directed the waitress to refill his glass.

He chewed away while gazing out the window past the Holiday Inn at a neon sign on Main Street. It said Uncle Lewy's. He got a tingle down yonder. What was that chick's name he was gonna bang before Uncle Asshole pulled him away to stand around that empty hole with two Indians? Oh, yeah. Sylvia. Maybe she'd be there.

He'd save room for dessert.

As he stood to leave, a hostess escorted Bucky and Kindra to a booth. Harman grabbed a toothpick from the counter, stuck it in his mouth, and sauntered over as they sat down.

"Howdy, Kindra." He tipped his hat. "I see you have good taste in dining. Wouldn't hurt to be a little pickier about the company."

"Oh, Bucky's not so bad," she said, "once you get to know him. It's my birthday." She beamed. "I'm eighteen."

Harman made his eyes wide. "*No.*"

"That's right, Chief," Bucky said. "Flirt all you want and no one will call you a pervert."

Harman put on his best icy stare. He turned to Kindra and loosened his face. "Don't forget what I taught your civics class. It's your right to disagree with a policeman, but it's your duty to obey him. Something injun-lover here never learned. He almost got himself shot once. Next time, he may not be so lucky."

Bucky stretched both arms across the back of the booth. "You've been pretty lucky yourself—So far."

Harman pulled the toothpick from his mouth. "You threatenin' me?"

"I make it a rule not to threaten officers of the law. Especially those I assume will soon arrest a murderer."

"No assume to it. Already made my arrest, but that's a good rule for you to stick to."

Bucky and Kindra exchanged glances. "Well," Bucky said, "was it Kansas?"

"Nope. It was Hector."

Bucky shook his head slowly. "I'll be damned. So the toe impression was Hector's."

"What do you mean, toe? It was the whole goddamn foot."

Harman turned to Kindra and touched his hat. "You have yourself a nice birthday dinner." He tramped off feeling damn proud of himself. It had only been a few hours since he arrested Hector, and the news—even if details were off—was already being talked about.

When he got to his car, he found Johnston sitting in the passenger seat.

"Hop in, Chief. We're going for a ride."

෨෨෨

"Park up ahead across from the school," Johnston said. Potter Elementary School, Harman's alma mater.

"What the hell we doin' here?"

"City Attorney Lovelace says you stirred up a hornet's nest by arresting Hector Manfield."

"I should give a flying fuck? He's got an open-and-shut murder case. What's his problem?"

"Maybe your case is weak. If so, he gets his ass reamed by Jefferson Davis."

Harman glanced at Johnston's face in the dim moonlight. Wrinkled as a dried leaf. "He's got nothin' to worry about. Is that why you dragged me out here and fucked up my evening?"

"If the mayor gets reelected Tuesday, you'll have more to whimper about than lost pussy. You'll be out of a job."

"What, out of a job?"

"You've got enemies, I told you that. I can only protect you with the mayor gone from office. He's not exactly a fan of yours. But don't worry, I've taken out an insurance policy—one you'll deliver."

"Huh?"

"The voting polls close at six p.m., and you, being chief, will transport the ballot box from that gymnasium," he pointed across the street, "to the courthouse for ballot counting."

"Am I supposed to stuff it with phony ballots?"

"The box will be locked. But I like your thinking. To-night, I'm giving you a boxful of ballots."

Harman flinched. "What are you talkin' about?"

"A duplicate ballot box."

"You crazy? I ain't switching no ballot boxes."

"Why, don't like your job?"

"Jailhouse food don't agree with me."

"Okay." Johnston faced forward and flicked his wrist. "Let's go."

Harman reached for the ignition but had a bad feeling. "We don't have a problem, do we?"

"*We* don't have a problem, but I'm afraid the council won't be pleased to learn the army charged you with rape."

"Bullshit! That charge was dropped."

"Only because the parents of the underage girl didn't want her name in the paper. Don't be a fool. They stuff ballot boxes down in Texas every goddamn election. It couldn't be simpler. When the polls close, you take the box and put it in your trunk beside the one I'm going to give you. You drive to the courthouse, park in the underground structure, and deliver the replacement box to room 101."

Yeah, and prune-face's hands stay clean. "What about the boxes from other polling places?"

"Those will be legit and taken care of by others. It's customary for the police chief to deliver the first box. You'll get your picture in the paper."

"Suppose someone's around, comes up to my car?"

"Don't worry. I'll be at both ends to run interference if necessary."

He fucking well had better be.

CHAPTER 39

The next afternoon, Alsop got a call from Harman begging him to come to the station right away. Ten minutes later, Hazelwood greeted Alsop with a smirk. "This is good, *really* good."

"What?"

"You'll find out."

Alsop found Harman standing at his window looking as if his dog had been run over by a truck. "Hello, Chief."

"Good, you're here. Have a seat." Harman flung himself into his chair. "That lawyer Davis has been here all morning. Met with Hector, checked my note pad, then saw the judge. Now he's back with Hector again."

Mrs. Rheingold's voice came over the intercom. "Chief, Mr. Davis is here to see you."

The door opened, and a hefty man of about sixty strutted in. Big and round-jawed, he carried a belly that battled against the buttons of his dress shirt. "Sorry to interrupt you boys," he drawled. "But Chief, you really must let my client go home. He's not at all pleased with the accommodations."

Alsop stood, out of politeness and to not be looked down on.

Davis's black eyes went to him. "Don't believe we've

met, suh." He extended a hand. "I'm Jefferson Davis."

"Councilman Alsop. How do you do?"

So, this was the famous lawyer known to see around corners.

"Well, now." Davis scanned the room, apparently unsure where to sit.

Harman bolted from his seat and rustled up an extra chair.

"I've just conferred with my client, Mr. Manfield," Davis said. "He's agreed to plead guilty."

Harman's eyes lit up like a cat's in a car's headlights. "Really, p—plead guilty?"

"Yes, suh," Davis said. "Guilty of voyeurism."

The cat just got run over. "Wait a minute!" Harman snarled. "You can't pull this."

Davis turned to Alsop. "I believe it was at your home, Councilman, where an occurrence took place. Mr. Manfield is greatly ashamed and wishes to express his deepest apologies to you and your wife."

"Listen here," Harman exploded, "I have an eyewitness who saw him enter Councilman Alsop's house after he cut a goddamn brake line."

Davis pulled a small tin from his coat pocket, picked a mint, and dropped it in his mouth. "Go on."

"Nothin' to go on to. You want us to add the charge of peeping Tom, we can do that, but the witness saw your client enter a house, not peep through windows."

Davis smiled and showed his well-kept teeth.

Alsop sensed a bombshell about to go off. "Mr. Davis, you have something else?"

Davis smiled. "I do, indeed." He produced a notebook from a breast pocket and crossed his legs. A pant leg rode up, exposing pasty skin. "Now, Chief Harman, according to your police report—" He slipped on tortoiseshell glasses and read from his notebook. "—Mr. Kansas Karradine told you that while he was pissing in Councilman Alsop's bushes—" He raised his eyebrows at Harman. "—I'm quoting your notes here, 'he saw a tall shadowy shape enter the house through the side door.' Is that correct?"

Harman swiveled his chair. "Kansas knew it was Hector—worked with him."

"'Worked with him.' I see."

"Had somethin' in his hand, too, if you keep reading."

"Did you not threaten to destroy Mr. Karradine's house, tear it apart plank by plank?"

Harman stopped swiveling. "That didn't mean—"

"And did you not attempt to conceal the fact that Councilman Alsop had reported a peeping Tom at his residence?"

"No concealment. Hadn't done the official report yet, is all. Besides, that has nothin' to do with nothin'."

"Councilman Alsop," Davis said. "Wouldn't you assume that if someone walked into your bathroom with a muddy shoe they'd have left a little something on the floor?"

Alsop had been wondering about that. "Sure, unless they wiped up."

"Of course," Davis said. "You would've had a mop and bucket there for them." He turned to Harman, his face having lost its country-boy charm. "Chief, this reckless charge of yours brings shame to your town and its citizens. Your witness—your *only* witness, a pervert who pisses in backyards—didn't see my client's face and only invented this cock-and-bull story because you threatened to demolish his home. You have not a shred of credible evidence, and to withhold the peeping Tom incidents is both unlawful police work and a disgrace to your profession."

Harman had bled enough.

"You've made your point, Mr. Davis," Alsop said. "What do you want?"

Davis snapped back on his friendly smile. "Of course." He got to his feet. "If you would be so kind, Chief Harman, as to escort my client to the courthouse, you'll find Judge Thompson waiting to accept his guilty plea to the charge of voyeurism. After that, Mr. Manfield will pay his fifty-dollar fine, and we can be done with this whole business. I think that would be the best outcome for all of us, wouldn't you agree?"

✁✁✁

Alsop grabbed a bowl of chili at Sally's while trying to come to terms with Hector as a Peeping Tom. Of course, Alsop would have to fire him. It would hurt business not to. Besides, Jo-Dee would be too embarrassed to ever look him in the eye again. As for Harman, he almost felt sorry for him, but definitely not sorry for Kansas. He was still a prime murder suspect.

The election was tomorrow, and Alsop would leave for an automobile conference the following day. He had much to do, including a trip to the polling places to ensure the ballots were ready.

After finishing his meal, he saw Hector and Millie getting out of Harman's squad car across the street at the police station. Millie spotted him, said something to Hector, and dashed over.

"Cal, I'm not going to apologize for Hector because he's not a peeping Tom, and *certainly* not a killer. But I want you to know if you fire him, we're still beholden to you for your kindness. It was right good of you to hire him after he lost his hand."

"What do you mean, he's not a peeping Tom? Didn't he just plead guilty and pay a fine?"

"My brother, Jeff—lawyers, who knows how they think? Something's wrong, and I assure you, I'll find out what."

CHAPTER 40

Harman squeezed his eyes shut as if trying to wish away a bad dream. A tap came at the windshield. A mustached man in a blue suit wearing a badge that said *Voter Registrar* motioned him hurriedly to pull forward. Every instinct in Harman's body told him to back out and get the fuck outta there.

The man kept gesturing. Now energetically. "Come on, Chief, it's been a long day."

Harman shoved his car in reverse and glanced into his mirror. Shit! A car had pulled up behind him. Light glinted off the Cadillac's logo on the car's hood. Heat simmered inside his chest. Up ahead, a crowd of people lined the steps leading into the school auditorium.

Harman put the car back in drive and moved on, his hands sticky on the wheel. He checked the crowd for Johnston's ugly face. The registrar paced alongside. A slap on the car's roof. "You're good here, Chief."

Holy shit! There was no way he could park here, open his trunk and not have someone see the phony ballot box. Johnston must've been out of his fucking mind. Harman slid from the car.

The registrar took his arm. "Let's go, Chief. We'll get a picture of you carrying the ballot box out."

Harman's eyes darted around. Where the fuck was Johnston and his so-called interference?

They entered the auditorium. It smelled exactly the same as always—like a jail cell. Harman jammed his hands into his pockets. The place was smaller than he remembered. Same paint color. Same flip-up wooden seats. Same stage from where he received his sixth-grade diploma. Near the flag stood two voting booths. Temporary cubbyholes with open fronts, tan canvas sides and backs. Harman eyed the ballot box on a table. As Johnston had promised: a dead ringer for the one in the trunk.

The registrar signaled over an old man with a camera who was eating soup at a table.

Harman hit on an idea. "Hold up there, podna," he said to the photographer and grabbed the registrar's arm. "What's your name?"

"James. Tommy James."

"We've got a change of plans, Tommy."

The man, his face sunbaked leather—probably a mailman or tractor driver—glanced at his watch and sighed. "What change of plans?"

Poor bastard. Worked twelve hours, feels beat as a rug, and wifey wants him home. Harman leaned in close. "We got a security problem."

"That's ridiculous."

Harman reached up and tugged Tommy's lapels like reins. "Caddos. That sound ridiculous?"

Tommy wrinkled his brow. "You're not serious."

"Another bomb threat. Serious enough?"

"Oh, my Lord!"

Harman strolled out onto the steps. "Hey, everyone. Come on in and get your picture taken."

The crowd streamed in with their smiles ready and gathered behind the box. Harman stood front and center, arms folded, grinning.

"Thanks for coming, folks," Harman said when it was over. "The ballot box won't go to the courthouse until morning, so you can all go home and look forward to seeing your picture in tomorrow's paper."

Everyone except Tommy filed out the door, happy to have been photographed and chattering about adding the picture to their scrapbooks.

"Turn off all the lights, both inside and out," Harman said to Tommy. "Then open the door and be sure it's all clear."

"Then what?"

"What do you think? I'll take the ballots to the courthouse."

"But what about the Caddos and the bomb?"

Harman winked. "We outfoxed them."

෨෨෨

It was only four miles to the courthouse, but to Harman it felt like a hundred.

How could that bastard Johnston decide not to show up at the auditorium? Maybe he wouldn't be at the courthouse, either. Maybe he got in a fucking car accident.

Crap! Harman slapped the steering wheel. The courthouse was now only a block away. A young couple stood in front, reading the placard by the buried Belvedere.

Wait a minute! Why didn't he think of this before? Dump the real box *before* going to the courthouse. Or—fuck it! Dump the phony one, and screw Johnston royally. Better not. Wouldn't be cool to cross him.

He sailed past the courthouse and turned north onto Simpson Road. He pulled over and stopped to weigh his options. Toss it in a dumpster? Too risky. Bury it? Not enough time. Besides, he didn't have a shovel. Bingo! The abandoned excavation site at the end of Wheeler

Road. Lots of places there. He flipped on the ignition just as a squad car pulled alongside. Officer Sparks cranked down his window.

"Hey, Chief. Whatcha doing? They're waiting for the ballots."

Harman let loose a sigh, taking his time on the exhale. He hit on an idea and opened his window. "Larry, I want you to go to the courthouse and clear the parking structure of all personnel."

"How come?"

"Just do it, goddamnit! I'll give you five minutes head start."

Harman sat drumming his fingers on the wheel. Good. Let Johnston get rid of the fucking real box. He pulled his cruiser over the humped entrance and down into the dimly lit garage. No one in sight. For a dipshit, Sparks did a good job.

He drove to the farthest corner, backed into a slot, got out, and closed the door.

Across the way, maybe a hundred feet, a chunky man in a dark suit leaned against a car, looking at him. He pulled out a pack of smokes.

Harman's legs wobbled. Where the fuck were Johnston and Sparks? His eyes darted around. He gripped the trunk key in his hand. He needed to get the phony box out before—He glanced again at the man by the car. Shit! That's the Caddy that pulled up behind him at the school. He squinted. In the car, a faint figure sat at the wheel talking to the man leaning against the door.

Harman started for the trunk.

"Hey, Chief. Got a match?"

Harman didn't look back. "Be right there."

The man's footsteps echoed.

Harman opened the trunk, took out the second ballot box, and set it down. The stranger ambled up holding a cigarette as the trunk slammed shut. He had dark wavy hair and a flat nose.

"Hey, asshole," Harman said to him. "Didn't I say I'd be right there?"

The man glanced over his shoulder, then back at Harman. He put his hand to his ear. "You talking to me, Chief?"

Jesus Christ. The guy was deaf and had a fucked up eye. "Listen retard, you're not supposed to be down here. Now get the fuck out."

The man raised his hands. "Whoa, Chief. Is that any way to address a citizen?"

Harman glanced around. No Sparks, no anybody. He swallowed. "Who the fuck are you?"

"Just a messenger, Chief."

A muscle tightened in the back of his throat. "What are you talkin' about?"

The man turned around. "Hey Willow, what was that guy's name?"

A blonde-haired woman stuck her head out of the Caddy. "Mr. Johnston."

"That's right, Mr. Johnston."

Harman felt as though he was plummeting down a dark shaft. He'd been set up.

"Don't you want to know the message?" the deaf-fuck asked.

Harman drew his gun. He didn't think about it, just did it. He had to get outta there and dump the original ballot box. Come up with a good story later. He nodded toward the box on the ground. "Pick that up and take it into room 101."

"Sure, Chief. But don't shoot the messenger."

A car door slammed, then a rifle cocked.

A woman stood by the Caddy, her rifle pointed right at him. He almost wanted to laugh until he met her hard gaze. He couldn't feel his legs. His hands tingled, and the dark shaft turned black.

The man reached out and took Harman's gun. "Don't you want to know Mr. Johnston's message?"

Harman nodded.

"He said to tell you crime doesn't pay."

CHAPTER 41

Polling booths had been closed two hours when Bucky escorted the elderly couple outside into the crisp evening air to take ownership of their new Plymouth Belvedere.

"Pastor Agnew," Bucky said, "if you drive safely and provide regular service, this beauty will still be around in fifty years."

The pastor chuckled. "You mean even if I'm not?"

"You'll be here in spirit, and you and your car could celebrate with its sister hibernating under the courthouse lawn."

"I guess I'll have to take your word for it, Bucky."

Sam drifted up and extended his hand to the pastor. "You're a lucky man, sir. Since the commemoration, the whole country's scrambling to snatch up these one-of-a-kind models. Everyone craves this marvel of tail fins and chrome." He turned to Bucky. "Cal wants to see you. But stick around for this." He turned to the pastor. "A guy goes into a bank and says, 'Give me all your money, this is a—'"

"Bucky!" Alsop whirled his arm. "Hurry up, and grab your camera."

Bucky retrieved his camera from his desk and jumped

into Alsop's Imperial. "Where are we going?"

"To the courthouse. I just got word the FBI has cleared the vote-counting room and locked the doors."

"How come?"

"That's what we're going to find out. And it had better be quick, because I'm leaving in the morning for Kansas City and the Western Dealership Conference."

Bucky had learned about Hector's innocence and realized that there were two shoe impressions: the still unidentified toe print they found in the berm, and Hector's footprint discovered outside Alsop's bathroom window.

"Before you go," Bucky said, "I'd like your help. Chief Parker told me he called someone the day of the celebration. That person confirmed his suspicion on the identity of the killer. Harman doesn't know who he is, otherwise we'd have heard. Can you get your hands on Chief Parker's phone records? You being a councilman, I'll bet the phone company will give them to you."

Alsop shook his head. "I doubt it."

"Then ask Mrs. Rheingold. She was the chief's secretary."

"That might work. When she gets the records, I'll have her contact you."

Alsop pulled into the underbelly of the courthouse. It smelled of car exhaust and dried oil. Inside, a crowd mingled at the door of room 101. Butcher paper covered the windows. A man in a blue suit and wearing an FBI badge blocked the door.

"This is an outrage," the mayor protested, riding up on his tiptoes. "I'm the mayor."

"I don't care if you're Napoleon, *sir*. No one enters."

Bucky raised his camera to the agent. He clicked the shutter and almost dropped his camera. The agent was the one in the photograph of Willow and Bart entering the courthouse during the celebration.

"Are the ballots being counted?" A woman shouted. "When will we know the results?" Others fired off similar questions.

The agent raised his hands. "The vote counters have been sent home. That's all I can say."

"Excuse me—pardon me."

Willow's luscious voice. Bucky turned. No wig covered her short brown hair. She wore a tailored black suit, and a black bag hung from a shoulder. She edged past him—without the wiggle—like he was invisible.

Bucky's heart practically thumped him out the building and down the stairs. He followed at her heels through the crowd to the door.

The agent opened the door enough for her to slip in, but held his hand in Bucky's face.

Bucky sidestepped, raised his camera above his head, and fired off a shot through the open doorway. The agent reached for the camera. Bucky dodged his grasp and tore out of the building.

ลงเงา

Bucky returned to work, unable to concentrate—nerves frazzled after seeing Willow. She looked so different. That must've been how she looked when Kindra saw her in the motel room with the gun on the table.

Maybe the couple from hell worked undercover for the FBI. But why would they have blueprints of a racetrack and risk their lives by crashing a brand new car?

Pictures of Willow kept popping into his head, and he took his time looking at them. Pictures of her in the dealership that first day, and there at the car crash. He could even hear her saying to Bart, "You almost got us killed and ruined Bucky's life." She had said it like she really cared.

Bucky played that one over and over.

✇✇✇

The next morning, Bucky developed the courthouse pictures and was shocked by one of them.

He tried to call Alsop, but he'd already left for Kansas City. He stared at the picture again, the crooked high angle through the doorway into room 101. People in dark suits with FBI badges stood around, and seated in handcuffs were Johnston, Overstreet, and Harman. Bart hovered over Johnston with a finger thrust in his face.

Bart and Willow must really work for the FBI. Wait—they *are* the FBI.

Bucky's phone rang.

Mrs. Rheingold said that Chief Parker had called the Tulsa Police Department on the day of the celebration. She gave him the number and he dialed. The receptionist asked for a name or extension. He told her Chief Parker had been working on a big murder case and had talked to someone at this number.

She asked the date and said she'd try to find out who the person was.

He gave the date and his number. To add urgency, he added, "Please find out soon, otherwise, the murderer might kill more people."

✇✇✇

When Bucky returned from lunch, a *While you were out* note was on his desk. *Call Sergeant Grady*. The Tulsa Police Department's phone number and an extension loomed at the bottom. Far out! That was the guy Chief Parker must've talked to about the berm evidence. He dialed the number with an unsteady hand.

"Crime lab, Sergeant Grady." He sounded like he was gargling rocks.

Heat shot all the way to Bucky's ears. He tried to sound official. "Bucky Ontario calling from Defiance. I understand you spoke with Chief Parker about evidence in our murder case."

"Goddamn shame about Parker. That idiot Trigger should have his balls cut off. *Killer dogs.* Don't get me started."

"Absolutely. I was there, just awful. Now about that impression…"

"I wondered when someone would pick it up."

"Yeah, well, we've been kinda busy. But with Chief Parker dead—the dogs and all—I wonder if you can give me a quick summary." Bucky tightened his grip on the receiver.

"Like I told Parker, the imprint at the crime scene was made from a shoe with an unusually thick sole, made by the Elevator Shoe Company. Right foot, size nine narrow. And as I recall, a five and a quarter-inch elevation. I told Parker my theory."

"Uh-huh." Bucky remained completely still as he listened, as if waiting to hear the correct time.

"Whoever owns it has a short right leg."

CHAPTER 42

"You boys have dug yourselves into a deep hole," Jefferson Davis the fourth said to his two clients. "Ballot stuffing went out with two-dollar whores and nickel cigars. Lyndon Johnson did it in Texas back in '48, but, unlike you, he got away with it." Davis popped a mint into his mouth. "It always gives me a bad taste when the federal government meddles in a state's affairs."

"Couldn't chance losing," Johnston mumbled behind his grand desk.

Overstreet, who had an Adam's apple the size of a horse's eye, sat stiffly under a portrait of Davis's Confederate grandfather generations removed. He straightened his paisley bow tie and brushed imaginary lint off a tweed sleeve. "When you're close to the wire and behind, you don't pull the reins."

Davis wondered if perhaps he should have boarded the train home this morning instead of sitting here, talking to these pompous featherweights. As he was standing on the station platform, Doc Little had shuffled up to him, huffing and puffing. He claimed to represent the Defiance City Council and persuaded him to stay and defend these "esteemed citizens."

"I talked to Clyde Tolson at the bureau," Davis said.

"He's second to Hoover. We went to George Washington University together back in 'twenty-seven. He agreed to put the brakes on this thing—for now."

Johnston and Overstreet exchanged nods.

"Don't breathe too easy," Davis snapped. "You've been like minnows swimming through razorblades. The feds didn't set you up to help you get rich in the racetrack business."

"Set us up?" Johnston blurted, bouncing in his seat. "What in tarnation does that mean?"

"They'd been watching you boys for two years."

Overstreet's Adam's apple took a ride up and down. "Two years!"

Johnston shifted in his chair. "The hell you talkin' about?"

"Tolson said he has proof of you both having ties with the Chicago Outfit. He also believes there's someone local working with you, but he doesn't know who."

Overstreet's voice hardened. "That's *absurd*."

"I'm *telling* you what the man said." Davis narrowed his eyes at Johnston: *and don't-you-start.* "The Outfit has been fixing horse races for years, and now they've been caught muscling into the racetrack operation itself. Through phone taps, the feds learned of your partnering up to operate the track's pari-mutuel betting system."

Johnston put his palms on the desk and rose a foot off his chair. "Tolson actually *told* you this?"

"Only because the bureau had just indicted the Chicago bunch. The feds hadn't planned to move this soon. They wanted to wait until you boys got your racetrack business going, but something pushed up their schedule, and Tolson wouldn't say what."

Johnston stared blankly at Overstreet, then to Davis. "I don't follow."

"Since the racetrack wasn't built yet, they had no case

against you." Looking at Johnston, Davis added, "That's why they maneuvered you into committing voter fraud."

Johnston winced.

"They had to charge you with something. They knew all about the political machinations you'd pulled to get the racetrack built in Tulsa County. And they knew it was imperative for you, Mr. Overstreet, to win the mayoral election. The feds wanted you two to believe with certainty that the governor was backing the mayor and preparing to build the racetrack here in Garfield County."

Johnston stared at his gnarled hands for several moments. "It was that blueprint fella."

Davis nodded. "An agent pulled in from New York with stage experience and a knack for eccentricity. He'd behave outlandish enough that folks would pay attention to him, take note of his blueprints, and spread the word. They picked Councilman Alsop's car dealership to set it up. An outside female agent added to the ruse."

Johnston removed the wet cigar from his mouth and studied it. "The governor in on this?"

"The feds had asked him to state publicly that he would veto the bill. He declined, inferring that it would depend on the election's outcome. But later, he agreed to tacitly support the mayor by attending the anniversary celebration." Davis wiped his glasses with his crumpled tie.

Johnston grabbed three cigars from his desk drawer. He passed them around and everyone lit up. He leaned back in a fog of smoke. "So, Mr. Davis, how do you intend to pull us out of this hole?"

CHAPTER 43

Harman stood anxiously shifting from one foot to the other while holding the door for a woman dabbing her eyes with a hankie as she came out of the police station.

"Sparks wants to see you," Sergeant Hazelwood said when he entered.

Harman raised his palm. "Not now." He blew past and through Mrs. Rheingold's office. The FBI had grilled him again. This time, two hours' worth.

Mrs. Rheingold followed him in and pointed to his new uniform hanging on the hat rack. "How do you like it?"

"It's great." He hauled a phone book out from a desk drawer.

"I took it home and ironed it. I'll be leaving now."

"Wait. Do you know a lawyer? I need a lawyer."

"*Well*, there's Mr. Caldwell." She put a finger to her chin. "*Noo*, I think he died a few years back."

"Never mind. Here." He thrust the phone book at her. "Take this and see if you can find a live one who'll take on a new case. But make sure he's good. Call tomorrow, and check references."

Harman slogged to the window and gazed out. That

bastard Johnston and his bastard lawyer. He pulled a card from his shirt pocket and studied it. *Agent Paul Saunders, FBI.* Seemed like a nice guy. He said Johnston's lawyer was trying to get his client off the hook by pinning the ballot box switch on him.

Saunders also said he could free Harman from the bear trap if he'd come clean with the identity of Johnston and Overstreet's third partner. If not, Harman could chew his own leg off. But Harman didn't know any third partner. Saunders didn't mention anything about those two Indians getting plugged. Thanks for small favors.

"Chief!" someone called at the door.

Harman flinched and turned. "Hey, Sparks, didn't hear you there. Someone should put a bell around your neck. What do you want?"

"I don't think you're going to like this." Sparks eased inside, got this look on his face and says, "It's about that Peeping Tom."

"Jesus Christ, Hector back at it?" Harman crumpled into his chair.

"That's just it. It's someone else."

"What?"

"A kid, seventeen. Caught him this evening. He admitted everything. Five houses, including Alsop's. His mom just left the station to see the judge."

Harman clutched his head in his hands. "But Hector fucking *confessed!*" A moment later, he raised his head. "Wait a minute. That means Hector *did* leave the house, and *did* cut that goddamn brake line just like I said. Get your ass over there, slap the bracelets on him, and bring him in." Harman spun a three-sixty in his chair. "Screw you, Mr. Jefferson Davis, the fucking Fourth."

CHAPTER 44

Alsop had been home less than an hour from his Kansas City trip when the doorbell rang. Jo-Dee rolled off him, covering herself with a sheet.

"Who's that?" she said in a near whisper.

Alsop reached above the headboard and peeked through the blinds. "Can't see. Middle of the afternoon, maybe the Fuller Brush Man. He'll go away."

"We can't be doing this with someone at the door."

The bell rang again. Jo-Dee scooped up her clothes and fled into the bathroom.

"Dammit!" Alsop got off the bed. "Where the devil's my other sock?" He threw on clothes and trudged to the door. It was Millie, Hector's wife.

"They've arrested Hector again," she said.

"Again?"

"I thought you should know."

"Of course, come in." He led her into the den where Jo-Dee now sat knitting, cheeks flushed. "Please sit down, Millie. I'd like Jo-Dee to hear this."

Millie, eyes glossy, sat perched like a sparrow on the sofa's edge, her hair perfectly coiffed. "They made me swear not to tell, but now, now that Hector's—"

"Who made you swear?" Alsop sat down, uncomfortably conscious of wearing his shoes without socks.

"Jeff and Hector. Mainly Jeff." She looked at Jo-Dee. "Jeff's my brother, Hector's attorney."

Jo-Dee gave a nod and fleeting smile before turning back to her knitting. Alsop suppressed a grin.

Millie clenched her hands. "Chief Harman was right. Hector did go out your side door, but not to cut any fool brake line, but to fix your blasted bathroom doorknob."

Jo-Dee looked up from her knitting. "What?"

"You see, after using the bathroom, Hector couldn't get out. He said the doorknob was broken, so he left through the side door to get a screwdriver from the car."

Jo-Dee's needles froze mid-loop. "My gosh, she's right. After Josh got stuck in the bathroom at the party, Hector said he had tried earlier to fix the doorknob."

"If he'd have gone out the side door and came back in again," Alsop said, "he would've stepped in mud and left a mess on the bathroom floor." He turned to Jo-Dee. "Did you clean up any mud after the party?"

Jo-Dee shook her head.

Millie jutted her chin out proudly. "Hector knows *not* to leave messes. If he made one, he cleaned it up."

"Why the hell didn't Hector just say so?"

"Jeff convinced him a jury wouldn't believe his story. Better to be an admitted Peeping Tom than a convicted killer."

"This is awful!" Jo-Dee cried. "Hector's life is going to be ruined because of a broken doorknob."

Alsop felt sick to his stomach about all the trouble Hector was in—If only he'd listened to Jo-Dee and fixed that damn doorknob! He couldn't let Hector go through all this alone. "Don't worry, Millie. We'll find a way to help Hector, I promise!"

CHAPTER 45

Kathy's voice drifted through the intercom, "Bucky, I just got a call. You'll be receiving a visitor soon."

Visitor or potential car buyer? Bucky straightened his tie and checked for the handkerchief in his right pocket. Minutes later, a dark blue '55 Caddy screeched to a stop outside.

Willow.

She got out and waved through the window.

His heart thumped—as usual. She looked different than in her tight, low-cut dress, but still a knockout in a skirt and sweater.

He hurried outside in a restrained gallop, as an orange sun settled on the horizon.

"Hi, Bucky." Willow smoothed her skirt and touched her hair. Her voice sounded so friendly, he'd roll over like a puppy and let her rub his tummy. He glimpsed Bart in the car and heard a ball game on the radio.

"Well, look at you," he said. "FBI, huh? I heard about the voter fraud."

She winked. "Bart's FBI, I'm on loan from Treasury. We were undercover."

"And you got your man. Or I should say men?"

She socked his shoulder. "We *always* get our men. We wanted to thank you for…well, for being a good sport. You came through for us, though you didn't know it, and we appreciate it."

Bucky forced a smile. Willow probably wasn't even her real name.

"Yea!" Bart yelled from the car. "The Knicks clobbered the Celtics!" He heaved himself out and came flying over. "Bucky, you sonofagun, put 'er there." He threw out his meaty hand and they shook.

"Hey, what happened to your eye? Looks normal."

"Hadya fooled, didn't I? Used one of those contact lenses made special for when I starred in *The Hunchback of Notre Dame* off Broadway."

"Wait a minute. You mean you made up that story about crashing your jeep in a ditch?"

"On the spot. Called *im*provisation. I hand it to you, Bucky-boy, you conducted yourself like a man in them there badlands. Called me an asshole. Beautiful. I almost broke character and split a gut." He looked at Willow. "Willow, didn't I sniff the air and say—wait a minute—" He raised his chin. "—and say, 'I'm smelling sarcasm?'"

She gave a faint smile. "A star performance."

"Did you guys crash the car on purpose?"

Willow shook her head. "Bart's got good eyes, but horrible driving skills."

"My kid sister's a G-Man fiend," Bucky said. "The comics. She'll flip when I tell her about you guys. Especially how you had me going."

"We'll be down in Oklahoma City for a couple of days," she said, "but when I check in at Quantico, I'll send you a Junior G-Man badge for your sister."

She kissed his cheek and got into the car. The crime fighters waved farewell and, with a cloud of dust, rode off under a fiery sky.

Bucky sighed. She never said her real name.

ᴇᴈᴇᴈ

Bucky waited in Kindra's living room for her to finish chores, so they could start their math tutoring session.

A silver framed photo on the mantel caught his eye. He picked it up. A man in a military uniform held a little girl in his arms. His foot rested on the running board of a '32 Chevy Roadster, similar to Bucky's '32 Ford. Bucky heard the soft patter of footsteps in the hallway and put back the picture.

"That's Kindra and her father," Gustafson said, shuffling in from the hallway.

"Hi, Mr. Gustafson."

He shook Bucky's hand and actually smiled for a change, then turned serious. "You probably know about the car accident. Kindra was three."

"Yes, awful. A wheel came off an oncoming car." Bucky had never been inside his ex-boss's house before, and Gustafson looked tinier and more rounded in his casual wear of slippers and a bathrobe. Even more like Mr. Magoo than he did at work.

Kindra stuck her head in the doorway, a bundle of clothes in her arms. "I'm almost done, Bucky. This is the last load. Grandfather, I'm going to throw your overalls in with these whites. They're so faded it won't matter." She disappeared down the hall.

Bucky slid his hand across the slick Magnavox TV cabinet. "Beautiful television."

"I never got into the TV habit," Gustafson said. "Like to let my mind visualize what the radio's talking about. I understand Hector's locked up again for the Will and Miss Iris murders. Having Harman as police chief is depriving Defiance of a village idiot. Dollar to a doughnut says Kansas did it."

Maybe Gustafson knew something Bucky didn't. "What makes you think so?"

"You know what he's like. Way he treats his own daughter."

Bucky wasn't sure what he meant. Kansas had seemed controlling of Marybeth, but he also bought her magazines and made sure she got her favorite ice cream at the store. Besides, even if Kansas was a child molester—of course, that was bad enough—but that in itself didn't make him a murderer—or the father of Marybeth's baby. Though he probably was the first thing and possibly the second.

"Gus. *Gus!*" came shouts from upstairs. "I'm starving up here. Where's my lunch?"

Gustafson made a face and waved his arm. "That's Mrs. G. She eats the same stinking soup every day." He cupped a hand to his mouth. "In a minute, dear." Then he waddled out of the room.

Searching for Kindra, Bucky passed by the kitchen. Gustafson was dishing up a bowl of soup, and Bucky caught the eye of some dark-haired girl eating at the table. Kindra stood in the laundry room running a sheet through the ringer.

"Who's the girl in the kitchen?" Bucky asked.

"That's Abby. Help me hang these sheets before we start on my geometry. I *really* appreciate your help. Math isn't exactly my strongest subject."

They headed outside to the clothesline. The yard included an orchard with several kinds of trees. Apple and peach that Bucky knew for sure. The first thing he remembered tasting and wanting to taste again was Gramma's peach pie made with a crispy graham-cracker crust. He supposed he was about four.

Kindra handed Bucky clothespins from her apron. "Clean sheets smell *so* good." She handed an end to Bucky and he sniffed. "Not now, silly, when they're dry. Hey, don't let it hit the dirt. Gosh, that's all I'd need."

"Is Saturday chore day around here?"

"I wash and vacuum."

"My daddy used to make me do more than that. I had to—"

"My grandfather can't *make* me do anything. Not since I was twelve-and-a-half."

"Was that your emancipation age or something?" *Ha, there's a fancy word for her.* "You don't know this, but a foot impression was made in the dirt near where Will had parked his car. Whoever cut his brake line wore a special shoe. A real thick one. And guess what? Kansas wears a special shoe because of his foot problem. You know, otherwise he'd walk around lopsided."

She handed him more clothespins and a pillowcase. "Maybe both shoes are special."

"Doesn't matter, because the foot impression will prove who the killer was."

"You really think it was Kansas?" she said lightheartedly.

"I'll know once I get that foot impression."

CHAPTER 46

If Harman could keep his mind off going to jail, it could be a bitchin' afternoon. He was about to be indicted on several counts of voter fraud, but figured, fuck it, he'd take the rest of the day off. Tomorrow he'd meet with some lawyer Mrs. Rheingold had lined up. Let him worry about that bastard Johnston and his lies.

Harman threw a leg over his newly outfitted motorcycle. Perfect. Lights, siren, and a glossy black-and-white paint job with a red star on the tank. He slid on a pair of aviator sunglasses and tightened the chin cord of his powdery-white Stetson. It complemented his new uniform with collar pins, gold stars, and eagles on each epaulet. He fired up his machine, and the pipes let out a gargled roar. With his arms stretched forward, his blue shirt felt comfortably snug, like skin on a sausage.

He zipped his leather jacket and spun north under a clear sky with scattered white clouds, past pungent earthy fields, over an open highway.

At the little town of Lamont, he caught a light at Miles Avenue in front of a pink hotel. He nodded to the old biddies on the porch who seemed to flicker in the breeze while waiting out their lives and boring the pants off anyone stupid enough to sit beside them.

A nice long stretch of road allowed him to throw open the throttle. The speedometer tickled eighty. He soon found himself in the feathery wake of a slow-moving truck stacked high with chickens.

Good time to test his new lights and siren. Yeehaw!

He bore down on the farmer like a screaming freight train, gumballs flashing, siren wailing—the whole shit-load. He shot past, and the rickety truck bounced off the road and banged wildly along the rough shoulder. *That ol' boy will need a new axle and a change of shorts.*

After three hours on the trail, Harman arrived back in Defiance, stopped at the Ranch Road Speedy Mart to stretch his legs and down a cold one.

He grabbed a Pabst from the cooler and placed it on the counter.

"With you in a sec," a voice called.

Harman eyed the cigars on display and glanced around before slipping the biggest one up his sleeve.

An Indian appeared. His nametag said Tony. "Anything beside the beer?"

"Matches."

"They're free."

Harman took two packs. "Thanks a bunch."

He emerged from the store humming *Peggy Sue,* planning to down his suds in the parking lot. He leaned against his bike and let the brew do its magic.

A gold Studebaker pulled in across the lot. A little girl jumped out, then stopped and yelled back to the driver, "What kind did Daddy say?"

A blonde with a fur coat and frilly blouse stuck her head out the window.

Hello, sugar tits. They bulged like the hubcaps of her Stude.

"Chesterfield," she hollered. "If he asks for a note, tell him I'm here in the car."

Harman looked at her and strutted his stuff. Waitress—could spot 'em anywhere. He'd had lots of them. Only one thing bothered him more than the company of an ugly waitress, and that was the company of the same ugly waitress the following morning.

She caught his eye and winked. He waved his cigar. Very cool. The little girl came out and hopped in the car. They drove off, leaving Harman in the mood for something more than a cigar. He threw it down and moseyed inside for another beer. He wondered if the alcohol or the woman gave rise to the little voice in his pants. He opened his second bottle and said to the clerk, "Haven't patronized the wigwam house in a while. Any fresh fillies to break in?"

Tony grimaced. "I don't think you ought to be going to the reservation."

The man had a point. Fuckin' injuns might like nothing better than to cut off his balls. "Wait a minute. Your people are Cheyenne. Why should you give a shit about a couple of Caddo gettin' shot up?"

"We're all brothers, that's why."

"Well, fuck 'em. Where's the can? I wanna sit with my beer."

Ten minutes later, Harman left the Speedy Mart feeling *really* in the mood for one o' them Indian maidens with firm, brown titties.

Then Marybeth popped into his mind.

Harman rumbled north along Simpson Road, feeling a buzz from the beers, not much caring about the pleasant cold wind in his face, the lovely white clouds, or the delightful smell of waving wheat fields.

His mind was on Marybeth's pants and what was in them.

Three-thirty. She should be home from school. To make sure, he pulled into a filling station and called her house from a phone booth. She answered on the second ring. He hung up and grinned.

He opened the booth's door and found a bent-over old lady staring at him with a curdled face. "Aren't you able to use the phone on your motorcycle?"

He raised his sunglasses. "Call was personal. Wouldn't be right usin' it to phone my poor sick mother."

"Oh, I'm sorry. Has she been ill long?"

"Screw you, lady, and the broom you rode in on."

He mounted his bike, and the seat settled down on its springs. Passing Alsop's dealership, he slowed with an engine rev, hoping Alsop might catch sight of his bike and new uniform. He figured Kansas had at least another hour's work before knocking off.

As he waited to make a left onto Valley Spring Lane, he saw Gustafson in his gray Packard turn onto Simpson Road. Eager to show off again, he tried to switch on his flashing lights but fumbled, missing his chance.

Five minutes later he enjoyed watching Marybeth prance down her porch, perky as a chickadee and looking like a cheerleader. Plaid skirt, green sweater, and itty-bitty pigtails poking up from her head like pineapples. She bounced up to him on his growling machine.

"Su*per*." She circled the bike, taking in every detail. "Dinger of a bike."

"Check this." He flashed the red lights. "Got 'em jus' like you said."

She squealed, her face bright with excitement. She grabbed his waist and swung a leg over the back. "Let's tool out."

"Whoa," he said, killing the engine. He didn't want to waste time doin' that. Besides, how'd it look, him being police chief? "Maybe later."

She jumped off and pouted. "Why'd you come, then? To arrest Papa?"

He removed his sunglasses and slipped them into his shirt pocket. "Got *no* problem with your papa."

"He hates your guts."

"That's his problem." Harman slid off his bike and tugged the seat of his pants to loosen the wedgie. "I came to see you."

"That's nice. Goodbye." She started toward the house. "I got homework to do."

"Now wait up, little girl." He pinched his throat. "Can ya offer me somethin' to rinse the trail dust?"

"I'll get you water. You stay out here." She trekked inside.

Harman waited a moment, then followed, swinging his arms high. He settled on the living room couch, hard as stone and covered with bearskin. After building the cabin, Kansas probably made the furniture using every leftover except the sawdust. It even smelled like sawdust. A history book sat on the coffee table. It pictured an Indian on a horse with buffaloes grazing in the background.

Marybeth came in from the kitchen and stopped short, splashing water on the floor. It looked like it could use the rinse. "You shouldn't be in here."

"I promise not to steal nothin'." He glanced around. "Nothin' I'd want, except maybe that buck head your papa probably bagged."

"He wouldn't like you being here."

Harman stood. "Well now, are you a good little girl who tells her papa everything?" He took the water from her.

She stared at her feet. "*No*, but still—"

He gulped a few swallows, belched, and handed her the glass. "Somethin' I notice about you, Marybeth, is your posture."

She set the glass on the mantel beside a tin of shoe polish. "What about my posture?"

"Don't get riled, it's a compliment. Lots o' girls slouch, you know, bend over." He demonstrated. "Their soft bones harden like those prehistoric dinosaurs in that museum over in Tulsa. Makes girls unattractive." He ran his hand down her back. Feeling her bra strap made his groin tingle. "See, yours is straight, makes you attractive. I read that girls in them fancy finishing schools back east walk with a book on their heads to get their backs to do what yours does naturally."

"Really?" She straightened more.

He sat back on the couch. "You could be a model like in them fashion magazines." He patted the spot next to him.

She plopped down and slouched. "I don't read those types. Well, sometimes, but mainly I read mystery magazines like *Ellery Queen*. I want to be a writer like that."

"Murder stories, robberies, that whatcha mean?"

"Yeah, different kinds."

"Must be exciting knowing a real bank robber. Heard you went to visit Tyburn there in jail before he relocated down south for trial."

"So? No law against it."

"Not unless you slip him a hacksaw." He draped his arm across the back of the couch, lifted his knee and turned to face her. "You kinda go for older men, don't ya?"

She shrugged. "Depends."

Now we're getting somewhere. "You won't be seein' Tyburn for a long time unless you visit him at El Reno. Me and him are the same age, case you didn't know."

"I know yous went to school together."

"Went everywhere together. Me and him was like this." He crossed his fingers. "Funny how life works out when ya think about it: me bein' a policeman—chief no less—and him facin' a prison stretch."

"Papa would say it's God's plan. Not me. I believe if people sin they should pay."

Harman didn't come here to goddamn philosophize. Time to get her warmed up and screw her socks off. "Not everyone pays for their crimes. Betcha didn't know I got files of unsolved crimes right here in Defiance. Confidential files goin' back fifty—a hundred years. Thievery, gunfights, rapes, murders. Got one nobody even knowed about. Way back, Mayor Potter's wife, she shot and killed a woman fer seducin' her husband."

"Maybe she shoulda shot him."

"Don't matter. She was never charged. The police chief and city council didn't want to embarrass the town, so they hushed everything up. Those files are confidential, you understand." He took her hand. "Can ya keep a secret?"

"*Sure*."

"The mayor's wife was a klep*to*maniac, maybe even a nym*pho*maniac. Files got all them details. I'm thinkin', maybe you could write a story about it, change the names, like on that TV show, Dragnet. You know, protect the innocent."

Her eyes got all big. "You'd let me?"

He rubbed his chin. "Wouldn't be legal exactly, but, maybe. Tyburn told me somethin' I was supposed to keep secret. And I intend to. I'm a man o' my word. But seein' that he won't be around anymore—least for a long time—I'll tell you."

"*Okaaay*," she said cautiously.

"He said you had the most beautiful sugar titties he'd ever seen."

A blush spread over her face, down her neck, and maybe all the way to her ankles.

"I'd be real grateful if you'd give me a peek at 'em."

"*No*. I can't be doin' that. You're the police chief."

"It's because I am the police chief that you can. If I say it's okay, it's okay."

"Wouldn't be right."

"You wanna see them files, don't ya?"

Her eyes shifted to the floor. "You'd let me read them and write a story about Mayor Potter's wife?"

He snapped his fingers. "That's a deal."

"And I only have to show 'em to you?"

"Whatever you say." He felt blood pump down where he'd need it.

"Just a look."

He nodded. "Just a look."

She lifted the front of her sweater for a split second, then lowered it. He glimpsed the top of her breasts bulging deliciously from her white bra. A tiny pink bow sat smack in the center.

"That don't count," he said, laughing.

She giggled.

"Besides," he said, "let's go in your bedroom for better light."

"We're not doin' sex!"

The hell we're not. He felt like a balloon that had been filled with an intoxicating gas. He nodded, stood, and held out his hand.

She ignored his hand and got up. He followed her down a short hallway and turned into her room. The bed's footboard was near the door. Clothes covered the bed and draped over every piece of furniture. In a corner sat stacks of magazines, a broken vase, and some dead flowers.

He back-armed a heap of clothes off the bed, and they sat.

Their knees touching, he said, "Let's start over, nice and slow."

She exhaled and lifted her sweater, this time pulling it

over her head. Her tits filled her bra with lots of over-flow.

He reached around her to undo the clasp, then paused. "May I have the honor?"

She rolled her eyes, and he undid the strap. His heart banged like drums as he lowered her bra. He gaped at those creamy whites with brown nipples the size of silver dollars.

"There, you've seen 'em."

He cupped one in his hand and squeezed. Squishy, not firm like them wigwam girls, whose nipples came up fast under tweaking. Not that he gave a shit one-way or the other. He put his lips around one of them and gave it a good hard suck. Chicks dug it.

"*Ouch!* That hurts. And you're only supposed to look."

He peered up at her, his breathing shallow. He visualized that dark wedge deep between her white thighs. "Lemme see what's under them undies."

"I can't do *that*." She grabbed her sweater. "Shouldn't be doing this. Besides, that wasn't the deal."

"Just a peek. I'll pull down your panties only a little." He pushed her onto her back and reached under her skirt all the way up her thighs.

She raised her hips. "But that's all."

He slipped her white panties past her knees and off one foot. Her lower territory was so thick with brush, it needed clearing. He dove in nose first and made a part. Her scent filled his nostrils. He straightened and hastily unzipped his new blue slacks.

She pushed up onto her elbows. "I told you, *no sex*."

Ah, fuck this shit. He whacked her once across the snout, then threw himself between her legs.

She let out a series of piercing screams, each with pulsating contractions. Seconds later, he exploded inside her.

Then something hard and cold pressed against the back of his neck. Everything went black.

CHAPTER 47

Jo-Dee relaxed on the sofa, nursing her first sherry, while Alsop poured his second. He took the drink and paced back to his leather chair. A roast could be smelled cooking in the oven.

"How about after supper," Alsop said, "we turn in early and don't answer the door no matter what?"

Abashed, she cooed, "Oh, you."

Ten minutes later, the phone rang. Alsop stood.

"Are you sure you want to answer it?" Jo-Dee asked, eyes fluttering.

He hesitated another ring. "I'd better. Could be Bucky wanting to throw in a free radio for someone."

He picked up the receiver. "Hello?"

"Cal, it's Sparks. We got another double murder. I think you might want to—"

"Whoa, hold on. Double murder? Where?"

"Kansas's place. Could you come over? Someone from the council should be here."

Alsop swallowed a lump. Kansas and Marybeth? He couldn't bring himself to ask. "The chief there?"

"Uh, yeah. You could say that. Can you bring that Bucky fella with his camera? We still don't have a photographer."

Alsop hung up and turned to Jo-Dee. "There's been a double killing at Kansas's house." He grabbed his coat. "Call Bucky at work and tell him to meet me there with his camera."

∽∾

Kansas's property was crammed with cars. Alsop parked on the gravel driveway and hurried to the house, oblivious of the freezing cold. A light flashed in the hallway. Bucky had already arrived with his camera.

What the devil was retired Chief Trigger doing there, talking to Officer Sparks in the living room? Harman would never have the good sense to ask for help in a murder investigation. Marybeth sat slouched in a chair, her face a mask of tears.

Alsop went to her and knelt down, relieved the young girl wasn't one of the victims. Her eyes were red as cayenne pepper. "Marybeth, are you okay?"

She nodded and turned away.

Trigger, standing with Sparks by the fireplace, motioned Alsop over.

Alsop patted Marybeth's knee and went to him. "What happened, Chief?"

Trigger scowled and popped the knuckles of his fingers. "This should win a medal for the most fucked-up crime scene of the century. Until I looked closely, I thought Kansas and Harman had a shootout. And since this amateur—" He tossed his head toward Sparks. "—fooled with the bodies, it'll be impossible to know exactly how it went down."

Sparks bristled. "I told you, Chief, I only covered them with sheets."

"I know, I know," the chief growled, in obvious frustration.

Alsop nodded toward Marybeth. "Did she witness what happened?"

"She's our prime suspect."

"Excuse me, Chief." Bucky approached from the hallway. "I got pictures of the gun and powder burns on the back of Harman's neck. I also found a partial footprint in the blood. I need a shot of Marybeth's bloody shoe before she walks around and rubs it off."

"Sparks, give him a hand." Trigger turned back to Alsop. "Where were we? Oh, yeah, the girl claims she blacked out while Harman raped her, and *vaguely* remembers hearing two gunshots. Says afterward she gets up from the bed, drags the two bodies out into the hallway and puts Kansas's revolver over there on the table."

"She say why she moved the bodies?"

Trigger shot a glance at her and leaned in. "Says she can't remember." He hoisted his eyebrows. "Real fuckin' believable. What she does remember is getting porked by Harman."

"Where were they shot?" Alsop said. "I mean, on their bodies."

"Harman got it in the back of the neck, Kansas in the heart."

Bucky came up to Chief Trigger again. "I've got pictures of everything. Bodies, bedroom, hallway, the works."

"Did you get those blood stains in the hall?"

"All of them. Chief, I have a suggestion." Bucky lowered his voice. "I went into Kansas's room to take pictures and found his nightstand open."

"Yeah, what about it?"

"Since the gun belonged to Kansas, whoever used it—" He nodded toward Marybeth. "—may have taken it from the nightstand."

"And how the hell are we going to know that?"

"Have Officer Sparks dust it for fingerprints."

Doc Little scuffed in from outside with a black bag and a white-gowned nurse. Chief Trigger pointed down the hall. The doc shuffled to the bodies, the nurse to Marybeth.

Trigger turned to Alsop. "If you and the council would like me to fill in until you find yourselves another chief, I'll do it. You're going to need all the experienced help you can get."

Alsop's mind raced. Trigger had been forced to retire because of his use of smoke bombs and killer dogs at the celebration. But Alsop couldn't think of an alternative. "That's probably a good idea."

"I'll finish up here and set up headquarters in Chief Harman's office. I suggest you check with your council, see if they want me to stay on. If so, let's meet there tomorrow afternoon and review what we've got. I should know a lot by then. And Bucky, be there with your pictures."

CHAPTER 48

Three men gathered around Johnston's desk, and two of them laughed heartily. Overstreet nodded to Johnston and poured a second round. "Another toast to Mr. Jefferson Davis, who, as promised, dug us out of a mighty deep hole."

"Hear, hear," Johnston chimed. Everyone threw down their drinks.

"Well, Mr. Overstreet," Davis said, stroking his wrinkled red tie, "you forfeited the mayorship but could've done worse. As operators of the Tulsa County racetrack's pari-mutuel betting, you two should earn enough in commissions to buy your own racetrack."

Overstreet smiled. "Running for mayor was simply a means to an end."

Davis set his glass on the corner of the desk. Better to warn these clowns or he might have to deal with them again. "You boys got off because the FBI didn't want to justify wire taps all the way to the supreme court. The last thing the feds want is to argue a fourth amendment search-and-seizure case before Chief Justice Warren. Besides, they bagged the Chicago Outfit, and that was their prime goal anyway. But they know of your accomplice with the Outfit, and if they ever get their hands on him, and he talks, you can bet they'll make him a sweet offer to give you boys up."

Overstreet smiled confidently. "We understand."

Davis picked up his drink and peered into it. One thing still puzzled him. "Tell me, Mr. Overstreet. Why didn't the governor veto the racetrack bill? It was assumed he would with the mayor in office. What changed his mind?"

"Everybody wants something, Mr. Davis. And we knew what the governor wanted most." His eyes flicked to Johnston. "You want to tell him, Maynard?"

Johnston blew a thin stream of smoke peacefully at the ceiling from his freshly lit cigar. "My problem, Mr. Davis, is I never learned to accept defeat. Instead, I've learned to whisper in all the right ears, especially in Washington. That, and to sprinkle a few dollars around like Christmas candy. So you see, come the 1960 presidential election, the Republican candidate will be none other than our own Governor Alvin Wishbone."

CHAPTER 49

Bucky stared at the dried pictures on the clothesline over his sink. Pictures of two dead bodies. Bodies alive twenty-four hours ago. Bodies of people he knew, though didn't particularly like. Now he might never find out if Kansas was guilty of killing Miss Iris and Will.

Still, grief had snuck up his chest, making for a long and sleepless night. He tossed and turned along with every different scenario he could imagine resulting in two deaths. It seemed to boil down to the question of whether Marybeth did all the killing, some of the killing, or none of the killing.

Though unlikely, it could also have been an intruder. Bucky didn't see evidence of one, and he hadn't had time to study the photos for clues, but Chief Trigger would.

A horn beeped outside. It was Alsop.

Bucky climbed into the car. "Well," he said, "have any theories?"

"I'm guessing Kansas caught Harman raping his daughter and shot him." Alsop shook his head. "But for the life of me, I can't imagine why Marybeth would then shoot her own father."

If Harman was right about Kansas having abused her,

that could explain why. "Hopefully Chief Trigger will figure it out."

❦❦❦

Bucky entered the Defiance Chief of Police's old office to find Trigger at the desk, his steel-gray hair cut plain and blunt, and the third to occupy this room within only a week. A few others were sitting around waiting for Trigger to begin.

"Hello, Chief," Bucky said and laid a stack of photographs on the desk. "All the bloody footprints belonged to Marybeth." He offered the chief a magnifier. "Take a look."

The chief brushed the pictures aside. "Any other footprints?"

"Only hers."

"Take a seat. Okay, everybody, let's get started."

The chief would probably want to study the pictures later, Bucky assumed though he didn't like being brushed off.

"We're here to review the alleged rape of Marybeth by Chief Harman and the shooting deaths of Chief Harman and Kansas Karradine. For the record, it's now three-fifteen p.m., January 19, 1957, and we are assembled at the Defiance police station."

His gaze swept the room. "I'll state the names of those present. Councilman Alsop, Councilman Doc Little, Officer Sparks, and Mr. Bucky Ontario. Taking notes is Mrs. Rheingold. I'm Cosmos Trigger, acting chief." He glanced at Alsop, who nodded. "I'll preface by saying that I questioned Marybeth extensively this morning and will have much to say about that interview. She is now under foster supervision with Mrs. Rheingold."

Chief Trigger heaved himself to his feet, lumbered to a

blackboard in the corner, and wheeled it around. "Both victims were shot with a Colt revolver owned by Kansas Karradine. Listed here are four possible ways the two men were killed. All subsequent to, or during, the sex act between Harman and Marybeth. First, Marybeth shot Kansas, then Harman. Second, she did it the other way around; she shot Harman, then Kansas. Third, Harman shot Kansas, and then Marybeth shot Harman. And fourth, Kansas shot Harman, then Marybeth shot Kansas."

Bucky put up his hand. "Suppose a fourth person shot them both?"

The chief shook his head. "I questioned Marybeth, and she said Kansas kept his pistol in his nightstand. If someone else did the shooting, he would've had to enter the house, go down the hallway, past Marybeth's bedroom—while she was being raped—go into Kansas's room, get his gun, and shoot Harman. Then maybe Kansas comes home and that same person shoots him. The problem is, there's no evidence of that occurring. As your photos confirm, the only footprints on the bloody floor were Marybeth's."

The person could've stepped around the blood, but Bucky didn't think Chief Trigger would appreciate him saying that. He probably didn't even dust the drawer knob for prints. Bucky raised his hand again. "Chief, which way do you think the shooting happened?"

The chief crossed an X through all four scenarios, put the chalk down and swiped his hands. "I'll tell you how the killings were done, but first some background." He strutted to his chair and cracked his knuckles. "Since retiring from the Edmond police force, I've been contracting with the marshal's office to escort prisoners to and from various locations both in and out of state. Recently, I was transporting Tyburn Newgate from the Defiance jail to Oklahoma City for trial. During transport, Newgate talked about Marybeth and said that I, and I quote, 'Oughta get some of that...ass,' sorry Mrs. Rheingold, 'because she'll really go for someone with a badge.'"

Mrs. Rheingold shivered her rump into the cushion.

"Yesterday afternoon, Chief Harman drove to the home of Kansas Karradine with the intention of having sex with Kansas's sixteen-year-old daughter, Marybeth. She invited him in, he drank a glass of water—his fingerprints are on a glass—and they had sex in Marybeth's bedroom. Consensual sex. Her father came home, saw what was happening, went to his bedroom, got his gun, and shot Harman in the back of the neck."

Sparks's eyes went wide. "Then Marybeth shot her own father?"

"You're jumping ahead. Sex with Harman was consensual. Sex with her father was not."

Mrs. Rheingold put a hand to her mouth.

"Years of it," he added. "Marybeth told me her father had been molesting her since she was ten. I think when Kansas shot Harman, something snapped in her head. She somehow got hold of the gun and shot her father in the hallway. In an effort to create confusion, she dragged Harman's body from the bedroom into the hallway near her father's."

Doc Little coughed into his fist. "The chief's theory is entirely plausible. I've known Marybeth a long time— brought her into this world. It saddens me to say this, but Marybeth has always been a troubled child. Had my suspicions about her being molested, but—Anyway, I witnessed Chief Trigger's interrogation of her this morning, and I believe she acted without forethought and truly has no recollection of the entire episode."

"That may be true," Chief Trigger agreed, then added, "or she may be a goddamn good liar."

"Chief," Bucky interrupted, "did you ask her if Kansas cut Will's brake line?"

"I did, and she said he used wire cutters. I released Hector this morning. All charges against him should be dropped."

Bucky wanted to know how Marybeth knew that. He'd find out later. And with Kansas dead, she might even be willing to talk about what happened to her baby.

"What happens next?" Alsop asked.

"If you put Marybeth on trial as a minor, she'll stick to her story and no jury in the state will convict her. Her lawyer will play up the sexual abuse. On top of that, he'll claim she's an orphan. You do what Defiance always does when its good image is on the line—bury the whole damn business. All the murders are solved. Kansas killed Will and Miss Iris, then Harman. Marybeth killed her abusive father. Make a fuss about this and the press is going to pounce like flies on shit. Best to not charge Marybeth, close the case, and forget this mess ever happened."

სთცა

Later that afternoon, Bucky watched a father and son wheel onto the car lot in a snazzy new Lincoln. Mister big-bucks, the father, wanted to buy his son a used car for his birthday and steered him toward a stodgy 1940 black Packard.

"That's a fine automobile," Bucky assured them, then took the kid aside. He was sixteen, Marybeth's age. Even had her same red hair. "No girl," Bucky went on, "wants to be seen in something her father drives. You want chicks, you'll get that cobalt blue '55 Ford Coupe with glass pipes and spinner hubcaps."

Bucky made an extra two hundred smackers on that

one. Know your customer—that was his philosophy.

As he watched the boy drive off, his thoughts turned back to Marybeth. Now would be a good time to question her claim that Kansas cut Will's brake line—and bring up a few other matters.

Bucky strode to his desk and dialed the phone. "Hello, Mrs. Rheingold, this is Bucky. How's Marybeth doing?"

"Under the circumstances, surprisingly well."

"There's some things you should know. I'd like to come over and talk to both of you. Will in a half hour be okay?"

"She's been through a lot, Bucky. But if you think it's important, I suppose it'll be all right."

✌✍✌✍

Mrs. Rheingold lived in a small duplex on East Whipple Street. An older neighborhood with narrow streets, overgrown trees, and cracked sidewalks.

Bucky sank into a wingback chair with upholstery as soft as a flower petal and took in the scent of Vicks Nose Drops. He faced a wall-setting of porcelain ducklings waddling after their mother. Marybeth sat slouched on a sofa wearing a green sweatshirt and stroking a tortoise-shell cat shaped like a feather duster. Mrs. Rheingold occupied a cushioned rocker, a shawl draped across her shoulders, her brown spotted hands curled around the armrests.

A vase of orange poppies sat on the coffee table, along with graham crackers arranged in a circle on a plate. "Marybeth brought the lovely poppies, Bucky," Mrs. Rheingold said. "Help yourself to the graham crackers."

Bucky reached for one. "My gramma used to make—"

"What do you want to talk about?" Marybeth interrupted.

Bucky snapped his hand back and rubbed it down his pant leg. "Oh, yeah, right." He cleared his throat. "Now, as I understand it, you told Chief Trigger that your father cut Will's brake line. I'm just wondering how you know that."

"I know lots o' stuff."

"Did he tell you he did it?"

"Yeah, Papa told me."

She didn't sound very convincing. She had told Chief Trigger that he used wire cutters, but the anonymous note said tinsnips.

"What'd he use to cut them with?"

"Those wire cutter thingies."

Being a girl, she might not have known the difference. He'd move onto something else. He cleared his throat. "What happened to your baby?"

Mrs. Rheingold's head jerked back.

"It was a girl, and she was murdered," Marybeth said calmly.

"Murdered!" Bucky yelped. The cat jumped off Marybeth's lap, and he felt the blood race to his toes. He had always assumed the baby died, but *murdered?* "Who—who murdered her?"

Her lips quivered. "Papa did."

Bucky glanced at Mrs. Rheingold, her mouth open in a tight circle. "Why on earth would he want to murder your baby?" he said to Marybeth.

"He'll burn in Hell for it."

"Okay, let's back up," Bucky said. "Where'd you give birth to the baby?"

"Up in the loft."

Mrs. Rheingold's eyes went wide. "Oh, my!"

Bucky remembered seeing the stairs up to the loft when searching for Kindra's ring. "Were you alone?"

Marybeth nodded. "I was gonna do it by myself, but

couldn't help screaming because it felt like a cow comin' outta me. Papa heard and came up."

"Your papa didn't know you were pregnant?"

"Only VO and Kindra knew."

"You were screaming, then what?"

"Like I said, Papa came up and helped pull it out."

"Then you say he killed it?" Bucky cringed just saying the words.

"Not then. When the baby was born, I told Papa my plan to go to Tulsa with VO and give it up for adoption. He thought that was a good plan."

Mrs. Rheingold's eyes were back to normal. "For heaven's sake, why didn't you?"

"I changed my mind."

"What do you mean?" Bucky said.

"She was so cute and helpless, the next day I told Papa I wanted to keep her."

Bucky sucked air between his teeth. This was all hard to imagine. "Go on."

"Papa got mad and said he couldn't live under a bastard curse. I got scared and wrapped my baby in a blanket and ran to my secret hiding place inside a hollow oak tree up behind the house. I heard Papa comin' after us. The baby started crying, so I held her little mouth so Papa couldn't hear. I was so scared. When she stopped crying, I tried to feed her, you know, with my milk, but she wouldn't take it. Then Papa caught us and took her away. She was a good baby. She didn't even cry." Marybeth pressed her chin to her chest and whimpered.

Mrs. Rheingold leaned forward in her rocker and waved a hankie. Marybeth snatched it and scrubbed her nose.

"When I came back to the house, Papa was diggin' a grave. He said the baby was dead. He killed my baby!"

Mrs. Rheingold asked gently, "Did your papa say he killed your baby?"

"O'course not."

"Do you think, perhaps," Mrs. Rheingold continued, "you accidentally smothered the baby by holding its mouth? We understand, dear."

"No! *He* killed her."

Bucky and Mrs. Rheingold exchanged glances. Bucky felt it was obvious how the baby died. "You saw me watching you at the baby's grave the day your papa caught me, didn't you? That's why you moved the baby."

She blotted tears with the hankie. "Uh-huh. Papa and me."

"Where's the baby now?" Bucky asked, holding his breath.

"Papa took and hid it."

"*Hid it?*" Mrs. Rheingold cried. She fanned herself.

"It's in that car."

The Belvedere! That's why Kansas guarded it like a tiger. His car. Bucky wanted to hear it from Marybeth. "What car?"

"That buried one. Papa put it in the trunk."

CHAPTER 50

In the goddamn *trunk*?" Alsop blurted.

"Believe me," Bucky said, having expected Alsop's shock. "I'm as surprised as you are. Kansas didn't want it found."

"*Jesus keyrist.*"

"Adds up when you think about it. Kansas was protective of that car. He barked my head off when he caught me and Kindra taking pictures. Seemed worried I'd opened the trunk. I don't think he took his eyes off that car once at the courthouse."

Alsop launched from his chair. "The jack! Come with me."

They scurried outside to the back. The sky had turned gray, and a thin layer of last night's snow blanketed the ground.

They entered the repair shop, and Alsop pointed to a jack on the floor near a stack of tires. "Look. That's gotta be the one to the Belvedere."

Confused, Bucky asked, "Why would Kansas take it out? Babies are no bigger than a breadbox."

"Before the chief and his men arrived to search the car for the bomb, Kansas had already unwrapped it and emptied the glove box and trunk. He forgot to put the jack back with the baby." He shook his head. "It's a shame, but the council will never allow the baby to be exhumed. The story would reflect poorly on the town. They'll let future generations figure it out."

Bucky's muscles tightened. "No disrespect, Cal, but I've got to say, that baby needs a proper burial now, not in fifty years. Chief Trigger and everyone else seems to worry about the town's precious image, but what's right's right."

Alsop raised his hands. "Point made. Let's go back in the office."

Back inside, and feeling less angry, Bucky said, "I've been thinking. As disgusting as it is that Kansas would hide the baby inside a car trunk, I'm not convinced he cut Will's brake line."

"You know something I don't?" Alsop lit a cigar.

"Only that there's no hard evidence that he did."

"Kansas made no secret about wanting Will's job. That's motive. Plus, there's Marybeth's testimony."

"Testimony that he used wire cutters when the anonymous note said tinsnips. And another thing, that yellow rag I found near the crime scene, hell, everyone knows Kansas wipes his hands with one a million times a day. He would've been stupid to leave it there."

Alsop nodded and puffed his cigar.

"And as for suspects, who's to say the killer was even at the party?"

Alsop twirled his cigar ash into his piston-shaped ashtray. "Maybe you should talk to Trigger."

Bucky almost laughed. "Are you kidding? Trigger's mind's already made up. Besides, I figured out how to prove if Kansas did it or not."

"Oh, and how's that?"

"By getting my hands on that foot impression."

❧❧❧

While at his desk, waiting for an open phone line, Bucky thought about how much he liked being an investigator. Taking crime photos. Asking questions. Like the ones he posed to Marybeth that led to his finding out what happened to her baby. Although he hadn't done so hot, trying to find Kindra's ring. But like Marybeth said, she probably lost it hitchhiking. The important thing now was to prove whether or not Kansas sabotaged Will's car. Because, if he didn't, a murderer was still out there.

A line cleared, and Bucky dialed.

"Sergeant Grady, Bucky Ontario here from Defiance. About that foot impression Chief Parker left with you—"

"What's with you blockheads?" Grady sounded like someone was stepping on his throat. "I heard Trigger's back on payroll. His damn dogs killed Parker, for Christ's sake! Never mind. You want that impression or not?"

"That's why I'm calling. Appreciate it if you'd leave it at your front desk and we'll have someone come by."

"What'd you say your name was?"

"Ontario. Hold on." Bucky didn't want to answer more questions. He held the phone at arm's length. "What? A murder? Be right there." Into the phone he said, "I'll send someone. Thanks, Sarge."

❧❧❧

At four o'clock, Bucky topped off his engine with oil, hopped in his roadster, and headed east for Tulsa. He hoped Sergeant Grady had left the foot impression at the front desk. The roads had been snowplowed, making it clear sailing all the way. The low afternoon sun shafted through dark clouds. More snowfall would hit soon.

Ninety minutes later, he pulled up to a stoplight in

front of the police station at 401 East Fourth Street. A kid about twelve launched from the curb and shuffled between lanes of cars, waving newspapers and shouting headlines. Bucky shook his head at him as he scuffled past, then parked around the corner, and dashed inside the station. A desk sergeant sat in a cushy black chair, working on a newspaper crossword puzzle. He had a mouth shaped like the top half of a circle and thumb-sized shadows under his eyes. Bucky put the man at about retirement age. Hopefully, he wouldn't be interested in asking too many questions.

Bucky lowered his chin and used his best baritone voice. "I'm Ontario from Defiance. Here to pick up a package."

The old sergeant glanced up. "What package?"

"Sergeant…" Bucky almost forgot the name. "Sergeant Grady left one here."

The sergeant removed his silver-rimmed glasses and glanced around. Not finding the package, he set the paper down and checked under his desk. "Don't see anything. What is it?"

Bucky swiped sweat from his brow. "A plaster foot impression. It's supposed to be here at the front desk."

The sergeant spread his hands. "Well, it's not. And Grady's not here, so you're out of luck." He picked up his paper and shifted awkwardly in his chair, as if hemorrhoids were giving him trouble.

Drips of sweat rolled onto Bucky's ear. "But the Defiance police need it tonight."

"Sorry about that," the sergeant said, not looking sorry. He put his glasses back on.

"Please call someone," Bucky begged, forgetting his baritone and swiping at his ear. "It's really important."

The sergeant blew air through his lips and made a big production of dropping the newspaper by first hovering it over his desk a few seconds. He ran his finger down a list of extensions taped to the desk, picked up the phone and punched in numbers. "Hey, anyone still in the lab?" He peered over his glasses at Bucky. "They're getting someone." Into the phone he said, "Frank, you know about some plaster…" He looked at Bucky again. "What'd you say it was?"

"A foot impression. And it's *real* important."

"Oh, yeah. A foot impression belonging to Defiance PD. I'll hold." He eyed Bucky. "He's checking. Who'd you say you were?"

"I'm—"

The sergeant raised his palm. "What, you've got it? Bring it on down. Someone's here for it."

∽∾∽

The temperature had dropped below freezing, making 412 slick with ice. Bucky had already seen two cars in the ditch. He crept along, thinking about how he needed to do wash at the Laundromat.

He looked at the shoebox on the seat and smiled. The foot impression would prove once and for all whether or not Kansas had killed Miss Iris and Will. There at his house, Gustafson had said he'd bet a dollar to a doughnut that he had. Wonder if the old guy was holding something back. He seemed different at home than he had at work. Maybe it just appeared that way because he was in a bathrobe and slippers. Bucky reeled their conversation back in his mind like a movie in reverse, mentally examining each frame.

Snowflakes fell on the windshield, wispy ones. A sign ahead said Glencoe, pop. 358. Bucky's stomach grumbled. He'd pull off and find a place to eat. He stopped at a light. When it changed, someone honked at him. He turned into the intersection giving too much gas and fish-tailed on an icy patch. The jerk honked again, or maybe another jerk, and he honked back. Something he'd picked up from Kindra.

An adobe building emerged in the snow. Christmas lights hung from two windows that were probably kept up all year. A splintery wood sign stood out front with carved letters that looked old enough to predate state-hood. The sign read *Rusty's Hacienda, Fine Mexican Food*.

He pulled into the lot between the diner and a small nondescript motel. His headlights swept across the front of a cream-colored Duesenberg pulling out from the mo-tel. Bucky's head lurched forward. *My God!* Doc Little was behind the wheel, and beside him sat Kindra, shaking snow from her hair. Bucky shuddered, as if a spider had crawled up the back of his neck. They were in the motel together.

His mind spinning, he slogged inside the diner and collapsed on a stool at the counter. A blackboard on the wall said *Today's specials. #1 Menudo Soup 40 cents. #2 Combination Homemade Tamales, Chile Rellenos, and Salsa. $1.40.*

A big-hipped waitress wearing a sombrero came by. Her skin looked freshly coated with a fine dark polish. Bucky ordered the combination.

He finished up and dropped a bill and some loose change on the counter. He had barely tasted the meal, wondering why Kindra would shack up with an old gee-zer like Doc Little. And Bucky had thought her too young for Harman and Peter!

"How was the special?" the waitress asked.

"Food's great. Say, I thought I saw someone I know drive off. An old, white-whiskered guy."

"You must mean Doc Little." She laughed nervously. "He got angry with me."

"Angry?"

"I served him the wrong special. He'd ordered the combination, but I gave him the menudo soup."

"He come in often?"

"Every Wednesday. Checks out of the motel and eats before—"

A tray full of food crashed behind her and splattered all over the place. She swiveled her big hips around to the busboy behind her. "Manuel! Watch where you're going!"

Bucky had heard all he could stomach. He needed to get out of there.

He drove off, wipers whacking against the now heavy snow that came down as if thrown from the sky. Ahead, the eyes of a cat flashed green in the headlights. For what possible reason would an eighteen-year-old girl want to be with a dinosaur like Doc Little? Money? Excitement? Whatever the reason, it was enough to make Bucky puke. He would call Kindra the minute he got home and let her have it. But after thinking some more, he wondered if maybe Doc Little was coercing her. Bucky would talk to her and find out. But first—he placed his hand on the shoebox beside him—he would photograph the impression and then find out once and for all if Kansas was a murderer.

ᶜ⌒ᵉ⌒ᵓ

At his desk the next morning, Bucky's thoughts jumped around like grasshoppers. Boy, would he be screwed if Kansas was already buried.

He dialed, and a woman answered. "Fromm Mortuary."

"I was wondering if you've buried Kansas Karradine yet? He got shot the other day in the heart." Hopefully he had on the same shoes he wore at the party. If not, Bucky would check his house later.

Papers shuffled. "That with a C or a K? Oh, you mean Keifer Karradine. He's scheduled to be buried this morning. Both he and the police chief. Hell of a thing." She made a little breathy sound, like she had pursed her lips.

Bucky's heart stopped. So did his lungs. Would he have to dig up another grave? This time with a casket in it? He glanced at his watch. "It's only eleven o'clock. Maybe they're not buried yet."

"No telling," she said. "Stopped snowing, but the ground's hard, making for slow digging. They're both going to the same place. Cemetery up on Boot Hill."

"Boot Hill?" Bucky had never heard of it. He knew of only two graveyards, neither of them called Boot Hill. He'd been to Green Hill, the Negro cemetery where he took the picture of a body sliding from a casket into a grave.

She gave a high-pitched laugh. "That's a joke around here. You know, we've got Green Hill. Boot Hill—Gunsmoke? Forget it. The real name's Quiet Oaks over on—"

"Thanks." Bucky slammed the phone down. Grieving relatives must love her humor. Quiet Oaks was on the way to VO's house. He put on his coat and went to Sam reading a Popular Mechanics magazine. "Cover me, will you? I'm taking an early lunch."

Sam turned a page and double clicked his tongue. "Gotcha covered."

഑ഌഌ

The sky was charcoal ash, the color of tombstone, and

the temperature dropped fast. Bucky reached the graveyard. A sign read:

Quiet Oaks Cemetery
Where Peace is Eternal

The driveway curved and ended in a gravel parking
lot. A walkway bordered with snow-covered flowers led
to the entrance. The graveyard lay behind the building.
He drove through an open gate, eyes peeled for men with
shovels. At a rise, he stopped. There! His heart sparked
with hope.

Two Negros stood behind an old pickup, heads bob-
bing, arms swinging. Strange that there were no mourners. Awfully cold. They must've all gone home after the
services. Bucky glanced at the shoebox on his seat and
pulled alongside the pickup. It contained one casket. He
hoped Kansas lay in *that* one and not the one getting
shoveled over with dirt.

He crawled out of his car, knees wobbly. "Which one
did you bury?"

The tubby one shrugged while the guy with a kerchief
covering his neck put down his shovel and pulled a paper
from his pocket. "Says C386."

Bucky studied the paper. Beside the number, it said
Raymond Harman. Bucky let out a breath of white steam.
Kansas was in the other casket. He grabbed the shoebox
from his car, climbed onto the pickup, and opened the
casket.

"Jesus Christ!" He dropped the lid with a bang and
jerked back, almost tumbling off the pickup. Kansas was
staring at him with one eye, and a circle of blood covered
his heart. Man, you'd think Fromm would've had the decency to close the man's eyes and give him a clean shirt.

Tubby threw down his shovel and marched over to Bucky. "Whadaya think you're doin'?"

Bucky pointed to the casket. "This man is a murder suspect. And I'm here to prove his innocence or guilt. Search warrant's in my car," he said, hoping the lie didn't show on his face. "Now if you boys could give me a hand and hold up this lid for a minute, you'll witness the crime of the century solved before your very eyes." The two men looked at each other. "Don't just stand there shivering," Bucky snarled. "Hop to it."

Bucky had worked with colored folk all his life—shrimping, doing chores—and knew if he acted like a boss, these men would follow reasonable instructions.

The two men jumped aboard and opened the casket while Bucky took the plaster impression from the shoebox and held it up. "This toe impression came from the right shoe of a murderer. Now if one of you fellas could separate the feet, we'll just see…" He bent down and held the impression against Kansas's right shoe. "Well, boys," he said as the two men bent in close, "what do you think?"

"Wouldn't fit," Tubby said.

"That's right," the other one said. "This man's shoe is way too wide." He stared at Bucky, eyes bursting to know. "That mean he didn't do it?"

Bucky straightened tall, jutted his finger skyward, and declared, "This man is innocent!" He put the impression back in the shoebox and hopped from the truck bed. "Bury him."

❦

Bucky shook with excitement. Clearing Kansas of cutting Will's brake line left him with a pretty good idea of who the real killer was. But to be sure, he had one more thing to check out.

He marched into the Holiday Inn and slapped down on the counter a picture of Kindra posing on the Belvedere. "Have you ever seen this person?" The clerk had little cowboy boots for earrings. She put on pink-rimmed glasses, which hung around her neck by a shoelace. She shook her head and her cowboy boots took a twirl. "Should I have?"

"She may have come in a day or two before the fifty-year celebration. She'd have asked for someone's room number."

The woman paged through a calendar on the desk and scrunched up her face.

"What's the matter?" Bucky asked.

"Nothing. I was adjusting my glasses. I worked nights that week. Henry had the day shift. I'll get him."

Something burrowed in the pit of Bucky's stomach. If he was right, he couldn't just let a killer walk free.

Henry appeared at the counter. Bucky had seen him before when he picked up Peter to sell him the Fury. He was one of those guys who combed his hair over to cover baldness. Bucky would rather show his scalp than try to cover it with a few scraggly cat whiskers.

"You were asking about someone?"

Bucky tapped Kindra's picture. "Her. Look familiar?"

"You a cop?"

"Special investigator. Maybe she asked for a room number."

"Like maybe that reporter's? The one you picked up here in that jazzy car."

"Yeah, like maybe him."

"The guy was pretty proud of himself. Danced in here whistling. Said he had met with the mayor on Friday and was here on secret assignment."

Bucky thought Peter had talked to the mayor on the phone. Now it seemed Peter came to town the day Will's brake line was cut, then left and returned Sunday, when he ran out of gas.

"The secret assignment," Bucky said, "was our anniversary celebration. Back to my question." He tapped the photo. "Did she ask for the reporter's room number?"

"Yep, room 210, as I recall."

The beast burrowing in Bucky's stomach clawed into daylight. Now he knew. Kindra wrote the anonymous note that said *tinsnips* and slid it under Peter's door. She knew who the killer was. And now, so did Bucky.

CHAPTER 51

Kindra bounced into Bucky's room, cheeks pink from the cold, eyes blazing with anticipation. He got her there under the pretext of her helping him print pictures.

"Okay." She tossed her things onto a chair. "Roll the presses."

"That's a newspaper term. Want a Nehi or anything? I'd like to talk about something first."

Her light-green eyes turned a deeper, agitated green. "Talk about what?"

Bucky sat down at the table, unhappy that he sounded so serious. "Come here and have a seat."

She stood stiffly. "What's this about?"

Bucky wished she'd sit down. "Let's call it your extra curricular activities."

A shadow crossed her face. "Excuse me?"

"We'll start with why you were at the Holiday Inn the day you saw Willow's gun through her window."

She snatched a pencil off the table and wagged it between two fingers. "I told you, I was picking up Abby."

"Uh-huh. Problem is, I don't believe you. You slipped a note under Peter Thomas's door."

Her mouth dropped. "You're crazy." She tossed the

pencil on the table, grabbed her things, and shot for the door.

Bucky jumped up and blocked her. "Wait a minute." He held her shoulders. "I know everything. Well, almost everything."

She wriggled from his grasp. "You don't know anything."

"Maybe I don't. Please sit down, and I'll tell you what I know."

She stared hard at him, her glance sharp as knives. Then she sat with her arms crossed tightly, the way women do when they're aching to hit you with a rolling pin. "I want to tell you right now," she said, "I don't appreciate you getting me over here under false pretenses."

Bucky slid into a chair. "I understand. I've seen proof that clears Kansas of cutting Will's brake line. Kansas had an especially thick shoe, but so does the real killer, who also happens to have tinsnips. The ones belonging to your grandfather."

"You're funny." Kindra picked up the pencil again. "Who gave you that nutty idea?"

She wasn't giving in, but neither was she racing for the door.

"You did when we were hanging clothes, though I didn't realize it then. I told you the person wore a special shoe, remember? I said otherwise he'd walk lopsided. You said maybe both shoes were special."

She flicked the pencil again. "That didn't mean anything."

"But it did, and you said it without thinking. Just like I handed Kansas the button without thinking. Five minutes before you said that, I was talking to your grandfather in the living room, and noticed how different he appeared in a robe and slippers. Driving home from Tulsa with the foot impression, I realized your grandfather didn't just look tinier in slippers, he *was* tinier because he wasn't wearing his Elevator Shoes."

"Nonsense. Everyone looks tinier in slippers. Even so, what in the world possessed you to think my grandfather would want to kill Will?"

"He didn't."

Her head jerked back. "Then what are you talking about?"

"He meant to kill Kansas. He didn't know Kansas had sold his Desoto to Will. Miss Iris told me at Will's party that he had bought the car that same day. I even saw the for sale sign on the car's backseat. Your grandfather ended up killing two innocent people. The next day, you and everybody else in town heard there'd been an accident. That afternoon, doing your Saturday wash, you smelled brake fluid on your grandfather's shirt or overalls."

Kindra glared at him, her face hard.

"You probably didn't think anything of it until the next day when the paper said Will and Miss Iris died because their car's brake line was cut. You remembered your grandfather's shirt and overalls, and maybe thought back and recalled him stepping out for a while Friday night. You searched around and found the tinsnips with brake fluid on them. Maybe they were still in his overalls."

"You think you're so smart," she snarled.

"Not smart enough to know why your grandfather wanted to kill Kansas. But I know he planned it well. He threw his oily work rag in the bushes, expecting it to be found. Police would think it belonged to a mechanic. It's ironic that Kansas was blamed for a death intended to be his own, and crazier still that it was Kansas's daughter who, according to Chief Trigger's theory, gave him the old coup de grace." Bucky would now bring up his own coup de grace. "And why on earth would you shack up with Doc Little?"

Her chair screeched back, and she jumped to her feet. "What?"

"Don't bother denying it. I saw you two driving away from a motel in Glencoe."

"How *could* you?" She clenched her fists. "You're so full of it. I've known Doctor Little since I was born."

"I suppose you're going to say you weren't there."

"I was there, Mister Know-it-all, but not shacking up." She sat back down, keeping her chair a distance from the table.

"Okay then, why were you there?"

"Doctor Little rents a motel room—with his own money—for two hours every Wednesday to help indigent patients. That means poor, in case you didn't know." She pulled a hankie from her pocket and blew her nose, a soft girly blow. "And since I'm going to be a nurse, he lets me come and help."

"Oh…" Heat rose to Bucky's cheeks. He felt embarrassed, but relieved. "Guess I'm wrong on that one."

"Don't say you're sorry or anything."

"I am sorry."

"Forget it now."

Bucky drummed his fingers on the table. "How come you never said anything about helping him before?"

"That was the first time, but I'm going to help lots more times."

"Okay, but why'd you give Peter the note?"

"Contrary to your belief, I didn't slip it under his door. I saw him in person and told him what happened. He promised not to say or print anything. Then I typed the note on his typewriter."

Bucky thought a reporter's job wasn't to keep secrets, but to report news. Especially murders. "How come you told him, and not me?" Bucky felt hurt that she hadn't talked to him first.

She squeezed her eyes closed, as if holding back tears. "He was older. More experienced. Someone I could confide in." She opened her eyes and drew in a deep breath. "We made an agreement that if Grandfather was caught, I would give him an exclusive scoop."

"In exchange for…"

"I had him promise that he'd paint grandfather in a positive light. Then maybe the jury would go easy on him."

Oh, sure. Maybe even acquit him. "Was the note his idea?"

She shook her head. "It was mine. I had to do something, so I thought giving the police an anonymous clue would be a good idea. You know, put them on the right track without them knowing it was me."

That was what Chief Parker had thought. "Why not tell them straight out?"

"Oh, I couldn't do that."

"How come?"

"Grandfather would know it was me," she said, working her hands in her lap.

"So? What's wrong with that?"

She shrugged. "It just didn't feel right, that's all." She nodded toward the fridge. "I'll take that Nehi, if you don't mind. You're right about the brake fluid. It was on Grandfather's overalls. It probably squirted on him. I found the tinsnips in the toolshed."

Bucky got up and opened the soft drink, handed it to her, and sat back down. "Well, we have to report him. Dropping anonymous clues isn't going to cut it."

"Oh, no. Doctor Little insisted I forget the whole thing."

"What! Doc Little? How'd he get into the picture?"

"We had dinner at that Mexican restaurant by the motel. You know, the one where we were *shacking up*."

"And you told him?" Bucky got up and padded to the sink.

"He knew something was wrong and kept asking. So, I told him. He was really mad that I'd told Peter, so mad he yelled at the waitress for practically nothing. He told me to forget everything."

"But why?" Bucky poured a glass of water and downed it.

"Because I didn't have real proof, and if I was wrong, it would destroy Grandfather, and because he's on the council, hurt the town. After all, we're hoping to host the next County Fair."

Hurt the town. That again! "How do you feel? I mean, isn't it creepy that your grandfather's a killer?"

She closed her eyes. "I don't think about it."

"Doc Little's wrong, you know. There is proof." He shook a finger at her. "Real proof, and I've got it. Your grandfather murdered people."

"Grandfather didn't mean to kill those people. You said so yourself. We should forget it ever happened."

"To me, they were more than just *those people*. But besides, why did he want to kill Kansas?"

She shook her head.

"Anyway, you wanted your grandfather to get caught, remember? That's why you wrote the note."

Like a drop of honey, a tear exuded from the corner of her eye. "I shouldn't have done it. Besides, Doctor Little told me if I made trouble, I'd never get into nursing school. They only accept girls from good families. He said if I promised to forget the whole thing, he'd continue to let me help him with patients over in Glencoe, and I'd be guaranteed to get into a first-rate nursing school."

"Sweet Jesus, Kindra, you might buy his bullshit, but I

don't. He's trying to protect his friend, and if you're not going to report him, I will."

"Oh, sure, go ahead and mess up everything for the town. Not to mention my life. Thanks a lot, *buster!*" She got up and grabbed her purse and coat. "And you wanted to get into public service and help people. Ha! You don't care about anybody but yourself. Good*bye*."

CHAPTER 52

Bucky thought about what Kindra had said. Was she right to believe there was a greater good than turning in a killer? Daddy said corporations and crooked politicians had destroyed the lives of common fishermen. The citizens of Defiance were those same kind of folks. Bucky came to Defiance to one day become mayor and do good for the town and its people. Would turning in Gustafson mess up those goals?

He scooped up his dirty clothes to take to the Laundromat, and, while stripping the bed sheets, knocked over a picture of his kid sister. She had on a Robin Hood Halloween costume. Smiling, he dusted the picture with his sleeve and put it back.

By the time he returned from the Laundromat, he knew what he'd do. Alsop said he had integrity, and that he himself admired it. But he also said that in politics you've got to make judgments. *Nourishment for one fella may poison another.* The mayor's television speech was the same garbage, and so was Doc Little's message to Kindra.

Bucky had thought, after talking to Alsop, that if he were in office, he'd do things differently. But maybe he didn't have to wait until then. He opened his Carnegie book. *To win friends and influence people, one must be true to oneself.* He closed the book. Tomorrow he'd tell Chief Trigger everything.

෧෨෧෨

Thud, thud, thud! "Police! Open up!"

Bucky's eyes flung open. The clock hands pointed to one twenty, and someone was pounding on his door with fists, not knuckles.

A man's voice boomed, "Ontario! Open the door!"

"Hold on." Bucky's voice felt gritty with sleep. He rolled out of bed and stumbled to the front door. He opened it a notch, and it bashed against his forehead. "What the fuck!"

Mr. Johnston, Doc Little, and Chief Trigger barged past him.

"You're in a heap of trouble, asshole," Chief Trigger said.

Johnston began turning on lights.

Bucky's heart thudded against his breastbone. "What trouble?"

Chief Trigger yanked up a chair. "Put your ass down."

Bucky heard Johnston or Doc Little opening kitchen cabinets.

"You think you can waltz into the Tulsa police station, impersonate a police officer, and walk out with whatever the fuck you want?"

"You're crazy, I didn't impersonate anyone."

The chief grabbed a fistful of Bucky's T-shirt and raised him off the chair. "Get lippy, and I'll knock you through the goddamn wall."

Bucky decided right then that Chief Trigger was not the man to confide in about Gustafson.

Johnston placed a hand on the chief's shoulder, and

the chief backed up. "Bucky," Johnston said, "you're a good man. I'd hate to see you find more trouble than you're already in." He pulled a chair around, sat, and straightened out a few wrinkles in Bucky's shirt. "Let's do this the easy way. Hand over the item you took from the Tulsa Police, and I think I can persuade Chief Trigger not to arrest you."

Dammit! The minute Kindra left, she must've scurried over to Doc Little's and blabbed her head off. He spread his hands. "I don't have it."

"Come on, now," Johnston said with a smile, "we're all friends and want to do the right thing."

These bastards want to protect their buddy Gustafson and let dead Kansas take the fall. Bucky said, "Kindra convinced me not to mess with a case that's officially closed, so last night, I threw it over Half Chance Bridge."

"You lyin' son of a bitch!" Chief Trigger stepped forward and swung a roundhouse punch, knocking Bucky to the floor. "You'll be pricing crutches pretty quick."

Johnston knelt beside him. "You don't want to do this. You have a real future here, a chance to become a respected member of the community."

Doc Little ran his hand down Bucky's photographic enlarger. "Kindra said you see yourself as a businessman, someday a councilman, even mayor."

His head throbbing, Bucky glared at him, too angry to consider his future. "Kindra told me you'd help her get into a good nursing college, but if she told about her grandfather being a murderer, no school would have her." Bucky turned to Johnston. "Is that what it takes to be a respected member of this community, dishonesty and manipulation?"

"Now be nice," Johnston said. "Tell us where it is. Believe me, it's the best thing."

Bucky got to his feet and spread his hands. "Honest,

it's gone." He heard a crash and turned. His enlarger lay in pieces on the floor. "Hey, that was expensive!"

"You've had your chance, Bucky," Johnston said and nodded to Chief Trigger.

A blurred fist crossed Bucky's vision, and he slammed against a wall before the pain set in.

Trigger stomped over to Bucky's bed and flung it upside down. He grabbed the picture of Bucky's kid sister from the nightstand and drew back his arm.

"Okay! It's in my car—assholes."

ʚ৩ʚ৩

The morning was gray and cold when Bucky dragged himself to work. He felt hollow as a dug-out canoe. A throbbing jaw, itchy left eye, and broken bed made for a crummy night's sleep. He wanted to tell Alsop about his wonderful evening, but he wasn't in. Wanted to tell him what he thought of the people governing this town. Pretty damn disgusting.

The food truck had just left when Sam dropped by Bucky's desk, scooted up a chair, and placed a cup of something on the desk. He looked at Bucky's black eye and nodded. "Must've been a high doorknob."

Bucky didn't want to explain. "Found myself in the middle of a bar fight while taking pictures." He peered into Sam's cup. "What's that, soup?"

Sam crinkled his face. "When have you seen me eat soup? It's chili."

Bucky shot a glance toward Alsop's empty office. "Where's the boss?"

"Attending a special city council session."

The words felt like something driven against Bucky's chest. Were they talking about him? "They're probably discussing their next pay raise. You know how big shots are. Say, what's that joke you wanted to tell me about a guy robbing a bank?"

Sam grinned. "A guy goes into a bank and says, 'Give me all your money, this is a screw up.' The teller says, 'Don't you mean stick up?' 'No, screw up. I forgot my gun.'"

Alsop entered his office and closed the door.

"That's a good one, Sam. I gotta go."

Bucky hurried over and opened Alsop's door a crack. "Can we talk?"

Alsop waved him in. "The council wants me to fire you. Have a seat."

Bucky's knees buckled and he collapsed into a chair. "You're kidding?"

"Fuck the bastards. Don't worry about it."

"You mean—you mean I'm not fired?"

"Hell no, I've got a business to run." He pointed to the showroom. "Now get out there and sell cars."

"Wait a minute, Cal. Jesus, can we talk about this?"

"Look, no one tells me what to do. I've got Jo-Dee, and I've got my business. If it takes kowtowing to the old guard of this town to become mayor someday, then they can shove it." With a wry smile, he added, "Of course, I'm only thirty-three. Those old farts won't be around forever."

∽∾

The sun had fought its way through the clouds all afternoon, and Bucky was making good time getting to Tulsa. Feeling had returned to his jaw. Mostly painful. He wondered if every council member wanted Alsop to fire him, or just some.

The highway swept him right into town about two fifteen. He parked in front of the Fourth Street police station and approached the same desk sergeant he'd met when he picked up the foot impression.

"My name's Bucky Ontar—"

"What do you want now?" he grumbled.

"I need to see Sergeant Grady." Since Grady had expressed such dislike for Chief Trigger, Bucky figured he might be just the kind of person to report Gustafson to. Bucky would've talked to Willow, but she had said she was going down to Oklahoma City.

The sergeant reached for his phone. A minute later Bucky mounted the stairs to room 202.

He opened the door. Several cops sat at desks. The officer with jet-black hair and a snappy mustache that curled up like bird wings glanced up from his typing and motioned him over with a head jerk. The man wore a blue uniform that fit him the way a stall fits a horse. He had a weightlifter's burly physique, a hard, no nonsense face, and fast fingers. "I'm Grady," he said. "Have a seat. Be with you in a minute."

Bucky sat listening to the rat-a-tat-tat of Grady's typewriter, to the bell, to the shift. Line after line. Finally, the ratcheting sound of paper being yanked from the typewriter. Grady dropped the paper in the out box and leaned back in his chair. "Now, what can I do for you?"

For the next twenty minutes, Grady twirled his mustache and listened, while Bucky told him his belief about Gustafson cutting Will's brake line and all the subsequent events. He admitted not knowing Gustafson's motive, but believed the impression would match his shoe.

When Bucky finished, Grady got to his feet. "I'll take care of it," he said, like a magician about to wave a magic wand.

Thrilled at Grady's willing assistance, Bucky stammered, "Wa—what's going to happen?"

"The Garfield County Sheriff will get in touch with you. Go home and wait."

Bucky liked that idea. A county sheriff would probably have more authority than just a policeman. He could barely believe this fantastic turn of events. *Finally*, he would talk to someone trustworthy, a cop who would do the right thing and hopefully put Gustafson away.

CHAPTER 53

Around five o'clock that same day, a knock came at the door. Not as hard as last night's, but determined. "Who is it?"

"Sheriff Sweeney, Garfield County."

Bucky sighed with relief and opened the door.

"Bucky Ontario?"

Sheriff Sweeney hadn't mentioned the three deputies in green uniforms accompanying him. They all poured in, except the beefy one with the double chin who stayed out in the thirty-degree fresh air.

The sheriff placed his hat on the kitchen counter. The hat had left a crease along his hairline just above his ears. "May we sit?"

Bucky shuffled around the three men and pulled up chairs. The last time he stood crowded among policemen, he was looking down their flaming-red gun barrels, with bullets shooting out and whizzing by him.

The sheriff and the long-necked deputy sat; the other deputy, heavy-shouldered, stood at the door, parade rest, jaw fixed.

The sheriff relaxed his hands on the table. "Our Tulsa friends say you've got quite a story. I'd like to hear it."

The deputy beside him took out a notebook and ballpoint pen from his coat pocket and clicked the pen with his thumb.

Bucky figured Sergeant Grady had already told the sheriff everything, but he needed to hear it firsthand. When Bucky finished, Sweeney nodded to the deputy at the door, who left. The nod was probably a signal to go arrest Gustafson. Pretty exciting.

The sheriff asked for a glass of water, and Bucky poured three. The sheriff took a sip and ran the back of his hand across his mouth. He bounced his fingertips together, then flattened his palms against each other and slowly rubbed them up and down. "Now, Mr. Ontario, you say this Mr…" He glanced at his deputy, who checked his notes.

"Gustafson."

"Right. You say Mr. Gustafson was not at the party?"

"That's right. And he didn't know Kansas had sold his car to Will, that's why—"

"Right, you said he meant to kill Kansas, but screwed up."

"Well—" Bucky squirmed in his chair, "he just didn't—"

"But no one actually saw Gustafson cut the brake line. And, of all those people at the party, no one saw him outside, loitering around the car, anything like that?"

A small rock formed in Bucky's chest. "I guess not."

"You say someone wrote an anonymous note that said tinsnips, but you don't know who that person was or what the word really meant."

Bucky wanted to protect Kindra and not say her name. The rock was growing.

"And you don't know what motive Gustafson might've had?"

"No, but if you compare Gustafson's shoe to the foot impression, that'll prove it."

"Ah, yes, the foot impression Chief Trigger supposedly took from you."

"That's right, and I have—"

The door opened. The deputy who'd left stuck his head in and nodded. The sheriff nodded back.

In strode Chief Trigger.

The rock expanded against Bucky's lungs. He couldn't breathe.

The sheriff stood and stretched out a hand. "Thanks for coming, Cosmos. Have a seat and we'll straighten this thing out."

"No problem, Phil." They shook hands.

"I'll get right to the meat of things," the sheriff said. "Mr. Ontario here claims you and two others came in here last night and ran off with a plaster foot impression. He says the impression proved that some person named Gustafson committed a double murder by cutting some fella's brake line."

Trigger shook his head. "This guy, they call him Bucky, he—"

"Because that's my name."

The sheriff shot Bucky a stern look.

"Bucky here's been a troublemaker ever since I've known him," Trigger went on. "Been in and out of jail I don't know how many times."

"What?"

The sheriff turned to Bucky. "Keep your mouth shut unless I ask you a question."

Trigger put his forearms on the table and pulled one of his fingers until the knuckle cracked. "Facts are clear that the perpetrator in this murder left a unique shoe print, which Chief Parker believed belonged to Kansas Karradine, because he had a clubfoot or some damn thing and wore a special shoe. Nobody here knew Chief Parker had sent the impression to Tulsa for analysis. When I came onto the case, I investigated and determined with certainty that Kansas was indeed the perpetrator. Bucky here somehow found out about the impression, went to Tulsa, impersonated a Defiance peace officer, and took the damn thing as a souvenir."

"Not a souvenir, but as proof that Gustafson is a murderer."

"What did Sheriff Sweeney tell you, shitbrain? Keep your lip buttoned," Trigger snarled. "Last night was the first I'd heard of the impression, and that this guy—" he jabbed a finger at Bucky. "—had taken it. Being duty-bound to check new evidence, I confiscated it."

Sweeney rubbed an elbow. "Then what?"

"Well, I went to Gustafson's house and compared his shoes to the impression. None matched. His were several sizes too small."

"You have that evidence?" Sweeney asked.

"Yeah, sure. In my car."

"Good. I'd like to see this comparison."

Trigger turned his head and coughed. "There's a problem, Phil. I have the shoes, but not the impression. After I finished my analysis at Gustafson's, I instructed my officer to take the impression to the station and log it in, along with the shoes that I'd planned to return later. He placed the plaster impression on the roof of the squad car to unlock the door and the goddamn thing slid off and smashed to pieces."

Bucky raised his hand.

"What?" the sheriff snapped.

"I'd like to suggest that Chief Trigger bring in Gustafson's shoes, so you can see his thick soles."

Sweeney thought a moment. "Good idea."

Trigger hesitated then tossed his keys to the deputy at the door. "In the trunk."

The deputy brought the shoes in and placed them on the table with a thud.

"Jesus Christ," Sweeney said. "Soles must be four or five inches thick. What is this guy, a midget?"

Bucky took a deep breath. "Chief Trigger, you're an expert on these things. Can you explain how one goes about comparing a shoe to an impression?"

"It's simple. You look at tread marks and measure height and width."

"I'm not sure I understand." Bucky fetched a ruler from the counter. "Can you show us?"

Trigger placed the shoe on the ruler. "See, measures four and three-eighths inches wide."

"What did the impression measure?" Sweeney asked.

"Much wider," Trigger said. "Here, I've got it in my notes." He pulled a notebook from his pocket and showed Sweeney his figures. "Five and a half inches. A lot wider."

Bucky stretched around and read the notes. "It says the sole height is three inches. What's Gustafson's?"

Sweeney measured. "Four and a half. Big difference."

"There you have it, Phil." Trigger closed his notebook, with a satisfied smirk. "Let's go home."

"Chief Trigger," Bucky said, "you mentioned comparing tread."

Trigger got to his feet. "Different as night and day," he said.

"Sheriff, there's one more thing." Bucky went to his desk and brought back a folder. "I took these photos of the impression. As you can see, each includes a ruler. And look." He held Gustafson's shoe upside down and put his ruler on it. "Four and three-eighths inches wide, just like the picture. And here, the shoe's tread also matches."

The sheriff sighed and nodded to the policeman at the

door who whipped out his handcuffs and stepped forward.

Trigger's head swiveled back and forth, eyes flashing. "Now, now, wait a minute, Phil. Let's talk about this."

"Hands behind your back, Trigger."

CHAPTER 54

Bucky got out of bed around nine, hoping yesterday's big news made it into the morning newspaper. He may have even been whistling as he shaved on this very pleasant morning—which instantly went to hell.

On page four he read: *Having concluded his investigation of the Will and Iris Chambers killings, Chief Trigger is stepping down as temporary chief. The city council will be seeking a permanent replacement.*

That was it? Chief Trigger was stepping down? Holy Jesus! Pravda had more principles than this *Prairie Duster* rag. And the town put up with it! They should change the plaque next to the Belvedere. *Town of monkeys: see no evil, hear no evil, speak no evil.*

He threw the newspaper onto the floor and paced. Trying to predict the future, he threw himself onto the couch. If a jury found Gustafson innocent, no one would ever know why he wanted Kansas dead. Well, nothing Bucky could do about that. Nothing he could do about anything. Marybeth's baby had been entombed, Kindra's ring might just as well have been, and—oh, yeah.

He reached into his pocket, pulled out the button, and looked at it. Some clue that turned out to be. He tossed it onto a table. Getting up, he went to the window and chewed a hangnail. Kindra would have it tough. No matter what happened to her grandfather, there'd be no escaping the stares and snickers.

Bucky wasn't scheduled for work until that afternoon. Maybe he should go talk to Kindra. Be supportive, explain that he was sorry to have hurt her, but…

He couldn't think of a good but. He knew then what his daddy had meant when he said, before giving him a spanking, "This will hurt me more than you."

Of course, that wasn't exactly the same, but he'd go see her anyway. Even let her yell at him if she wanted to.

Ten minutes later, he turned onto her street just as a milk truck pulled away from her house. Gustafson's old Packard sat in the driveway, and a strange sadness washed over him. It felt like someone he had once liked and respected had died.

He parked, and as he got out of his car, the front door opened, and Abby, the dark-haired girl in the kitchen he'd locked eyes with, bent down for the milk bottle. As he started up the walk, she turned toward the house and suddenly whirled back around. "You!" She pointed, her eyes dark and cold. "You have some nerve coming here!"

His blood froze, and he stopped in his tracks, unable to speak. He felt like turning on his heels and getting the hell out of there.

Gustafson came to the door.

My God! He's not even been arrested!

"That's all right, Abby," Gustafson said. "Come on in, Bucky."

Bucky cautiously mounted the steps, while Abby glared at him, as if wanting to clobber him with that milk bottle.

"Go on into the living room, Bucky. Abby, perhaps you could see if Mrs. G needs anything." Gustafson gestured Bucky inside. "Have a seat," he said and settled on a chair across from the couch where Bucky sat. "I'm glad you came by because I'd like to explain myself to you."

Bucky's blood not only got back to flowing, but it rushed in his ears. "Yes, sir," was all he could think to say. He wondered where Kindra was.

"I met with Judge Thompson last night, and he's given me the day to get my things in order before turning myself in. I know this won't help, but I can't tell you how painful it is to have been responsible for the tragic death of Will and Miss Iris. I had no idea Kansas had sold Will his car."

Bucky folded his hands in his lap. Nothing new there. But why'd he want him dead? Still, he didn't dare ask.

"Of course, you're wondering why I wanted to kill Kansas, and I'll tell you. Because he killed Marybeth's baby—and mine."

Wow! So he's *the baby's father.*

Gustafson nodded, sadness written all over his face. "My relationship with Marybeth goes back a long way, and, under the law, I've committed a crime by having relations with her. I won't try to justify them. But I will say, and so will she, that I always treated her kindly and with respect. She was an emotionally scarred and lonely child. She'd lost her mother, and as for Kansas…well, everyone knows he was a tyrannical brute."

But did he have short eyes, *as Harman had put it? Gustafson might be just the guy to ask.* "A rumor has it that he was a child molester."

"Not *a* rumor. Harman's rumor. And I have nothing to say about it."

"Mr. Gustafson, you've admitted to murder and child molestation, I think you owe it to the town to be straight on everything."

Gustafson stared at his feet and puckered his rubbery

lips. "Okay. Harman once came into the storeroom and…well, after that I paid him every month to never open his filthy mouth about what he saw."

"What's that have to do with his rumor?"

"He claimed it was to divert attention away from me, but, in fact, it was his way of throwing it in my face. That ended when I killed the scumbag."

"*You?* You shot Harman?" That news also shot down Chief Trigger's theory that Marybeth did it.

"I had just left Marybeth's house when I saw him turn onto her street, riding that hideous motorcycle of his. I turned around and parked up behind the house, waited a while, then climbed down the hill and snuck inside to the sound of Marybeth's screams. Believe me, I saw red. Marybeth had told me where Kansas kept his gun. I got it and shot the bastard. Later, when Kansas came home, I shot him, too. Another bastard."

The front door opened, and Kindra dragged herself into the room. "Hi, Bucky."

He jumped to his feet. "Hi."

She looked understandingly wrung out.

"I've told Bucky everything," Gustafson said.

She gave Bucky a weak, but friendly, smile and threw her purse onto the couch. "I just completed all the paperwork at school. They'll send my transcripts to Jefferson Davis High in Houston."

"*Houston?*" Bucky erupted.

Gustafson stood. "I have much to do, so I'll excuse myself." He left.

Bucky went to Kindra and took her hands. "How are you doing?"

She sighed. "I'm managing. Let's get away from here, and we'll talk. How about a long drive?"

They climbed into Bucky's car and headed east on 412 toward Tulsa.

Kindra laid her head back and closed her eyes. "I don't think I slept two hours last night."

"What's with you going to Houston?"

"I'm moving into Abby's apartment, and she's going to live here and care for Grandmother. In return, she gets to own the store."

Bucky blinked and turned to her. "This was all arranged last night?"

"Uh-huh. Grandfather and Grandmother came up with the idea. I don't know, but it seemed like they'd already planned it out. I'll finish high school and then go to UH. Abby's thrilled."

That all seemed weird—but in a rational sort of way. Kindra wouldn't be happy sticking around, her grandfather being a murderer and all, and someone had to care for Mrs. G and run the store. "So, let's hear it from the beginning."

"About six-thirty last night, Sheriff Rakoff came to the house and talked to Grandfather for a long time in the living room. Abby and I were told to stay out. When we were called in, Grandfather announced they were leaving to see Judge Thompson. The sheriff took with him a pair of Grandfather's shoes."

Gustafson must have confessed and turned them over. "Then what?"

"An hour or so later, Grandfather came back and told us about the awful things he did, along with everyone's attempt to cover it all up. He's to turn himself in at six o'clock."

"Did he say why he was so cooperative?"

"He didn't want to put the town through the humiliation of a long trial. Wanted to get everything out in the open and be done with it, he said. He even allowed me to call Peter like I had promised, and tell him about the murders and the cover up."

"Did you mention the baby?"

She shook her head. "I think Marybeth has suffered enough."

"It's clear now that VO knew your grandfather was the baby's father. He hinted at it when he said to us, if anyone's related to the baby it wasn't him. He then glanced at you. That means you're the baby's aunt. Or maybe cousin."

"My gosh!" She put a hand to her forehead and slumped further into her seat. "That's hard to get my head around."

"Tyburn also knew what your grandfather was up to. He told me in jail that the *old man* got his way with the female gender, and that he was *very friendly* to Marybeth."

They passed the Glencoe turnoff. The town with the motel that Bucky thought Kindra and Doc Little had shacked up in. He smiled at the absurd thought, then frowned. Or was it? He glanced over at Kindra, who'd fallen asleep. Was Marybeth the only young girl the old man was *friendly* with?

Around noon, they arrived back in Defiance to crowds of people milling about the streets and talking to one another. As he slowed for a turn, Pastor Agnew hollered at him from the sidewalk, "Way to go, Bucky, we're proud of you."

Kindra's eyes sprung open, and she looked around. "What's going on?"

"I have no idea, but I need to get to work. I'll drop you off at home."

When he pulled into the dealership, Kathy came running out with a photographer at her heels. "Bucky," she cried, as he got out of the car, "where have you been? Everybody's looking for you."

"Hold it!" The photographer's flash struck Bucky's

eyes. People crowded around him. Many he didn't even know.

"*Bucky.*"

That word, that voice. Bucky's heart skipped and soared all at once.

Willow.

She threw her arms around him. "I had to stop and congratulate you."

"What's going on?"

"I wish I had time to talk, but I'm working and have to run." She kissed him on the cheek, and a warm light burned in the center of his heart.

Alsop sidled up to him. "It's in this morning's *Oklahoma City Free Press*. All about Gustafson and the cover-up."

Peter didn't waste time getting his story printed. "What's all this got to do with me?"

The photographer edged up to them and put a new bulb in his flash. "Hey, how about a shot of you two?"

"Later," Alsop said, ushered Bucky into his office, and closed the door. "It has everything to do with you and your photographs. Peter's story hit the town like last year's tornado. It told how you exposed Gustafson, and how Chief Trigger, Doc Little, and Johnston conspired to protect him. Folks were outraged. By noon an ad hoc Citizens' Committee demanded the resignation of the mayor and the entire City Council."

"Geesh. How come?"

"They felt there had been too much corruption going on, and your display of decency and courage convinced them the town needed a clean sweep. After much soul searching, I informed the FBI that Doc Little, who was originally from Chicago, was the link between the Outfit, Johnston, and Overstreet in their racetrack scheme. They sent Bart and Willow up from Oklahoma City to take all three away."

"How did you know about Doc Little? And wasn't he your friend?"

"He'd been a friend of my father's for years. Dad had told me about him. Reporting him was the hardest thing I ever did. He was always good to me. Sold me this very property."

"Then why'd you do it?"

"Well, I guess you could say I learned from you."

"*Me?*"

"Remember after we got you patched up at Doc Little's, I said it was important to protect the town's image?"

Bucky nodded.

"Well, afterward, I realized that you had principles that I lacked. I thought of how you had risked your life by standing up for the two Caddo, for example. After further thought, I decided that I could no longer worry about protecting the town's image, or Doc Little."

The photographer stuck his head in the door. "Can we get that shot now?"

CHAPTER 55

The next morning, Bucky went to work with the realization that he'd become famous. But he quickly discovered that being famous was a pain in the butt. All day, folks popped in, not to buy cars or anything, but to shake hands and chew the fat. Even Dexter, his replacement at Gustafson's, showed up wanting an autograph.

A car beeped. Kindra.

She jaunted inside and rushed up to him, eyes bright with excitement. "I only have a minute. There's oodles to do before I leave tomorrow afternoon. Grandmother gave me her car for keeps."

A sudden sadness swept over him. "It must be hard for you around here. Why don't you sit down?" Bucky hated when people just stood there while he sat, especially when he didn't feel like getting up just to be polite.

"It's not hard at all. Everybody's been really nice. I feel sorry for Abby because she'll have to make Grandmother's soup every day. Grandfather had to do it, and he hated soup. Anyway, before I left, I wanted to stop and say goodbye, and that, well, you were right about turning in Grandfather. I have a lot of mixed-up feelings that I haven't sorted through yet." She reached over and adjusted his front curl. "I'm going to miss you, Bucky."

The sadness deepened. "Yeah, me, too."

She brightened. "Don't worry, I'll come visit during vacation and stuff. But I am happy for you and your new job."

"New job? I wish you'd sit down."

She gave him a funny look. "Don't tell me you don't know."

"I'm telling you, I don't know."

"Uh-oh. Think I let the cat out of the bag. Well, you'll find out soon, I'm sure. Pretend you're surprised, okay?"

"I'll go like this." He bulged his eyes. "What is it?"

"The Citizens' Committee is appointing you—no, I'd better not say." She hopped on her toes and flapped her arms. "But it's really neat. I've got to run." She reached up on her tiptoes and kissed him smack on the lips. Before he had time to process what had just happened, she was gone.

Wow! That was some goodbye. And what did she mean about the Citizens' Committee and a new job? It wasn't fair to give hints and then leave. He glanced in Alsop's office, but he wasn't there.

Pastor Agnew came into the showroom with a bunch of people following in his wake.

Bucky pushed himself to his feet. "Pastor Agnew." He didn't know some of the others, so he just nodded. "Nice to see y'all."

They nodded back with big smiles, but he didn't think they planned to buy cars.

With a broad Methodist grin, Pastor Agnew said, "We the Citizens' Committee are drafting you to become Defiance's Chief of Police."

Chief of Police? Drafting? Bucky heard the words, but their meaning struggled to reach his numbed brain. The room felt cramped. It was hard to breathe. "I'm too young to be a police chief."

"Old enough in my book," Pastor Agnew said with a wink toward Bucky.

Miss Smits—the high school music teacher—smiled. "We did our due diligence. We know *all* about you."

"Then you know I have no law enforcement experience."

"I never went to law school," Judge Thompson snorted. "You'll read books and learn on the job, like I did. Besides, you'll have lots of help when you need it."

Miss Smits patted his arm. "You have the qualities Defiance needs in an honest police chief, Bucky. You get along with people and will set a fine example."

"And he solves crimes," the pastor added.

Judge Thompson added briskly, "Be at the courthouse ten o'clock tomorrow morning and I'll swear you in. There'll be spectators, so you might prepare a speech. A short one."

The Citizens' Committee traipsed off, leaving Bucky hardly remembering what they said, except that as of tomorrow, he'd be a police chief. Did they know he took gym instead of ROTC in high school?

Alsop came in and marched over. "Hey, hey. Man of the hour." He threw out his hand.

Bucky stood and caught it. "You've heard?"

"They grilled me about you last night. I told them you'd be a fine chief, as long as a certain undercover agent wasn't around to distract you."

"You really think I'd be a good chief?"

"Hell of a lot more honest than those of the last few days."

"When you put it that way—"

"You've got competent people in the department, who will support you."

"But what about you losing your council seat?"

"There'll be a new council coming out of next month's special election, and I have the full endorsement of the Citizens' Committee. Regaining my seat will help me in the 1960 mayor's race."

"Do you think I'm moving too fast, becoming chief?" Bucky still couldn't wrap his brain around it.

"You'll never be handed a plum this ripe. Do a good job, and who knows—in '68 you might very well succeed me as mayor."

∽∾∽∾

Bucky pulled into the courthouse at nine-thirty the next morning. He arrived early and waited on the bench outside Judge Thompson's courtroom. He'd stayed up late, working on his speech, discarding draft after draft until he finally worked out something good.

He couldn't wait to tell Daddy. His son, a police chief. He wondered if Uncle Rupert was ever a police chief. Bucky would tell him, too.

The bailiff stuck his head out from the courtroom. "Are you Bucky?"

Bucky nodded.

"Judge Thompson wants you to wait in his chambers. He has something to say to you before he swears you in." The bailiff showed him inside.

Bucky had never been in a judge's chamber before. The desk had carved legs. The judge's chair was made of brown leather like the couch Bucky sat on studying his speech. He got tired of doing that, stood and checked himself in a full-length mirror on a door beside a coatrack holding the judge's robe. He hitched up his pants and adjusted his blue tie, wondering if his red and green plaid sports coat was suitable attire.

Just then, the door swung in and thumped his foot.

The judge clapped his hands. "Chop, chop. Let's go." He led Bucky down a hallway. They stopped at a door, and the judge regarded Bucky with eyes that meant business. "Realize, young man, we expect you to prove yourself."

"I understand, sir."

"What you don't understand is that you'll have enemies."

Bucky swallowed. "Enemies?"

"As chief, you'll have access to certain files." He opened the courtroom door. "And they know it, so be careful."

They entered the courtroom and stood before a lacquered wooden rail. About fifty people sat on the other side, and the bailiff stood at the door. Bucky's hand clutched his pocketed handkerchief.

"State your name," the judge said.

"Bucky Ontario."

"Raise your right hand."

Bucky pulled his hand from his pocket, and the handkerchief fell to the floor. He stepped on it so people couldn't see.

"Bucky Ontario," the judge intoned, "do you solemnly swear to uphold the duties and responsibilities of police chief for the town of Defiance, Oklahoma?"

"I do."

"I hereby declare you the Defiance Chief of Police." The judge shook Bucky's hand.

Everybody clapped. The judge whispered, "Go ahead and give that short speech."

Something contracted in Bucky's chest. He'd left it on the couch. He stared at the judge, needed to tell him he'd be right back.

The judge leaned in close. "Come on, we haven't got all day."

Bucky looked at those friendly faces and found his voice. "Hi. Um, my name's Bucky Ontario. I guess some of you know me, but for those of you who don't, well, I'm now Chief Bucky." His heart fluttered. This was *really* happening. "I've never been a police chief before, or even a policeman, but I believe in justice and promise to always uphold the law to the best of my ability. Thank you."

CHAPTER 56

In celebration of Bucky's new job, Alsop and Kathy took him to Cattlemen's Steakhouse for lunch. They presented him with a plaque honoring him as Car Salesman of the Year. Alsop told him he had set a one-day record by selling five Furies to the police department.

After lunch Bucky had an appointment with Pastor Agnew. The pastor wanted to discuss spiritual counseling for prisoners. On the way there, Bucky felt sad that the baby never received a proper ceremony and sorry that Kindra never got her mother's ring back. She was a good friend, and he wished he could do something for her.

VOs words, *Find the baby, find the ring* whirled in his head. He pictured Marybeth kneeling at the baby's grave, tears rolling down her face. Her image began to dissolve, almost did, but slowly returned to normal as though a director had changed his mind about a scene's ending. Then an unexpected possibility occurred to him. What if Marybeth had lied about Kansas hiding the baby in the Belvedere? Would she have let him put her baby in a concrete grave she couldn't even visit, one to be opened in fifty years? What if *she* hid the baby? Without warning, an idea popped into his head, so simple and unimaginable at the same time, that he gulped for air. He checked his watch. Kindra may not have left town yet. He'd see Pastor Agnew later.

He tried to recall Marybeth's exact words at Mrs. Rheingold's. Oh, wait, he'd need a shovel. Kindra had one. Man, if she'd already left for Houston—

He turned onto her street.

Dammit! Kindra's car was gone. He squealed up to the house and stopped. Abby was lounging in a hammock on the lawn, reading a book. He hollered out the window, "Did Kindra already leave for Houston?"

She looked up. "I'm afraid so."

Bucky's heart seemed to stop, hope shriveled up.

"About five minutes ago."

Bucky's heart jumped with new confidence. The shovel! He leapt from his car and ran around the house to the toolshed. When he returned with a shovel, Abby said, "I'm sorry I was so—"

"Thanks, Abby, but I have to catch Kindra. I'll return this." He jumped back in his car. She would probably take I-35. He headed that way.

Wait. She wasn't the type to have filled up with gas the night before. He wrestled a U-turn toward Gustafson's grocery, his mind running on high octane. There she was, pulling out from the gas pump. He honked and screeched up behind her.

"Kindra," he shouted from the car, his heart pounding so hard his chest hurt. "I know where the baby is."

She stuck her head out the window and frowned at him. "Isn't it buried in that car?"

"We were wrong. Park your car and get in."

Bucky peeled out onto the highway. "Marybeth told me at Mrs. Rheingold's house that Kansas had hidden the baby in the Belvedere's trunk. But she also said that after the baby's birth, she was afraid Kansas would take it away from her, so she hid with the baby in what she called her secret hiding place, a hollow oak tree behind her house. Don't you see? She made up the hidden-in-the-trunk story because she knew no one would dig up the Belvedere sealed in cement. Ten to one it's in that hollow oak tree."

They pulled onto Kansas's deserted property and jumped out of the car. Marybeth was still staying with Mrs. Rheingold.

Bucky pointed the shovel. "See those two big oaks up the incline? I'll bet the baby's in one of them."

They reached the first tree. Bucky walked around it. "No hollows. Must be the other one." They trekked through the brush over crackling dried leaves, sidestepping thick blackberry bushes toward the second oak, a huge one. Bucky crossed his fingers, hoping he was right.

The side away from the house and road had a large charred hollow in the base of the trunk, spacious enough for a man. Dirt covered the bottom.

"Whelp, nothin' left but to dig." Bucky hunched inside the tree with his shovel. Kindra stood aside, and dirt flew.

They heard the distinct sound of the shovel hitting something hard.

Like a coffin.

Bucky got on his knees and scooped out handfuls of dirt. "This is it, all right."

A minute later, he backed out of the tree carrying a wooden box about two feet long and a foot tall. Crudely painted orange poppies adorned the dirt-crusted cover. It had a brass latch and tiny gold lock. He set the box down, and with a sharp blow of the shovel popped the lock.

"You want to open it, Kindra?"

She stood staring. Her eyes fixed on the box.

"Okay, I'll do it." He reached down.

"No!" She whirled in front of him. "Get away."

Bucky stepped back. "What's the matter?"

She put her face in her hands and sobbed. Real big ones.

"We can talk, if you want to."

She kept bawling, and he put his arm across her shoulders. "Let's go sit over there on the log." They sat down, and he handed her his handkerchief. He said gently, "I think I know what's wrong."

She shook her head. "No you don't. No one does."

"It was the diary. When you learned that Marybeth was having sex with your grandfather since age ten, you blamed yourself for not having protected her."

She looked up at him, her forehead wrinkled in disbelief.

"Your grandfather had tried, or maybe did, some funny stuff with you when you were young, so you knew what he was like."

She gasped. "But how—how could you—"

"You told me once that your grandfather couldn't make you do anything since you were twelve-and-a-half. Putting that together with your feelings about what you learned from Marybeth's diary, led me to figuring it out."

She dabbed her eyes. "It *was* my fault. I should have known why he treated Marybeth so special in the store. Letting her read magazines and eat free ice cream."

"Kindra, you were a child with no understanding. It's—it's great that you found a way to protect yourself."

She sniffled. "It wasn't anything that great. He touched me once, and I told him if he ever did it again, I'd run away." She took in a deep breath, as if after a good cry, and looked at him with a weak smile. "I'm glad we talked about it."

"Both your grandfather and Marybeth were wrong about Kansas killing the baby. Marybeth didn't know it, but she smothered the infant by mistake while hiding from Kansas in the tree hollow. Kansas buried the baby, but it had to have been Marybeth and your grandfather who moved it. And I'll bet he put Kansas's button in the empty grave as evidence against him if it was ever dug up. Poor Kansas. He didn't kill anyone, and, as far as we know, didn't molest anyone." He pointed toward the small box. "What should we do about the baby?"

Kindra heaved a sigh. "The baby should stay here, where Marybeth buried it. Do you think Pastor Agnew might be willing to come and bless the child in the grave?"

Bucky nodded. "As a Defiance pastor, I'm sure he's used to unconventional requests. I'll put the baby back, and we'll go ask him."

They paced back to the box with the painted orange poppies. Bucky bent down to pick it up, and Kindra grabbed his arm. "I want to see the baby."

"You sure? The poor little thing won't look very presentable."

Kindra got on her knees and slowly raised the lid. She flinched from the stench. On top of a red and blue checked blanket, Bucky saw it. Kindra reached in and picked up her mother's ring. She stared at it a long time. A tear or two rolled from her eyes. She carefully lifted the edge of the blanket and peeked under it. Then she replaced the ring.

"What are you doing?"

"Marybeth must have loved her baby very much." She lowered the lid. "It's only right that the ring stays with her baby."

THE END

Coming early 2018
from Bill A. Brier:

THE KILLER WHO WASN'T THERE

The 1950s Killer Who Series ~ Book 2

Turn the page to read an excerpt

CHAPTER 1

A Negro in a phone company vest sprinted onto the road, arms waving.

I slammed on the brakes.

He rushed over, pounded on my window. "A girl—a young'un—in the ditch! Ya gotta come!"

I flew out of my roadster and raced after the man, scrambling through knee-high grass into a ravine.

"I was on a pole, workin'," he hollered over his shoulder, "spotted an animal circlin' somethin' in the brush. Looked like a kid, all rolled into a ball. I ran over, and a coyote skedaddled, jus' as I heard your car."

I gasped. A Negro girl lay on her side, whimpering, welts on her arms and legs. Her blood-splattered gingham dress—a dress like my kid sister used to wear—in shreds. She needed a doctor, fast. I bent down to her.

"Leave her alone!" a harsh voice hollered.

Startled, I glanced up the ridge. Two state troopers. One small and muscular, the other large and muscular. The small one started toward the girl.

"We'll take care of it, fella," the other said, shooting his hand up like a traffic cop.

"Anything I can do to help?" I offered. "I'm the new Defiance Police Chief. First day."

"That's nice, but this is a family matter. You run along, she'll be fine."

What was he thinking? "She doesn't look fine to me."

"Hey, Chief!" he barked, his face grisly. "This isn't your jurisdiction. Now take off."

The small trooper lifted the little girl and started back up the ravine.

The Negro whispered to me, "Ain't no family matter. Was the Klan."

The hairs on my neck bristled. I stared at him. *The Klan? Here?*

About the Author

Bill A. Brier grew up in California and went to Hollywood High School. After serving in the air force as a combat cameraman, he hired on at Disney Studios, as a film loader, and advanced from there.

He earned a master's degree in psychology—a big help when working with *Trumpish* Hollywood producers—"You're fired!" During his more than twenty-five years in the movie business as a cameraman, film editor, and general manager, Brier worked on everything from the hilarious, *The Love Bug*, to the creepy, *The Exorcist*, to the far out, *Star Trek* and *Battlestar Galactica*.

Eight years ago, Brier switched from reading scripts to writing mysteries and driving race cars. After completing three award-winning novels, he signed with Black Opal Books. His first novel, *The Devil Orders Takeout*, published in April 2017, is a standalone mystery/thriller about a devoted father and husband who makes a deal with a real-life devil to protect his golf-prodigy son—after his wife and older son are killed in a mysterious accident—and pays hell for it.

Brier's second book in *The Killer Who* series, *The Killer Who Wasn't There*, will be published in early 2018.

Brier lives in Southern California with his wife, dogs, and chickens. He writes every day and golfs infrequently (that damn right knee!). His five children and eight grandchildren keep him busy going to birthday parties, and he never misses one!

The Brier Patch, Brier's humorous and engaging blog about his wild and woolly early days in Hollywood, is on his website, BillBrier.com, along with contests, which will award the grand prizewinners $1,000.

www.ingramcontent.com/pod-product-compliance
Lightning Source LLC
Chambersburg PA
CBHW060936120726
47910CB00002B/354